POSTCARDS FROM ONKEL HENRY

LOUISE LYNETTE BENDER

LLB PUBLICATIONS

ISBN 979-8-9932856-0-3

"Ganz allein durch
Aufklärung der Vergangenheit
läßt sich die Gegenwart begreifen."

*"Only by throwing
light on the past
can the present
be understood."*

Johann Wolfgang von Goethe
-Tag- und Jahreshefte 1811
Translation by Goethe Global (goetheglobal.com)

MAP OF LOCATIONS

1. MELDORF, GERMANY
2. BROOKLYN, NEW YORK
3. CHARLESTON, SC
4. CARTAGENA, COLOMBIA
5. PANAMA CANAL
6. SANTIAGO, CHILE
7. PUNTA ARENAS, CHILE

FAMILY TREE

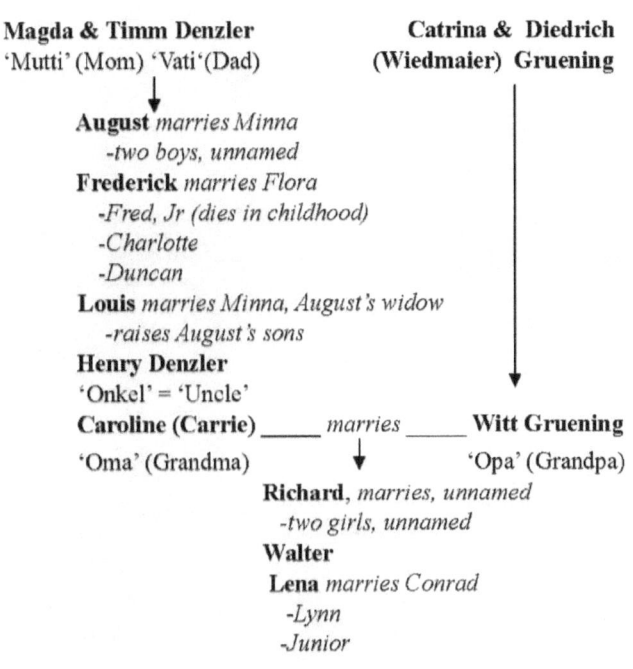

Magda & Timm Denzler
'Mutti' (Mom) 'Vati' (Dad)

       August *marries Minna*
         -two boys, unnamed
       Frederick *marries Flora*
         -Fred, Jr (dies in childhood)
         -Charlotte
         -Duncan
       Louis *marries Minna, August's widow*
         -raises August's sons
       Henry Denzler
       'Onkel' = 'Uncle'

Catrina & Diedrich
(Wiedmaier) Gruening

Caroline (Carrie) _____ *marries* _____ **Witt Gruening**
'Oma' (Grandma)   'Opa' (Grandpa)

           Richard, *marries, unnamed*
             -two girls, unnamed
           Walter
            Lena *marries Conrad*
            -Lynn
            -Junior

Retta Maasen 'Tante' (Aunt)
      Magda's lifelong family friend, Max's widow
      Peter, Amie, John, all young adults at births of Denzler children
Amalia Denzler *Timm's niece, comes to U.S. with mother & siblings*
Bridget *Carrie's co-worker in Brooklyn*
Rosie & Antoine Chapelle *Carrie's employers in Brooklyn*
Anne Carroll Moore & Mary Wright Plummer
      employees of the Pratt Institute Library in the late 1800's
Otto von Bismarck *German Chancellor/Prime Minister 1871-1890*
Abraham Lincoln *United States President 1861-1866*

– for Caroline Bender and Henry Braun,
who bear the names in their generations

– and for Joseph Morrissette McGowan,
always my first reader

Meldorf, 1883

O N A RARE SUNNY DAY, crisp and sparkling, Carrie Denzler pedals as fast as she can toward the usually dreary North Sea shore. She clings to the tiny bicycle all the boys learned to ride when they, too, were barely five. The vehicle is worn and a little rusty, but perfect for dodging rocks and holes in the path in pursuit of her big brothers.

Ahead, she watches seven-year-old Henry flying low on a bike both larger and newer than her own. She always has fun with Henry. He can make a toy out of anything. Today, he has a kite folded into a slim packet tied to his handlebars, string and a cross bar tucked neatly inside the paper body. He made her a kite, too. She knows he will put his kite together by the time she gets off her bicycle. She wishes he wasn't always fastest at whatever they do. But he loves to play, and she does too. She loves Henry.

Sixteen-year-old Frederick, trailing behind them, can be a little bossy, especially when he fills in for their mother. Still, Carrie is excited to spend time with him today. Frederick usually has to work at the candy store when he's not at school. 'I have responsibilities,' he says, when she wants him to play. Carrie doesn't need looking after, but if their mother insists on a grown-up in charge of their ride, then she is glad Frederick is the one who is with them. She loves Frederick, too.

"Hein-ry! Hein-ry! Look at meeeeee!" Carrie calls out to the brother ahead. He does not turn his head.

"Komm schon, Carolina! Come on, Carrie!" she hears Henry cry in return. "I'll look at you when we get to the bay!"

She turns to fix Frederick in her gaze, and nearly launches herself into the marsh alongside the dirt road. Frederick swerves to miss her skittering path, and slows to assure her safety. Her temper flares at the way her inexperience slows her progress in these moments.

"Weitermachen, Carolina! Keep going, Carrie!" Frederick urges. "We are almost there!" She pedals even harder, wanting desperately to overcome Henry. Finally, Henry skids to a stop in the rocks and sand. Carrie and Frederick follow suit in succession, abandoning their bikes to join Henry on the beach. Sure enough, he already has his kite assembled and runs to launch it.

"Sind Sie bereit, kleines Mädchen? Are you ready, little girl?" Frederick asks, to Carrie's eager nod. He pulls out the Henry-made kite he carries for her. Together, they tie the cross stick into place, and he eases some of the string off the wound bundle to create a long slack in the line, handing the bulk of the string to Carrie.

"Go on up ahead," he says to her. "I will fly past you in a minute." She scurries ahead onto the wide field that borders the beach, as far as the string will reach, and turns to gaze at her brother. The morning sun casts a golden haze around him, so bright she can see his form but not his eyes. She recognizes his stance and knows he will move soon.

He's off! She watches, poised like a cat ready to pounce, until he comes close, then she pivots to face the water. She feels the faint whoosh as he overtakes her, and holds tight to the string as the kite catches a breeze. He lets go. Magic. Pure magic, as the transfer between them puts her in control of what he has begun. The breeze in the cove keeps the string taut without mangling the delicate paper that covers the stick frame. The day radiates freedom. She looks over at Henry, who usually moves quickly to whatever is next. Even Henry looks content to keep his kite aloft, enjoying the peace at the end of his string.

Days are often fun, but seldom so carefree as this one. Carrie doesn't quite understand, but she often recognizes tension in the faces of her parents and oldest brothers. She hears the word "soldiers," and knows it means someone who fights. Her five-year-old logic dismisses the unease. Her brothers fight—all the time. They start out playing, and someone tussles a little too hard, and someone else twists a long ooooouch into a painful cry, and suddenly they are wrestling for real, the others cheering on one side or the other. They are playing. Why does the word "fight" place such pain on the faces of the grown-ups? What are they worried about? A fight ends in a minute!

Anyway, why would anyone want to fight, when they could come to the shore instead? She watches Henry steer his kite to land safely on the beach. No place on earth is as wonderful the North Sea shore. Her brothers would never fight here. This sun-warmed patch of happiness is the most magical place in the world.

But she notices, behind the smile in Frederick's eyes today, the hint of a grimace. She wonders what it means. She knows that he and August, their oldest brother, are going on a trip. She begs him to tell her the story again, and even Henry comes close to listen.

"Do you see," he says, "way out past the boats, past the dock and the ruddy fishermen? Where the water ends and meets the sky?" She nods as he points. "We are going even further than that, to the end of the sea, across the great ocean, to a place called New York."

"Why can't I go to New York?" Henry says. "Why do you get to go on a boat and I have to stay here? I want to go with you."

"New York?" Carrie ignores her youngest brother's familiar restlessness. She shivers, though the sun is warm. What does this New York have to do with her? What will her brothers do so far away? And why are they leaving the place where her family has always lived?

"New York," Frederick affirms. "The big city has a huuuuuge harbor, where hundreds or even thousands of people get off ships every day. We will work hard and send money back here to pay for your dollies and kites."

He understands that the money actually will pay for necessities like food and clothes. Eventually, it will buy steamer tickets for the two younger brothers to follow them to the far away city. He also grasps that the Prussian army's reach does not extend to New York.

But his sister is young. She can still escape the knowledge that even the basics of living require more money than they have. She can remain innocent of the fact that if he stays, he could die fighting for a cause which his family opposes. He is wiser than his years, but he resists imparting too much knowledge to his baby sister and her almost-twin brother. Not yet. The journey is an adventure, but it is no pleasure visit to see distant relatives. The younger children do not yet understand, but he knows he and August will stay in America.

They pedal their way to the house, a little less energetic on the return trip, sated by wind, play, and tales of the future. When they go through the kitchen, Frederick notices a letter from Retta Maasen on the kitchen table. The Denzler children call her Tante Retta and name her children as their cousins. In reality, the Maasen children are almost a generation older, and Retta is closer to their late grandmother's age than their mother's. They are actually related, but the kinship stretches so far back that none of them really remembers exactly how.

Not even their oldest brother, twenty-one-year-old August, remembers the Maasens. They left for New York before he was born. But Tante Retta is as well known to their family, through folklore and the post, as any close relation. She is the founder of the confectionery their family now owns and operates. Her letters arrive monthly, regular as rain.

October 17, 1882
Dear Magda,

I hear the news from Holstein, and am grateful we have a plan for August and Frederick. They both are in grave danger of conscription, as you must be aware. As difficult as I find it to believe, Bismarck is taking sixteen-

year-olds into battle in other cities. And of course, at twenty-one, August clearly falls within their scope of interest. I know you will be glad to see them safely abroad, even though I also know it breaks your mother-heart for them to go. Don't worry about them for a single minute. You get them on the ship, and we will take the transition from there.

We have held off hiring for the new shop until their arrival, so they both have instant jobs. Peter is ready with food, beds, and coats for the colder climate. You know my eldest—he thinks of everything! The boys obviously have all the skills for the job, especially Frederick. That child treated Maasen's Confectionery like home from the time he was in diapers! I predict he and his brother will have the first Denzler's shop open within the year.

How quickly can you save to buy tickets for your two younger boys? I do remember that Louis is only ten, and Henry barely seven, but the unrest in Germany will get worse, I fear. By the time you have the money they may be well within conscription age, too. We are ready whenever you are!

You poor dear, having to scurry for safety like you do. I remember how frightened we were when our children were small. When I tell people that our eldest was born in Denmark, the middle in Germany, and the youngest in Prussia, they don't believe me. But as you know, the different countries on their birth certificates were not because we moved so much. They were all born *in the same house in Meldorf, our family home for ten generations. The wars changed the borders with such violent speed that you never knew who would be in charge of your front yard when you woke up in the morning. You were a child and may not remember, but I was so terrified for you kinders all the time.*

I could not imagine ever leaving Meldorf, but as time goes on, I'm so glad we did. I hope you will come too, and bring both Timm and Carrie. But we must at least get the boys out of danger before they die in these hideous battles. How I look forward to giving them hugs! They have to be so big compared to the last time I saw them— young men rather than the boys I remember.

How is your sister-in-law coping with the death of Timm's brother? I know they wanted to come over here, too, but I imagine those plans are on hold for now.

I hate that my single topic today has been getting your family to safety, but that's where we are. I'm sure you are aware the officers are going house to house less than fifty miles from you. I don't want to frighten you any worse than you already are, but you need to be telling me those boys are on the boat.

Love to all,

Retta

Carrie misses her mother's affection in the rush to gather papers, clothes, and bags for the boys to leave. Loneliness cuts deeply as she absorbs the gaping menace of her brothers' impending absence. She watches them prepare. August moves deliberately, working his way down a list of items to pack, focused on his task. Frederick rushes about the house gathering his things in a pile, then organizes his bags carefully. Carrie shadows his every step, afraid he is so distracted that he will forget to tell her good-bye. She stiffens every time he leaves her sight, even if she can still hear his heavy feet on the wooden floors.

After he trips over her twice, nearly landing both of them on the floor each time, Frederick finally issues a stern command that she must stay next to the wall so she will not get hurt. Her lip trembling, she nods and becomes even more fretful. She remains still for a few minutes, simply because he says he needs her help. But soon, she silently slips away. She returns carrying a small parcel, which she tucks into the steamer trunk.

The next morning, Magda hands August a letter to post to Retta. It will likely sail on the ship with them, and may proceed them to her home by only an hour or so. She writes a mere week after the last letter she received:

October 27, 1882
Dear Retta,

August and Frederick sail today on the Rugia. *Check the schedule for their entry into the United States. Their departure was so hasty I can do nothing but pray they are permitted to enter New York rather than returned to the dangers of Meldorf. I'm not at all sure they have all the papers they need, and I will live in fear until I hear from them – or from you – that they have arrived.*

Timm and I already have begun to talk about the fastest way to finance a trip for the two younger boys.

My instincts tell me your words are true, and these terrible battles will become much worse. A tiny border scuffle on the world stage, but the world isn't living in the middle of it.

A simple "Danke" fails, but will have to suffice in the moment. Thank you. More soon.

Love you, too,
Magda

Just on the edge of morning, Vati hitches horses to the wagon and the boys heft their bags onto the back end. Carrie barrels out of her bed, rushes unseeing past a yawning Henry, hurls her small body into Frederick's arms, and sobs. Mutti tries to peel her away. They mean for the men alone to make the trip to the dock at Hamburg, but Carrie does not budge from Frederick.

Her father raises his eyebrows and shrugs at her mother, who yields to the iron will of their tiny hurricane of a daughter. Carrie remains in Frederick's arms as they roll away from the house. By the time they arrive at the ship, she only whimpers into her father's neck as Frederick hands her into Vati's arms and boards the ship.

"Your family is falling apart, isn't it, little one?" he whispers into her hair. "And nothing you can do can pull it back together."

Meldorf, 1883

I N THE TRUNK that Magda empties for the older boys to pack, she finds a crate of old books that she had long forgotten were in the house. She turns to them now, some poetry by Goethe, some novels by various authors, and ancient classics like *Beowulf* and the *Odyssey*. My, how her life has changed! She can't remember the last time that she—or Timm—read anything nearly as heady as this.

Now, as she sifts through the volumes, she discovers a smattering of Retta's letters to her, all bearing United States post marks. They must have used them in the old days as bookmarks, leaving behind a calendar composed entirely of correspondence. She can mark the date she read the book, and how far she read before she put it down, from where the letters fall between the pages. She arranges them in order and takes advantage of a rare moment of quiet to read.

April 5, 1856
Dear Magda,

> *The boys and Amie are doing very well. Thank you for asking about them; they're always first on my mind! They have settled in and seem none the worse for the wear and tear of moving so far away from everything and everyone they know. The store is up and running. Amie and Peter help out after school. John just hangs around, but soon he'll be helping, too.*

I barely got him birthed before we left Meldorf, but as you know, we put them to work early in our family! You will do the same someday.

Do you remember my very good friend Maria Wiedmaier from down by Hanover? Her daughter arrived here in Brooklyn today, enough years after the 1848 Revolts that you couldn't exactly call her a refugee, but fleeing the after-effects of the conflicts nonetheless. I so admire her courage, moving all by herself from one upheaval to another.

We're probably headed to war, too, although no one says those words yet. We can't seem to agree on the morality – or immorality – of pretending we can own another person and profit from the work they do without compensation. Here, at least, people are aware of the trouble and dedicated to addressing the problem. I feel weary to imagine moving from one warring land to another, but that's exactly what we've done.

Anyway, Catrina will stay with us until she gets settled. I already see so much of her mother in her that it's like having Maria in the house again. What a treat her visit will be!

I worry about you and hope the restlessness in Germany is not too harsh. We are relieved to be here, even as much as we miss Meldorf. Hope the chocolates on your side of the ocean are not giving you as much trouble as the soldiers. Thanks, as always, for stepping in for us!

Love,
Retta

January 26, 1861
Dear Magda,

Congratulations on your engagement! I knew that news would be coming! At times like this, I wish I were still in Meldorf, so I would not have to miss your big day. I will be loving you from afar, my girl! I wish your mother had lived to see this day. Such an intermingling of happiness and grief, for both of us.

The days have been interminable since Max's death, and yet I find so little time to write. I always knew I'd likely be left without him. He was a few years older than I, and suffered ill health from long before we left Meldorf. I hoped the reduction in stress would help him live longer, but alas, not long enough.

My children have been so sweet, but I am aware how very young they are. I hope my youngest remembers something of his father when he is older. I stay so busy, between them and the business, that you wouldn't think I'd have much time to feel lonely. But I miss Max fiercely, and the days are too long in his absence.

People have been unfailingly kind. My staunchest supporter, to my surprise, is Catrina Wiedmaier! I met her only once before she arrived at our doorstep, long ago and as a little girl. By the time she launched on her own here in Brooklyn, she became an extra older daughter to Max and me – a true delight.

Catrina stops by the shop almost daily since I reopened, dropping off a wurst and bit of sauerkraut, or a book, or some flowers. She says she remembers how hard life was when her mother died. I think she takes care of me the way she would have liked to take care of her mom. She is such a comfort, like the daughter she became to us, and makes this hard time feel survivable without forcing my own children into roles too old for their tender years.

Meanwhile, the national drama does not care who dies. South Carolina makes noisy threats to leave the union if they cannot keep their slaves. President Lincoln lets them know that the U.S. will not tolerate secession. How grown men can so closely resemble squabbling children, I will never understand. I've had enough of this foolishness for six lifetimes. They should listen to Tante Retta and stop this nonsense! But alas, they bicker on.

Much love,
Retta

Magda pauses to make a cup of tea. Most people in Meldorf paid little attention to the U.S. Civil War. They had their own problems in Germany, and the United States seemed too far away to affect their lives. But reading Retta's words, the other country's conflict fills Magda's imagination as if she had lived the experience herself. Human nature wreaks the same havoc everywhere. And yet life somehow goes on as usual.

April 18, 1862
Dear Magda,

I'm so cheered to hear your happy news! Your first child on the way! You and Timm will be wonderful parents. Enjoy every minute of your pregnancy. Your life, as they say, is about to change forever. I wish for less insanity in the world this child will inhabit, but I guess parents of every generation feel that worry. I know I did, and the world hasn't gotten any easier.

I hear mixed thoughts about your new prime minister. I hope he does better than I fear — I find him self-

serving and belligerent, but what do I know? I came over here to escape the anguish of daily assault by the so-called leaders of my ancestral home. I'm sorry you have to continue to make your way through the muck.

Over here, we are well into the war by now, a year since the Union first fired on Charleston, which I'm told is one of its oldest and most beautiful cities. Those streets may not look so beautiful right now. I have to give credit to the southerners – I may think they are misguided, but they are willing to fight for what they want!

I hear that we're having troubles in the west, too, something about disagreements over who has the right to occupy land in Minnesota, the settlers or the native peoples. Mr. Lincoln certainly has his hands full.

We've had interesting developments on the personal front, too. The kids and I had Catrina over for dinner tonight, and you will never guess what happened! Peter wasn't home, but stopped by to pick up some things he needed. He brought along a newfound friend, newly arrived from Germany. Diedrich (his name is Diedrich Gruening – you haven't heard of him, have you?) grew up in Hanover, just like Catrina! He arrived in Manhattan last week, and Peter has been showing him the town. You know Peter – never met a stranger!

How lucky that they happened by while Catrina was here – I think meeting each other was a taste of home for both of them. They never knew each other, but they knew the same places and some of the same people. They grew up on farms outside opposite sides of town. All this time I've teased Catrina that she should limit her interest in young men to German-born choices, and here she meets someone from practically next door! They got along famously, and of course my old matchmaking self can see

14

the sparks fly and wonders if anything will come of their introduction!

Take care of yourself and that precious little one on the way.

Love,

Retta

September 27, 1864

Dear Magda,

I woke up thinking of you this morning. How are you feeling? Sorry you are off to such a rough start on this second pregnancy. Hope the nausea fades.

The war goes on, but we are doing well. Diedrich remembers talk on board his ocean voyage about leaving one war-torn country for another. He thinks that scenario was overrated, and I have to agree. You would never know a war is happening here. We see no bombed-out buildings, no scorched countryside, no signs of earth-shaking division. Very different from the so-called scuffles that dot the Holstein countryside. I remind him that the actual fighting is much further south, so we are not in a place to see the destruction. Still, we will have quite the job cleaning the country up when it's all over.

Not much family news. Hope all is well there!

Retta

April 30, 1865

Dear Magda,

Another little boy! And what a lovely name, even if I did also choose it before you. My Peter Frederick is so excited to hear he has a little namesake in your Frederick

Nicholas. He's also so excited at impending nuptials that you'd think he was the blushing bride!

They say twice the children makes three times the work, but I know you're up for the load. You were made to be a mom. Is he sleeping at night now, or are you in danger of napping on the candy counter?

The drama in the so-called United States would certainly keep you awake! General Lee's surrender at Appomattox, President Lincoln's shocking and violent death, the assassin Booth trapped in death-dealing flames after stealing the attention from the actor Booth onstage. A novelist could not make up anything more exciting than the truth of our times. The nation has hardly breathed during this month full of action.

I sincerely hope this means the end of the conflict; I'm not certain my nerves can take any more excitement, and the nation certainly needs no more death and destruction. Part of me sighs in relief, and the other part wonders when the other shoe will fall, as they say. Emotion runs high.

And on an ironic personal note, Diedrich Gruening has been called up as a soldier! We think the decisive battle is over and the fighting will stop soon, but as long as war time officially continues, I guess they need soldiers. When he arrived in New York after the start of the war, he of course enrolled as eligible for the military. He says he had almost forgotten he was on the list; he's been quietly tending bar at the tavern in the basement of their apartment building and enjoying wedded bliss with his new bride.

Yes, he and Catrina finally made their love official! Now, they call him up and he has to leave her for a while. He is off to Charleston, where the war began, to guard the southern prisoners until their terms of release are final.

We don't believe he will face any danger, but of course you never know. We hope he will return to us soon.

Yours in hopes for a little less news next time,
Retta

In these days, Magda thinks, pausing in her reading to sip on her tea, everyone is going somewhere. Whether for worry or for love, to support a cause or to escape certain death, everyone is on the move.

June 2, 1866
Dear Magda,

Catrina and Diedrich have decided to move to Charleston! He will manage a farm that became available when one of the big plantations broke up from lack of available labor. They will be close to the city, but away from the center. They seem very content and excited about their decision.

They both are better attuned to the farm than to the city, and I see high irony in the fact that they came all the way from nearby plots of land in Germany to meet in New York City. Most of the farmers who enter the country through Castle Garden go directly to the western territories. But both of my young friends stayed in the city on arrival, at exactly the right time to meet each other within walking distance of the pier where they disembarked.

Their married life has been happy enough, living in one of those new tenement buildings on the Lower East Side and tending bar in their own basement. But now that they have a chance to return to the land and the water, I

17

can feel their excitement. The move will take them too far away for my taste (something I know you understand well), but I love the feeling that they are making their way home. Neither of them was meant to flourish among concrete and congestion.

Love,
Retta

Indeed, every generation believes they are bringing their children into the end of the world. Nothing has changed from that standpoint. And yet, they keep birthing those babies. Few actually give up hope. Magda sighs, feeling the full weight of her seafaring sons, and wondering when the next pair of boys will have to leave her. She reads on.

May 26, 1873
Dear Magda,

Another bouncing baby boy, ja? Quite the household you are establishing. Reminds me of when mine were little, all those little towheads running around the house. Congratulations!

I had a note from Catrina this morning, and they have a baby boy, too! Witt (pronounced in the English way, but I keep trying to say "Vitt" instead) was born in March — two months older than your Louis!

The last thing I want is to worry you, but I would be remiss if I did not warn you of the danger to your boys as they grow into men in Holstein right now. Please remember, if and when you want to move them safely out of Prussian reach, I am here with arms wide open, always.

Love,
Retta

Magda is still engrossed in the past when Carrie arrives home from Meldorf School for lunch. She and Timm enrolled their daughter in the spring, before they knew of August and Frederick's departure. Carrie started school the week after her brothers left. She wonders whether the changes are too much for her daughter, but in these first two weeks, adding school seems to be a helpful balm in the larger transition to a smaller family. Carrie loves her teacher, and the playful approach to learning suits her thirst for adventure. She seems to take comfort in the fact that Henry is just upstairs, and walks home with her for lunch.

"What are you doing, Mutti?" Magda looks up, a little startled to be brought back into the present by Carrie's voice. Carrie climbs up beside her mother and cuddles into her arm.

"I'm reading old letters from Tante Retta. You remember? She is my friend who lives in New York." Carrie greets Retta's name with obvious recognition.

"Does she talk about me?"

"Not in these letters. She wrote them before you were born, so you were not here to mention. But she loves you very much."

"I want to write, Mutti."

"Soon, my child, soon. Stitching teaches you letters, and you know how to write your name, don't you?"

"C-A-R-R-I-E," the child spells. "I stitched it last week."

"Smart girl," her mother says. "And I know you did a good job."

19

As they talk, they move into the kitchen, where leftover sausages need only a hot skillet to be ready for the children's lunch. As usual, Carrie brings her whole world of questions to the table. Henry folds his napkin into a tiny rabbit, while he waits to stab his wurst and make it strut across the plate to his mouth.

"Mutti, what is Frederick doing?"

"Frederick is still on the boat in the ocean. Maybe reading a book?"

"Maybe. Frederick likes books. He gave me one."

"I know he did. He's a good brother, isn't he?" Carrie nods enthusiastically. Henry settles into a rare pensive moment.

"I miss him, Mutti." Her body crumples a little.

"I know you do, sweetheart. When he and August get off the ship, they will work in Tante Retta's new candy shop in Brooklyn. Then you will be able to imagine where he is, and what he's doing. Everything will be just like it was here at home."

Chewing her sausage thoughtfully, Carrie replies. "Not just like, Mutti. Because he'll be there and we are here. We used to all be here. And that makes me feel sad."

"That's true, my child," Magda sighs. "Me, too." This child may be too precocious for her own good. She's always thinking. And as if to prove the point, Carrie goes on.

"Mutti, why is Amalia always so sad?" Carrie veers into a litany of questions often repeated since she first asked, over a year ago. "Does she cry because her Vati died?"

"Maybe," Magda answered. "But I think Amalia is having a hard time growing up, Carrie."

"Why?"

"I'm not sure, honey. She's different, I guess."

"I would cry a lot if my Vati died."

"I would, too, Carrie. We love your Vati, don't we?" Carrie nods seriously, her mind already off to other quandaries.

Carrie already knows, even at five, that her ten-year-old cousin is different from her and her brothers. Something is not quite right, not quite fair, about Amalia's life. And she will tell you so, every chance she gets. Carrie resents the way Amalia wiggles out of work and always seems able to snag both of their mothers' attention. Amalia is kind enough to Carrie, but her tears make Carrie impatient and angry, as if they are a greedy ploy to steal Mutti away from all the other children.

Carrie also senses a problem, something that pits Amalia against the wonders of the world. The older girl avoids taking action, and often fails if she tries. She feels unwell a lot, even most of the time. Nothing is ever right, everything produces complaints. Carrie doesn't understand her, and Mutti's explanations never make Amalia any easier to know. But Carrie persists in her efforts to arrange the pieces into a comprehensible picture, as she does with most things that confuse her.

Meldorf, 1883

I HOPE YOU CAN back that statement up with facts, and not some random, misplaced opinion." Magda's lips press tight after these words, and her eyes flash as she darts a glance toward her husband. The bells on the door handle ding as a customer enters the shop, interrupting their spat. Carrie whirls an impromptu dance, in her own world as the newcomer takes her sing-song voice for a greeting.

"Candy, candy, candy! Candy, candy, candy!"

"Well, aren't you the cutest little walking advertisement I've ever seen?" says the young man. "I would have to be cold-hearted to resist buying something in this shop!"

"May I help you find something?" Magda's greeting is cool, a little over-professional, no doubt a reaction to the young man's army uniform. Prussian. She stiffens, and then lets out a deliberate breath to calm herself. Speak of the devil.

"I'm going to see my girlfriend this weekend and want a gift to impress her," he says. "I understand your sweets are the finest Meldorf has to offer." Is he flirting with her? She shakes her head and maintains her aloof demeanor. She has no patience for him today, but manages a stiff smile.

"What do you have in mind?" she asks. "Does she prefer good, plain chocolates? Or perhaps you'd like a fancier option? My husband has a fine hand for decorative icing, as you can see." She sweeps her hand across the top of the glass counter that holds trays full of Timm's tiny creations. "They are very popular with the young women in town."

"I think the fancy ones. An assortment. A dozen."

"Yes, sir." She reaches behind her for a flat, lidded box and waxed tissue paper, then slides her hand under the glass lid of the counter to fill the cardboard void.

"I like that one with the lavender flowers. And that little butterfly." He directs her to particular pieces as she works, and the box quickly fills. She adds a ribbon. He looks pleased, and soon departs. She is not, and her husband is aware of the stiff tilt of her head as the soldier, oblivious to her disapproval, closes the door behind him. Carrie steals a glance in her direction.

"Mutti, can I go play? I want to play with Henry."

"Yes, dear. He and Louis were at their confirmation class at church, but they should be home by now. Careful you stay out of the road on your way."

"Alright, Mutti." Better to absorb the doting of the big brothers than to be ignored by her distracted parents.

"They are everywhere!" She sighs as the doorbell signals her child's departure. "I fail to understand how they are invisible to you."

"I see them. And of course I'm concerned. I just don't think that you have cause for panic."

"I'm not panicking. I feel . . . urgency. The soldiers are here looking for boys exactly like ours to join their

23

army. They are here to take over the resources of the land that has belonged to our ancestors for ten generations. And they are here to steal our sons to help them accomplish that mission. Our culture will undergo fundamental changes; our way of life will be gone. And for what? To line the pockets and puff up the self-importance of so-called leaders who don't care a whit for what's dear to us? I will not surrender my home to them. And certainly, I will not surrender my children."

"Magda, you are overreacting."

"I am not. The situation is gravely dangerous, and I will protect what matters to me—my freedom, my family, my homeland."

The chilly atmosphere infuses the room too thoroughly to dissipate quickly, but the absence of her daughter and the soldier ease her tension a bit. Timm reaches for his wife's hand.

"The Holstein region has weathered things like this before," Timm says. "Denmark and Prussia have been fighting over this land for years, and the battle amounts to little more than arm-wrestling over semantics. You know the routine; the addresses change on houses that remain exactly the same. We will survive the stresses again. I know you are worried about our soldier-age boys. I am too, but it sounds like even more than that. Why are you so sure the results will be tragic?"

"The raids are happening more and more often," Magda says. "Listen to the rhetoric. According to what Retta hears from her friends in Brooklyn, we are not getting nearly all of the news. But if you know what she hears, and you listen closely to the reports, you can hear the venom, the hatred.

"The fight has moved beyond a tussle over land, Timm," she goes on, "small boys wrestling for possession of a cherished toy. The fight has broadened into proclamations of good and evil. They show unbearable disrespect in speaking of us. Lies. Dehumanizing lies. This time, if we lose the land, our self-respect goes with it. The country's name has changed before, according to whose leaders have the upper hand. But they mean to take away our freedom this time, and they want to use our children to accomplish their aims."

"I don't know, Magda."

"You can discount my opinion," she retorts. "But I know what I know, deep inside me. I've been irritated at many of the officials who have volleyed our culture back and forth between them. But I have never been frightened, merely annoyed. Now, I am afraid."

Timm approaches her from behind as she stands at the counter, and cradles her body against his own. She struggles unsuccessfully to relax into him, and he persists in holding her, lightly and tenderly, a quick kiss on the wisp of hair that has escaped onto her neck.

The bell rings again, signaling a new customer's arrival. Another soldier, no doubt eager to please another girlfriend. This time Timm breaks away to assist, and Magda turns to restoring toppled boxes to order. A tray of molded butterflies, freshly swirled in pastel icing, goes under glass for display. But no matter how fanciful and delicious, these chocolates won't do young lovers any good. Chocolate absorbs too much of the angst of their makers for these candies to nurture joy today.

When the sun begins to fade from the sky, Magda leaves Timm to close the store and turns toward home. With five children—well, now three at home — and a husband to feed, she busies herself in the kitchen every day of the week. Tonight, she has the additional pressure of guests. Timm's sister-in-law and her brood will double the number of chairs around the table.

Time is short and the schnitzel is not going to make itself, so she calls Carrie to help. Strong-minded and capable, the child is infinitely helpful when she chooses to be. She arranges the flatware and napkins on the table in short order. When she finishes in the dining room, she moves into the kitchen and sets up a station near her mother to peel the potatoes. She feels helpful tonight, even serene, for now. Having the cousins to visit always brings out the competitive part of her nature, and sometimes leads her spirits to tumble into a tough ending.

An hour later, when her cousins arrive, Carrie's fragile contentment indeed fractures almost immediately to dust. Carrie suffers constant indignity over the amount of work that falls to her as the girl after four brothers. Her cousins, especially Amalia, increase that animosity ten-fold. Tonight proves the rule rather than the exception. Mutti knows Amalia's tendency toward helplessness irks her own daughter, and deliberately solicits Amalia's help on arrival.

"Amalia, Carrie has already set the table. Will you add glasses and water pitchers, please? They're on the shelf, here in the kitchen." Amalia picks up three glasses right away and takes them to the table, then hauls two pitchers to the sink and turns on the spigot to fill them.

Carrie shrugs and turns back to the potatoes. *Huh,* she thinks. *Maybe she's actually going to do a chore tonight.* Twenty minutes later, the potatoes are boiled and ready to drain and mash, but the two water pitchers are in the way, still in the sink.

"Frederick?!" Carrie calls out. She hears footsteps. "Frederick? Oh, Louis, it's you. I can't lift the pitchers. Will you put them on the table?"

"Of course, little sister!" Louis looks at her strangely, but promptly displays his bulking muscle by lifting both pitchers at once into their proper place. When he has also lifted the potatoes to the sink to drain, Carrie adds milk and salt, and expertly transforms them into mash. She adds a dollop of butter, stirs once more, and heads to the table, bowl in hand, ahead of her mother.

Three water glasses sit at one end of the table.

On an ordinary day, Carrie would squirm, but she would finish the work that falls to her by default. Both of her parents are hard workers, and their ethic prompts Carrie to follow suit. Today is different for some reason she can't explain. Her irritation with Amalia, her mother's tension, her father's deafness to her mother's fear, the overwhelming number of people in the house, she cannot narrow the knot in her swirling stomach to one cause.

And then she realizes, she assumed the footsteps belonged to Frederick, but Frederick is still gone. She becomes unmoored. Her body buzzes with the noise of a thousand soldiers marching through her blood. She dashes to the other end of the house seeking escape, hiding her blond curls under a blanket to scream into the pillow on her bed. She resolves to remain there, forever away from the cousin who antagonizes her very soul. But she is hungry, so she slouches back to the table when her mother sings out "Dinner!" The inevitable looms large, and the day ends more badly than anyone would think to predict.

After dinner, Mutti issues another invitation:

"Amalia and Henry, will you please help me remove the dirty dishes from the table?" They move to comply, Mutti right behind Amalia to keep her working. True to form, as soon as Mutti steps back into the kitchen, Amalia halts her efforts. She looks at the dishes piled in her hands as if she has forgotten what she is supposed to be doing. Just then, Carrie pivots to return to her bed, and very nearly crashes into her statue of a cousin. They narrowly miss ending up in a pile of broken china and skewed flatware on the floor. Carrie strains with the effort of keeping her temper contained.

Henry picks that moment to turn the chore into a game. Normally, his antics would pitch Carrie headlong into hilarity and dissolve all the tension in the room. Having deposited his stack of dishes in the kitchen sink, he returns to the dining room. He moves stealthily around the table in a circle wide enough to avoid detection. Rounding a chair where her back is turned to him, still restraining her desire to choke Amalia, he sneaks up behind her and gooses her in the sides, just below her arm pits. She jumps a good six inches into the air and stiffens like a thick rope suddenly jerked taut. He dissolves into laughter. She turns on her playmate in fury.

"Henry! Stop it! I hate you! Poking and laughing and laughing and poking! Don't ever touch me again! I hate you!" Carrie stamps her foot hard enough to rattle the dishes on the sideboard, then narrowly skirts her mother, who rounds the far corner with a large platter in hand. In another near miss to the family china, Carrie whirls around to continue a wail that, once begun, shows no sign of abatement.

"And Amalia doesn't finish her chores, and the boys leave me to do all the work in the whole house! And Frederick completely leaves me and never comes back! And then Henry laughs at me! And no one ever does anything about any of it. I hate you! I hate you all!" She spins around and heads for the door. Her father, hearing the commotion, sticks his head into the room to help. He scoops her up into his arms in a grand gesture of rescue. A family-wide roar of laughter at her dramatic aborted escape cuts the tension of the moment, for everyone except the star of the show.

Carrie's diminutive ire, born of sadness and dismissed by laughter, continues to grow. She struggles against her father's strength with furious displeasure, as if doubly determined to go her own way. She wiggles around to free her pudgy legs from her father's embrace, and kicks in blind wrath. Her feet narrowly miss her brother's head. She screams her indignity into her father's chest while he expertly wrestles her fiery ball of outrage to safety. And then in an instant, overwhelmed by a sensation of unwilling surrender, she collapses in defeat. She clings to her Vati as if he, too, will soon desert her and fade into the growing darkness of night.

Brooklyn, 1883

NEARLY SIX WEEKS AFTER the boys embark on their journey to New York, Magda finally receives a note from Retta. She confirms that August and Frederick are safely ashore and settling into an apartment with Peter above the new Columbia Street store. The details are harrowing, and Magda pales at the mishaps that mark their arrival. She imagines August's stoic face, mimicking calm, masking a core more cautious than his freewheeling brothers, and more afraid. Frederick, genuinely strong and steady, and the braver of the two, approaches the seafaring adventure with humor and grace. *So of course,* Magda thinks, *August is the one who suffers misadventure at the Port of New York.* She re-reads Retta's letter, and shudders again.

August disembarks at Castle Garden, the immigrant service center at the port. He and his brother exit the ship together. Choosing the shortest lines, they wait their turns to speak with agents at opposite ends of a long wooden counter. The high windows admit clear, natural light that is a welcome relief after two weeks below deck.

At the far end of the counter, Frederick presents his papers, receives half a dozen rubber stamped approvals from the agent, and glances over to see his brother step to the front of the line. The prospect of getting his first glimpse of the streets of the self-proclaimed land of plenty draws him out of the building toward his new home. He turns from his brother and steps into his new life. He and Peter Maasen, Retta's eldest, wait in vain for August to appear.

Inside, August discovers that he is missing one of the papers he needs to enter the United States. His brother is long out of sight. He moves to one side as requested, and waits for the agent's supervisor to arrive and explain what happens next. He shifts from one leg to the other, clutching his small bag and hoping that Frederick retrieves their shared steamer trunk.

What little courage he can muster fades out of him as he watches other passengers from steerage pass through the entry process without a problem. He trembles when he sees two of his bunkmates returned to the ship, and wonders what horrors they will face on the order of Prime Minister Bismarck and his terror machine back home.

Finally, after three nights of falling asleep in detention quarters, the last piece of the paper puzzle falls into place and he is called for final processing. He almost dares to breathe again, but his stomach still clutches around the icy knowledge of how close he came to being sent back to Meldorf.

August finally emerges from Castle Garden among hundreds of newly arrived travelers and those who are here to meet them. He realizes that the Maasens no longer have any idea when to expect him. Completing the chaos, he also sees that the written description of Peter is far too vague for him to identify this man he has never met. "Tall, fair, slender, with eyeglasses" could describe almost any man in the crowd. *I hope*, August thinks, *that Frederick will come, too, so we can identify each other.*

When no familiar person appears, August wanders the streets near the pier and finds a spot to curl up for the night. He returns by morning to the entrance of the pier in search of his brother. At twenty-one, his brain grasps that he is a grown man in possession of the skills to find his way through the city and meet his own needs. His gut doubts that truth. He coaches himself to have courage, to buck up in the face of this adversity, but he crumbles in his introduction to this new world. Through a supreme surge of bravery, he manages to remember that yes, he has a few coins to buy food, because no, he cannot wander far enough to find an orchard from which to grab a ripe pear, as he could back home. Not in New York City.

Only when he finds Frederick at the pier on the fourth morning in town does he allow himself to fully grasp his own terror. He fights back tears at the sight of his brother, then gives in, dissolving into the sidewalk. The introduction to Peter Maasen lacks the manly swagger he would prefer.

With newly dried eyes and the accompaniment of Frederick's teasing chuckle, they make their way to Peter's apartment. Frederick opens the trunk where their belongings are stashed. They are living in a corner of the living room, with little space for extra furniture beyond the narrow cots on which they sleep at night and stow during the day. The trunk functions as closet, chest of drawers, and bedside table, all at once. Frederick pulls out a parcel wrapped in brown paper, and hands it to August.

"I found this package tucked into our trunk when I began to arrange our things," he says to his brother. "I know we don't have much space, but let's unwrap it and find a place where we can see the inspiration. We could both use the reminder that everything eventually turns upright and helps us grow. Here, read the note."

> Dear Frederick,
> I made this for you.
> I know you like the saying.
> I love the book you gave me.
> I want to write a book.
> Mutti wants me to learn to
> sew, so I don't have time.
> I hope you like my sewing.
> Love,
> Carrie

Wrapped inside, he finds a slip of white linen, embroidered in green thread to spell the words "*Mehr Licht.*"

"'More light?'" August asks. "What did you give her for her birthday?"

"A copy of *Goethe's Correspondence with a Child*. Goethe wrote to Bettina von Armim when she was a girl, and she published the letters last winter. I had to save every penny to acquire a copy, but Carrie's smile was worth the trouble. Her face lit up a million shades of sparkle when she opened the package. She knows I love books, and now she has one of her own."

"But Carrie can barely read. Goethe? Really?"

Frederick shrugs. "She's bright. What better place to start?" He laughs, then becomes serious. "But really, I didn't know whether I would be at home for the next gift-giving occasion, so I went ahead and gave it to her early. Turns out I was right."

"Is the saying a quote from the book? If so, we must have a little genius back home! I've never known a five-year-old to quote Goethe."

"We do. But no, I doubt she has already reached the point of citing sources. She's five. The quote comes from a story I told her when she asked about Goethe. Supposedly, on his deathbed, he cried out, '*Mehr Licht!* Open the windows and give me More Light!' I told her that even in the last few minutes of his life, he wanted to understand more and more of the world, and she should use her mind and heart to do the same."

"Impressive conversation for a five-year-old. I can't seem to see the light on my path even at twenty-one."

"Indeed," Frederick says, suppressing a smile. "When Mutti made Carrie learn embroidery, she evidently decided on Goethe rather than flowers and alphabets."

He sets out the little piece of fabric, wrapped around a shim of wood and tacked with tiny nails, to occupy a place of honor on top of the trunk. And there the treasure stands during the entire time they are in their first, borrowed home in America. A haunting plea for growth and understanding, imperfect letters and lumps in the fabric where the knots line the underside: *Mehr Licht!*

August arrives at work the very next morning, ready to take orders from his Tante Retta. He never thinks to wonder why he didn't try to get a room by the pier, or why he didn't seek out a ferry to Brooklyn. He never stops to consider that his mother might like to learn of his safety. He stays in constant motion, almost devoid of sight. The letter from Tante Retta attempts reassurance but Magda knows Retta too well, and reads the veiled worry between her words.

In spite of the rough start, both brothers swiftly find their way, integrating themselves into the business and weaving themselves into the new configuration of family they all are creating together. They are always first to hear any news that later reaches Meldorf, and unfailingly included in every Maasen family event.

For a stretch of years after August and Frederick join the Brooklyn business, a new shop opens every spring, usually at the beginning of ice cream season. The original Maasen's Confectionery still stands on Atlantic Street, of course. But the Denzler's contributions so please Tante Retta that each successive store opens as Maasen & Denzler Confections, one on 5th Street, another on Pacific, one on Manhattan, and one on either end of Smith, rising to prominence as the premier confectionery in the borough. They concentrate on what Retta calls their "new basics," far beyond the artisan chocolates produced at the Meldorf store, but always within the scope of what they can do well.

Hard candies in apothecary jars line the shelves like a rainbow of jewels wrapped in cellophane, mimicking an edible church window. Gleaming counters and cabinets run the length of the showroom, alternating between marble work surfaces and transparent cases to show off specialty chocolates: seasonal designs and molds, nut clusters and caramels, dainty replicas of seashells and maraschino mice. Long lines of customers snake through the store to the back counter, where delicacies like sparkling sugar Easter eggs or Christmas marzipan are on sale in limited seasons. Grandparents stop to visit with grandchildren in tow, noisy youth congregate after school. Beaus find beautiful gifts for their loves. Maasen & Denzler's runs on love and chocolate.

And of course, the shops expand into one of America's favorite treats. Each morning throughout the hot summer months, the mothers and aunts who inhabit the shops make eggy custard, set it to cool in large metal bowls on ice, then pour it into giant tin cans. The fathers and uncles insert paddles into the mixture and nestle the cans into salted ice in small wooden barrels. The littlest children sit on top of the whole contraption as weights, while the biggest kids turn and turn and turn the cranks that rotate the paddles inside the cans.

Soon the middle-sized kids serve up creamy batches of ice cream, a single scoop at a time in a paper cone with a tiny wooden paddle of a spoon. The first batch never stretches to the end of the long line of customers eager to put down their pennies in exchange for a taste of the heavenly treat, so a second batch always follows close behind.

"We have to keep having babies in this family!" Retta is only half-joking when she says such things. "We have to produce enough little weights and strong arms to keep up with customer demand for ice cream!" When the lines spill out the door and onto the sidewalk, they spend the profits on more churns and hire neighborhood children to fill in the gaps. When the lines dwindle by even a few people, they revive interest by inventing new flavors. Melting German chocolate into the custard, or mashing fresh fruit from the farms outside the city, even stirring in the nuts and caramels left over from more conventional candies, all enliven the offerings. The variety increases the demand for the cool, sweet treat on the hot streets of the city in July.

The news from back home is not as sweet. The army comes around the house again, surveying the premises for new soldiers. When they find August missing, they issue charges for failure to appear for military duty, and threaten the same for Frederick if he is still absent at their next visit. The gaze that falls on Louis terrifies Magda beyond words. They ask his age more than once, as if to catch him in a lie.

That same night, she takes down the jar of cash they keep on the top shelf in the kitchen. Timm counts the money set aside for steamship fares for Louis and Henry. Together, they decide what they can sacrifice so the two younger boys can sail sooner than they had planned. Louis will not escape the soldiers' next visit. And Henry, with his wild streak, fearless voice, and love of the sea, always catches the attention of those who would force him into a mold of conformity. Even worse, if Bismarck's lackeys have a naval division, she can imagine him an eager volunteer for life on the sea. She shudders. Life eludes predictability.

Weeks turn into months and then into quick years, and they all ride the wave of adventure that joins them together across a treacherous sea. Back in Meldorf,

Carrie sometimes forgets about Frederick for an hour or two at a time. When she thinks of him in daylight, she laughs to remember tangling their kite string and chasing his shadow at the shore. When she says her prayers at night, a tear or two still escapes down her cheek.

But in the light of the afternoon, she smiles to remember his teasing, and recalls the times he spun out chocolate monsters at the shop in place of iced butterflies and flowers. The memories sustain her, and she fully embraces the wonders around her. Frederick remains her absent rock. But Henry is here, and he becomes her fullest joy.

Meldorf, 1887

ARE YOU READY to ride?" Henry reminds Carrie they have an excursion planned for the morning. Now ten, she has moved up two sizes in the family bicycle collection in the past year, and has gained so much height on her slender frame that she might be riding yet another size by the end of the summer. Her lengthening arms and legs transform her from a tot into a school-girl who looks like a full-fledged member of the family.

"Am I ever!" Carrie's enthusiastic reply brings a smile to Henry's eyes and a shout to his lips.

"Then let's go! We're wasting time!" And with that rally cry, Henry and Carrie jump on their bikes, his red and hers black, and take off to terrorize the good citizens of Meldorf. Her hair flies out behind her like a bridal veil, and his strong shoulders bake to a rich umber in the dwindling heat of the autumn sun. They bump along on the cobblestones, dodging pedestrians among the aging houses and businesses. Life is good. They are together as always. Today, they will end up at the shore for a picnic lunch that Carrie packed and Henry carries in a pouch across his chest. First, however, they head over to the store to tell their parents they are leaving.

"What is on your agenda today?" Vati asks, his question more from due diligence of ordinary parenting than from any specific concern. He and Mutti are more frightened for Louis, a near adult with broadening shoulders, the hair over his lip growing from peach fuzz into actual whiskers. They see the attention he attracts from soldiers in search of recruits. But Henry and Carrie are still clearly children, however gangly their limbs.

"We're taking a picnic to the beach," Henry says, "but on the way we are going to see the new building site in town. Louis says that it is huge!"

"Well, be careful and watch after your sister," Mutti chimes in. "And remember you need to help in the shop this afternoon, so don't be gone too long."

Carrie rolls her eyes and scoffs at the insinuation that she can't take care of herself. In her mind she can do anything Henry can do, and more. Henry winks at her and motions toward the door, grabbing a couple of conciliatory toffees on the way out. Soon they are rolling again, their schemes binding them together as thick as the honey on the combs out in the fields.

Their next stop is a new shop two streets over from the confectionary, where builders race against time to construct a rare new house right in the center of the village. The family who owns the property plans to live above the shop, as more and more people do these days. The new trend, imported from New York, is for business-owners to have dedicated work space attached below their homes. The confectionary, by contrast, rents space from the lawyer who occupies a large office above the shop.

The children prove Louis correct; the gigantic new construction stretches a full story, plus an attic level, higher than the surrounding two-story structures on the street. The owner is a barber. The family also plans a much-needed food market in the space. The builders work long days, hoping the residents can settle in before any snow flies. A wooden frame towers over the street, still open to the ground below. Henry and Carrie exchange a glance and a quick nod. The spot is perfect. They will be back when the builders' day has ended.

Carrie, of course, matures with the years. Nearly eleven, she stands tall and slender like her brothers. She wins prizes for her work in school, and still prefers adventure to housework or chocolates. Babies have been popping out like an epidemic in the neighborhood. She could escape the candy shop and earn a good living by babysitting like other girls her age, but she has little interest, especially if Henry tempts her with his latest flight of imagination.

When chores around the house become inconvenient for her, she borrows some tricks from her cousin Amalia. She seldom actually rebels anymore. If she objects to Mutti's request to plate the cookies or mind the visiting neighbor's baby, she simply slips out of the house without a word.

Carrie spends much of her time absorbed in books, preferring stories in equal balance with biographies of interesting lives. She keeps a journal in a safe place that she and Henry alone know, her words alternating between deep thoughts and the mundane events of her life. She and her family tolerate hard wooden pews and relish the sound of Bach on the organ as they worship in the local Lutheran cathedral. She sinks to her knees

41

beside her bed each night to quickly bless loved ones near and far.

She is a competent cook, can acquire groceries within a budget, and recognizes dirt on the floor or grime on the stove when she sees it. If temporarily undistracted by the hope of adventure, she might even clean the offending area without being asked. Occasionally, she stows her more forthright thoughts in a bubble in her head, instead of putting them all out into the universe. Nearing the tilting point from girlhood into young womanhood, Carrie gains the skills, if not the taste, for the traditional role of a woman.

She also reminds everyone regularly what she thinks of social convention. Today, forced to don a long cotton dress while her brother wears a shirt and trousers, she makes do by pulling on a pair of his short pants under her loose skirt. When she needs her legs free to pedal the bicycle, she simply billows the skirt around her waist and uses an old necktie to bind it out of the way. The neighbors will shake their heads, but she can avoid her clothing impediments in this fanciful garb. The wardrobe choice also works well for wading, in which she and her brother are sure to engage.

And so, with their lunch and their fishing gear, Carrie and Henry head out into the world, no thought in their heads for any day except today.

Five miles later, after dodging the ever-present soft sides of the road, Carrie and Henry abandon their bicycles in the grass approaching the sea. A random sheep sniffs out lunch among the grasses and wildflowers. Henry runs toward the ewe as she grazes, thinking to chase her. She raises her head and bleats at him, then returns to her meal. The children roll their own lunch out on a rock next to the water, downing the dark bread and cheese as if they had not eaten in days.

With everyone fed, they tackle the real business of the day. Each of them baits a hook with a bit of mackerel belly stashed away from last night's dinner, pitches a line into the water, and waits.

"It's late in the day for fishing, but you never know," says Henry, "maybe we'll get lucky."

"What do we hope to catch?" Carrie asks. "More stinky mackerel?"

"Maybe. Or cod, or bass. Something that Mutti can cook up for dinner."

"*Ja*, you know who will have to help with that," Carrie says. "I like catching them better than cooking them. But at least I get to trim off some raw belly for the next day's catch."

"You're pretty handy to have around, you know that?"

"I most certainly am, and don't you forget it, brother!" She punches him square on the arm.

"Yow! Now stop that. You're scaring the fish!"

Even as their fun subsides, however, they find few fish interested in what they have to offer. A couple of nibbles, some bait lost to the sea, but nothing ready for reeling in. They use up the raw fish to no avail, and move on to catching minnows in their bare hands.

"You want me to hook it for you?" Henry asks.

"I should say not!" Carrie replies. "I am as capable of spearing live fishes as I am dead chunks."

"Nothing squeamish about you. I should have known better than to ask."

"Yes, you should know better." Carrie says. "It's bad enough that Mutti is always trying to make me act like a girl. You don't have to join her."

"Yes, ma'am!" He salutes her.

"That's better. Now, have we given up on the fish yet?"

"I think it's time," he says. "I brought a ball. Run twenty-five paces!"

Each of them runs, then turns toward the other to throw and catch the ball until they collapse exhausted on the grassy expanse where the bicycles rest.

"This day has been the best!" Carrie says. "I could live my whole life biking and fishing and having lunch on the rocks. Listening to the water and breathing the scent of the flowers. Perfect."

"The best," echoes Henry. "And we're not done yet." He winks as they straddle their bikes.

Late that afternoon, when Carrie should be helping with dinner, she and Henry steal away to spend the sunset hour on the construction lot, emptied of workers for the day. The frame casts eerie shadows on the ground below. Henry begins to climb, Carrie close behind.

"We will capture the ship together," Henry proclaims, "and sail the blue oceans singing sea chanties and braving the tumble of the highest waves."

"We will say 'ahoy, mate,' and eat fish we catch in our bare hands!" Carrie echoes her brother's excitement.

"We will leave grown-ups behind," Henry goes on, "and play all day long. No chores, no studies, no long boring lectures about good behavior."

They reach the top of the building and stake their claim on its decks. They leap from beam to beam, as lithe as cats unconcerned for their own safety.

"Hein-ry! Wait, Hein-ry!" Henry, not even inclined to slow, much less stop, declines the request.

"You come on!" he yells in return. He makes her move faster and higher and lighter than she ever moved before, a thrilling quest for new freedom not often open to girls of her age.

Henry and Carrie attempt to sneak in through the pungent aroma of sausage and sauerkraut on their return home. But they drip with sweat and buzz with energy too bold to escape their mother's notice.

"Um-hmm. And where have you been, little miss? You are filthy dirty and I had to finish your dinner chores. You know how to act like a lady."

"But I am not a lady, Mutti. I am a pirate! I will save you from the robber barons!"

"You will do no such thing." Magda rolls her eyes as she speaks. "You are too old for such foolishness. Clean up and get to the table."

"You don't fuss at Henry when he wants adventures." The words pour forth past an uncharacteristic pout. "I like adventures, too. Why do you fuss at me?"

"Adventure for my girl involves dinner and dishes, not soiled clothes and sneaking through the streets to spy on the world. I need you to help me." Magda's body underlines the simple statement. Though sturdy and energetic, she is heavy with the round, weary evidence of another baby on the way.

"But—"

"No 'but.' I love that you and Henry enjoy each other, but his life is not right for a girl. Wash up and help me get dinner on the table."

"But Amalia doesn't—"

"No 'buts.' I need you to finish your job."

Carrie knows better, when her mother's mouth makes that line, than to reveal even a kernel of her spiciness. So, she hides behind the mask of a stilled body as her heart flounces from the room. She has no idea how much more will arise that she will need to protest.

Meldorf, 1890

THE DAYS OF CHILDHOOD roll past, and while Carrie still notices the occasional surge of soldiers through the street, they no longer inspire the uneasiness she used to feel at seeing them. Henry teaches her protective strategies, by playing at soldiers herself, that work for her in real life as well as in play. Stick and stocking cap become bayonet and helmet, and the two of them outwit the enemy by stalking unseen battalions on the streets of Meldorf and bursting from doorways to surprise unwitting slackers on the battle field. Their secret codes allow all manner of conversation, concealed both from their enemies and their parents, who hide their smiles at how well the two children get along.

To the parents, their play is only games. For the children, those games mimic survival training for the conflicts that rage all around them. As long as they are playing, danger cannot touch them. Comrades in arms, they regularly pledge undying loyalty to each other, always to be together, always to guard the other's back.

Clutching her beer bottle spyglass, Carrie surges on the enemy, hurling imaginary rocks to pelt them into oblivion and eliminate their threat. The memory of Frederick running with her kite evaporates like steam into the breeze. Joy abounds in the magical universe the near-twins create. They dismiss the dangers of the adult world as lack of imagination. The pair is inseparable.

The ordinary business of life marches through the streets around them, where dangers are less imaginary. For a few weeks in her eleventh year, Carrie finds herself doing all the chores at home. Mutti spends her time in bed, and Louis minds the chocolates while Vati worries over Mutti.

Carrie quivers at the look on her father's face while her mother drifts in and out of consciousness. Her usual grievances retreat into the shadows of her worry. After a brief season of bloody sheets and daily visits from the village doctor, Carrie learns that she will not have a new baby brother or sister after all. She at least has the good grace to feel guilty for being relieved, and does not complain about the increased burden of chores.

One evening, as Carrie peels carrots for dinner, working side by side with her newly risen mother, she finds herself remembering how much Frederick loves the brightly hued vegetable. She wonders if he still calls carrots the paintbrush among the winter doldrums, and looks forward like a giddy child to the carrot harvest from the summer garden. Suddenly she realizes that she hardly even thinks about her oldest brothers anymore, except in her darkened room, where she prays at night before she drifts off to sleep. The thought saddens her. Even so, she enjoys a rare serenity unknown since before she entered kindergarten. She has remade her world around their absence. She still thinks of them fondly, but her life feels steady and complete. She sighs deeply, a picture of recovered contentment.

Serenity melts into astonishment, however, when Vati approaches her that very night. He seeks to prepare her for changes still ahead, bearing down like rabid dogs. He has no time to waste. "The soldiers," he announces, "are coming to take your brother."

She freezes, dumbfounded.

"Henry?"

"Louis. And yes, eventually, Henry, too. We have to help them leave, to keep them safe."

"But I know how to fight soldiers. Henry taught me." Even she finds her assertion ridiculous. And yet imagination is all she has to protect her heart. Nonsense. This moment uncovers all the nonsense in her life: the connection that she requires from those she loves best; the deep, rich play that feeds her soul like fertile soil; the notion that she can reject motherhood and the womanly arts in favor of adventure. Her life is complete nonsense. And the nonsense never ends.

"He taught you how to fight pretend soldiers. Real soldiers are different."

"But he can't leave."

"I know. Your Mutti and I don't want him to go, either. But we are the parents, and it's our job to keep him as safe as we can."

"No, I mean Henry *can't* leave. I will die without him."

Carrie falls silent as Timm waits. And waits. She eventually crawls up into his lap, something she has not done since she was a little girl. He opens his arms, and waits some more. Sometime later, Magda calls them to dinner, and they go. Carrie still does not speak a word.

At ages even younger than their brothers, Henry at thirteen and Louis at fifteen prepare to retrace the route to Hamburg that swallowed their older brothers. They will board the next ship to the United States. Hastily packed, they leave behind things they mean to take, and take a few things for which they have no use. Their mother is unconcerned with their packing. She focuses on the need to avoid August's paperwork misad-ventures, which haunt her anew as she prepares to send the younger boys to their new home.

With all of Mutti's focus on legalities, Carrie finds herself free to wander, free to wonder what gift she can slip into Henry's bag that will bind him to her forever. She comes up empty. He will be gone, and she will not be there, no matter what she does. And so, unable to reach decisions in matters over which she has no say, she removes herself to the role of silent observer.

Louis, the rule keeper in the family, has the hardest time of any of the brothers leaving Meldorf. Where August was old enough to understand the argument for leaving, and Frederick was willing to trust his parents, Louis has neither clarity nor a steadfast model. He hears his parents' fear; he even understands and accepts their misgivings. But calling out above their words, he hears the loud claim of the soldiers that his duty lies in fighting for Prussia.

Louis packs, but he remains fretful. He cannot see what his parents see, their hesitation to risk his life to fight against himself, against his own self-respect, against the vile and childish grabs for their home. He teeters on the miserable border between duty to family and duty to country. Carrie cannot even try to help him. She has her own tightly twisted affections to keep her occupied.

Henry, the youngest of the brothers, is the true explorer of the family. He has salt water in his veins. Generations of sea-adjacent living coalesces in one thirteen-year-old body, one childlike soul stretching toward adulthood. He can't help himself. The same wind that lifts the kites on the beach at Meldorf ruffles his hair with restlessness for foreign shores. He packs in a flurry of excitement, looking only forward towards adventure.

Carrie watches Henry as he leaves her, day by day, long before he ever boards the ship. Helpless to catch his attention in any significant way, she knows he looks only toward the wildly exciting future before him. The craving for adventure that he and Carrie share suddenly collapses into play. Henry gets to go and live the life they've dreamed of, and she will no longer be a part of it. Oh, he still proclaims all for one and one for all. He still pledges they will be together forever. But here is the point where their paths diverge. She knows. And something in her breaks.

Once aboard, Henry quickly befriends half the emigrant population of the ship, and would no doubt win over the nobility upstairs if he could get to them. The slap of the waves on the side of the ship provides both pure enervation and lullaby to Henry's being. The sea calls his name, and nothing can prevail against it, least of all the voice of his brother.

Nothing improves for Louis when he stows his pangs of conscience in steerage with his luggage. Balancing a bowl of indeterminate mush on a lap made hazardous by the ship's unpredictable rocking, his gut is in an uproar. The challenge of holding on to one's stomach without the aid of a steady horizon increases the level of difficulty. And then there is the matter of his brother.

"What are you talking about? You can't go off on your own into a strange city! You are only thirteen!"

"Yes, I can," Henry says. "If I stay on the ship and sail on through to the port at Hoboken, I can go directly to the naval yard and get a job."

"No, you can't!" Louis' dander rises. "You are too young. I told mom I would watch after you, so you have to go ashore at New York Harbor!"

"My new friend Wilhelm — uh, William — and I are going together. We can look after each other. Besides, if I'm old enough to be running from Bismarck's army, I'm old enough to support the navy in my new home."

"But Mutti told me to — "

"No disrespect to Mutti, but she's not here. And you can't make me." Henry's eyes sparkle, knowing both that he has the upper hand in the conversation and that disobedience drives his brother to distraction. "I now have the freedom to do as I want, and I want to sail the seas. I won't go in a boat to a new home; I want a boat to be my new home."

Louis flushes shades of scarlet rage. All the numbskulls on the briny, and this one has to be his brother. His mother will be furious. And what will he tell Carrie? Louis gets off the boat in New York Harbor, his fear for his brother battling against his desperation to be off the ship. Where Henry is concerned, Louis is defeated.

Henry remains steadfast in his refusal to bend to expectation. He dismisses his brother in New York with a wave of his hand and a nearly imperceptible lift of his chin. True to his word, he sails right past the impressive New York City skyline to disembark in Hoboken. Once off the ship, the rebel pirate slips between the sails. He darts in and out of the lives of his relatives, who never know if or when he will appear. Allergic to roots, he prefers motion, the rolling stone in a concrete family. Life on the sea is the only life for Henry!

Louis readily transfers his dutiful energy to Maasen & Denzler Confections, engaging in a barrage of sweet-making that honors his mother's wishes for life in the new world. If he retains any loyalty to Prussia, no one sees the effects. He joins the other brothers in the apartment above the Columbia Street store. He pens a letter to Mutti as soon as his bag is empty.

Not even a note arrives in the post from Henry. And Tante Retta can send little news from the tidbits she so seldom receives. Carrie spends her afternoons writing daily epistles addressed to the brothers' apartment. She posts huge packets each week, which is as often as her parents will buy postage stamps. She never receives any indication that Henry reads them. When Carrie gets no response, she closes her salty eyes against nausea and despair. She does not want to be here any longer. She does not want to be anywhere that Henry is not.

Carrie returns to school eerily devoid of interest in her studies. For six years of school, she has never suffered a teacher's reprimand for anything beyond her daydreaming. Now, she knows that her teachers call on her parents at the store to discuss their concerns. The silent treatment, for adults and peers alike, spreads from home into the classroom. She stares at the clock every afternoon, wondering when she can go home, or when she has to go home. She really doesn't like either place. Her work becomes wildly inconsistent, her handwriting sloppy and spelling atrocious. Sums she has known since kindergarten suddenly disappear from her brain. She submits her papers wrinkled, or, more often, not turned in at all.

At home, Carrie dissolves in tears every morning, inconsolable at waking to Henry's absence. She mopes like a grieving slug around the edges of the house and lashes out over the slightest word of concern. Her room clutters with so much trash that Magda eventually gives up nagging and cleans the mess herself. Fortunately, a smaller family reduces the cooking, because Magda also handles every meal alone. Carrie sees the worry in her mother's eyes, knows the anguish she is causing, but she cannot help herself. And her mother cannot help her.

Carrie hears Mutti and Vati talking in the night, again and again, when they think she is asleep. Her parents' voices are easy to distinguish amid the creaks and groans of a dark house too quiet without the boys.

"I'm really worried about her, Timm. She honestly believes she cannot live in his absence. I shudder to think what she could do. I watch how your niece struggles, your sister-in-law always fearing she will harm herself, and I cannot imagine that life for us, especially for Carrie."

"But will giving into her antics save her," asks Timm, "or teach her to use emotional blackmail against us? Amalia has no emotional resilience, that is true, but I think my brother and sister-in-law helped create that monster. We are Carrie's parents. The consequences for giving in can be just as devastating as the consequences for holding the line." Clearly, Timm and Magda have had this same conversation before.

Magda shakes her head. "Carrie is more independent than Amalia ever has been. I think she knows what she needs, and we would help her best by honoring that knowledge."

"That's a lot of trust to put in an eleven-year-old."

"But we're not going to live forever, Timm. Isn't the child better off supervised by her brothers in a place of opportunity than stuck here in Meldorf where she could wither without hope? Rather than leave her alone, we have a chance to secure her future in the company of people who love her."

"Maybe you are right. But she is so young to set out alone."

"The youngest departure of them all." Magda's voice is full of tears as she speaks. "I don't think I can let her go."

And Carrie bites her lip as she thinks to herself, *Oh, yes, you can. And I'll see that you do.*

Meldorf, 1891

CARRIE STANDS FIRM for a full year of shenanigans before her mother gives in. She is twelve when her break comes, directly on the cusp between childhood and adulthood. Her mother repeatedly proclaims her too young to be away from home. But Carrie mounts a formidable campaign to join Henry's adventure. The battle volleys back and forth between the child and her parents, escalating into outright hostility as Carrie's usual quiet withdrawal becomes raw rebellion. Ordinary childish angst reaches new heights in the form of assault on every requirement of the home. She renders life unbearable in the Denzler household. Carrie's determination will see that she gets her way. Magda holds firm for a long while. But finally, in glorious victory, Carrie's steely, unalterable persistence prevails. She will reunite with her brothers. The deciding factor for enacting travel plans comes, predictably, as a letter from Tante Retta:

October 3, 1891
Dear Magda,

One of my customers tells me about a shipping company that reminds me of Carrie and your predicament regarding the safety of a child traveling alone. The Holland Amerika Lijn sails out of Rotterdam, which I know is a further journey from

Meldorf, but the benefits sound worth the trouble.
They provide some extra services that could make you
feel better about launching your baby girl into the
world . . ."

Shaking off inertia as she reads, Magda speaks with her husband, and then calls her daughter into the room.

"How would you like to go to New York to see Henry?" At the question, Carrie's mouth drops open in speechless shock. Although she knows the conversation has been happening in the background, she has never been included in the talk. Gaping disbelief is her first reaction to the question. Her second reaction is a burst of joy she has not experienced since the last ship sailed. She answers, of course, with a raucously enthusiastic "YES!"

The ship sails in four weeks, so they begin preparations right away. Carrie will carry her mother's own bags, one hefty leather with buckles, the other sturdy fabric with a loop to secure everyday needs over her shoulder. Most of their nonessential household goods have been sold to pay for passage, so she needs little space to pack. As the days fly on, they gradually broach the unspoken truth together. Like the boys, fleeing for their lives from the repressive regime, Carrie will not return to Meldorf.

She finds a thousand tiny ways to say good-bye. She swipes one of the boys' old bicycles from the shed and spins her golden hair into a frenzy racing through town. She pedals past the old pirate ship, construction now complete. She sits in church, listening to Bach as if his liquid tones exist only there, and nowhere else in the world. She waves at the old brick school and writes a thank-you note to her beloved teacher.

Hoping against hope that she might continue school in her new world, she stuffs her small library amid the clothes and girlish trinkets in her mother's leather bag. She pedals off to the shore to enjoy one last Meldorf breeze in her face, the taste of salt on her lips. She loves her home, but she loves her brother more. She is ready almost before she begins to pack.

"Do you think Henry would like some candies from the shop?" Carrie can taste her eagerness for sweet reunion, and it suits her palate. Magda smiles. Henry, and the rest of the brothers, have access to enough candy to make their bellies ache. But Carrie wants to take him something from home, and picks the family treasure.

"I'm sure he would love a sweet treat," Magda says, laughing. "But don't load your bags with presents. You also need to take your clothes, summer and winter. And your shoes and coat. Your Bible, prayer book, and other books. What else do you want to take? Your doll?" Carrie initially rejects the doll as too babyish to bring along, but finally slips the well-worn cloth creature into the smaller bag when her mother isn't looking.

Two bags are a full load when she finishes, ready to begin her adventure. Tears flow mostly from Mutti's direction. The traveler's eyes look only forward. Carrie, for all the wreckage of disconnections she has experienced, refuses to grasp the concept of forever.

The trip begins on land. The emigrant passengers spend a week at a specialized hotel near the Rotterdam port. During that week, advisors inspect every scrap of paper and help travelers obtain any missing documents. Once at the brand-new immigrant processing site on Ellis Island, the company brags, a full 99% of petitioners go smoothly through immigration procedures without delays in entry. A crash course in basic English language and American culture occupies guests bound for New York. In one of those sessions, Carrie befriends an older woman, whose entire attention trains on Carrie in a way her own mother never has time to offer. Frau Schlech, in turn, enjoys the girlish chatter that she misses in her daughter-less home.

The ship is barely out of Germany's waters before Carrie's first letter, posted before embarkment, reaches her mother:

November 3, 1891
Dear Mutti,

I made a new friend today. She is Frau Schlech, who has three grown-up sons and a husband already in the United States. Her mother died in Hamburg last month. Isn't that where we went to put my brothers on the boat? She is going to Nebraska where the rest of her family lives. She says we are both going to catch up with our boys!

We visited our ship yesterday to learn our way around. When we go upstairs to eat, we will be able to see the ocean. Frau Schlech says that we are sure to eat goulash more often than the people upstairs do, probably whipped up from their leftovers. Last night the ship's chef made us wiener schnitzel from the yummiest, tenderest veal. MMMmmmm! They told us most ships serve only two meals a day to downstairs guests, but we will get three.

They also say that on most ships, people sleep hundreds at a time, in one huge room downstairs. I visited my room, and found only about thirty beds and hammocks. I got a hammock – the rocking is great fun, and I feel like a real sailor! I left my big bag for storage, like you said, and I will keep the small one in my hammock.

Tomorrow, we sail. I will write to you again from New York.

Love from your Caroline

Carrie hears dazzling tales of the Rockefellers and the Vanderbilts, the Krupps and the occasional von Liebig, all the big names swathed in silk and satin and glittering jewels, who occupy the private berths on the upper decks. She realizes that they, not she, enjoy pretty linens and a constant view of the sea. But she still thinks she is the lucky one. Carrie remembers the tension surrounding her brothers' travels, and her mother's wails of distress on hearing the tales of ships and crews that treated the boys like human cattle.

Her experience is different. She eats three meals a day in the dining room, coming up from below to fresh air and real cloth linens. She sits at a table like the one at home, instead of balancing her dinner in a swinging hammock below deck. Unlike her peers, who all have parents aboard, she sails alone, aside from Frau Schlech. But she is not lonely. She enjoys friends, even if in the short term, for the length of the sailing. She spends her afternoons among other children of the ship, drawing pictures, completing English lessons, and slinking between bow and stern in a sea-bound version of hide-and-seek while the smallest sailors have their naps.

Perhaps most important to her feeling of security and well-being, Carrie has four brothers already in America, who will vie over meeting her ship at the harbor, and will stay faithfully in place until they find her. Her days are pure adventure. Still, crisis will always find a place to land.

Carrie is terrified, injured, bleeding, maybe dying. She has never seen blood like this, coming from her core, and yet from no place in particular. In her panic, she fails to recognize in the mess anything her mother said before she set sail. Her head spins. *What do I do? Where is a doctor? My stomach hurts. I'm pretty sure my insides are coming out in bloody slices. I will not survive this, I know it. What do I do?* She sobs, and Frau Schlech notices.

"My dear, what is wrong? Why are you crying?" Carrie shakes off Frau Schlech's touch. Frau Schlech's eyes meet Carrie's with empathy as she squats to the girl's level.

"Do you miss your mama?" Carrie shrugs, still bawling.

"Does something hurt?" Carrie continues her tears, but nods tentatively.

"What hurts?" Carrie gulps and places her hand on her stomach, then ducks her head and lifts her skirts. Frau Schlech nods.

"Are you afraid?" Carrie nods her head vigorously and renews her wailing. Frau Schlech puts her hand gently on Carrie's arm.

"Carrie, listen to me. Can you listen for one minute?" She sniffles, but quiets noticeably.

"Carrie, you are alright. Can you trust what I tell you?" Her lip trembles, but she nods.

"Carrie, did your mother tell you where babies come from?"

"Mama's tummy." Carrie is a youngest child, but plenty of younger cousins and neighbors have arrived in her dozen years.

"That's right! Mama's tummy. And there's pain involved, and blood, right?" Carrie nods. She's been around enough births to know the work is noisy, full of painful screams and even anger, and requires lots of towels and hot water. Her eyes light up in recognition, then shift rapidly into a horrified wince.

"I'm having a baby?" She wails again. "How will I take care of a baby on this ship?"

"No, no! You're not having a baby! Your body prepares to have babies later, at the right time, by bleeding. The blood that would go to keeping a baby alive, if one were in your belly, comes out when no baby is in your belly to need it." Carrie pauses.

"Oh. My Mutti told me about that, but I forgot. I thought I was bleeding to death."

"No, this kind of bleeding leads to life, not death, and later, not now. Did your mama pack some rags in your luggage? She might have said they were 'just in case.'"

"Yes. They are in my smaller bag, in my hammock."

"Get your bag and I'll show you how to use them."

"Alright." Carrie scurries off, then returns with a small bundle in her hands. Carefully following Frau Schlech's instructions, she secures a set of rags in her clean bloomers and sets aside the bloody underthings to wash.

"You're not a little girl anymore, Carrie. Today you are a woman." She unfastens a tiny silver heart on a chain from around her own neck and places it around Carrie's neck.

"My mother gave me this necklace the day I became a woman," she says, wistful. "My children are boys so they won't have need for it. Will you wear it for me, woman to woman?"

"Oh, yes!" Carrie's face shines as she rushes into Frau Schlech's arms. "Thank you! I am glad to be a woman with you!"

"And I am glad to be a woman with you, child. I'm glad to be a woman with you."

Carrie exits the Ellis Island maze easily, entering a blinding flash of sunlight. She hears the excited fervor of people greeting new arrivals, but for a moment she cannot see anyone to greet her. Before the glare even clears from her eyes, an unleashed collection of hugs envelops her. In the interminable months they have been apart, Henry has changed from a slender slip of a boy child into a strong and substantive young man. Frederick hovers close, less changed but still eager to care for her. He swoops in for the next long hug after Henry's. No doubt he is there, in part, because no one is ever sure whether Henry will arrive as promised.

They bundle her off to Retta's apartment above the original Maasen's Confectionary, schlepping her huge bag through the streets between them. All the people she knows in the United States, except of course Frau Schlech, cram their bodies together in one space to welcome their heroine. In the middle of the excitement, Henry reaches for her hand and she squeezes his. Forever separated from the land of her ancestors, Carrie has left her mother and father behind. Still. Henry is here, so she is home.

Carrie drifts off to sleep that night in the shadow of her brothers' steamer trunk. Atop the hulking, multi-functional furnishing in the corner of their dark living room, her "More Light!" embroidery holds a place of honor, still speaking its truth. As her last dregs of apprehension relax into pure excitement and then into contentment at the arc of her journey, she breathes deeply the rich air of New York adventure.

"More Light!" proves a fitting refrain to bring this long day to a close. From raising her blinded eyes to seek out the newly installed Statue of Liberty beyond the island, to the shining glow of her face surrounded by those deeply loved and long unseen, to the first glimpse of her new home, reflected in Henry's eyes. She is home, and surely the light will become stronger, shining into her future.

Brooklyn, 1891

CARRIE'S PLANS STRETCH as far as seeing her brothers, and no further. After she satisfies the yearning for that reunion, she fails even to comprehend the choices before her. She is a child making grown-up decisions. Frederick and Tante Retta, as experienced adults, are ready to take up the slack. Carrie begins by spending her days at Maasen & Denzler's on Columbia Street helping Frederick, doing what she already knows how to do: spinning out taffy, imitating her father's fine hand with decorative icing, expanding her English mastery by waiting on customers in a halting tongue.

"A special customer is coming by today, Carrie," Frederick says one morning a week or so into her new life, "a French businessman named Antoine Chapelle. He has an American wife named Rosie, and they live a few blocks from here. Their home is much larger than the one we brothers share."

Carrie looks at him curiously. He seems to be taking the long way around to telling her something. She nods slowly. He goes on.

"The last time they were in buying candy, they asked whether we knew anyone who would be available to work for them in their home. I thought of you. Now that you are here, I invited them to meet you. Would you like to live close by?"

"I like living in your apartment."

"And we love having you there! But a young girl living with a bunch of adult men, as Mutti would say, is simply not suitable."

"I am a grown-up now. I will be fine in your home. I came all this way because I want to be with you."

"You are so much more mature than when I left Meldorf," Frederick answers carefully, "that I have to check twice to be sure of who you are. But Mutti, you know, she worries. And Tante Retta agrees."

"I am so tired of Mutti's worries keeping me from doing what I want to do!" Frederick laughs. In his head, he hears her feet stomping, a sound from her little girl life.

"Yes, I imagine you are. I bet Louis rejoices now, that he chaperoned Henry, The Wild Thing, rather than you. You would have worried him clear to death! And we all know that Henry came close enough."

Carrie lets out the breath that she didn't realize she held. She had expected Henry, as one of the brothers, to live in the brothers' apartment. But after a couple of days, he returned to Hoboken. And now she apparently is to leave, as well.

"At the Chapelle's house you will have a little room of your own instead of a cot in the living room. And you will be right down the street, and can visit whenever you please. Will you meet them and give them a chance for me?"

"I like sleeping in the living room. Your apartment is cozy. I like living here."

"I know. And I love that you are so adaptable. I need you to meet them when they come by today, though, and then you and Tante Retta and I can talk about the best solution for your housing and work."

"Do I have to?"

"I really need you to."

"Then I guess I can meet them."

"Thank you. Would you like some ice cream to celebrate growing older and getting to make decisions like an adult? I made a churn while you were still sleeping."

No matter how grown up she might be, a girl has a hard time resisting ice cream. Since her brother needs her cooperation, she nods her head and seals the deal over a scoop of vanilla with streaks of chocolate fudge.

Early in the afternoon, the bell on the door of the shop rings. Carrie startles at the familiar sound, as if her imagination has settled her back into Meldorf and she is surprised to be in New York instead. She quickly recovers her wits.

"*Hallo,*" she says to the couple as they approach the counter. "*Willkommen*—ah, welcome. How can I help you?" Frederick, returning from the storeroom at that very moment, also greets the customers.

"Antoine! Rosie! How lovely to see you again. Please meet my sister, Carrie Denzler. Carrie, remember, I told you about Mr. and Mrs. Chapelle?"

"Oh, how lovely to meet you, Carrie! Your brother has told me such nice things about you. How are you?"

"*Mir geht es gut, danke.*" Carrie blushes and goes on after a hitch of hesitation. "I'm sorry. I am well, thank you. I am glad to meet you."

The conversation continues, mostly between Frederick and the Chapelles, as Carrie looks to her brother for translation. She steals glances at Mrs. Chapelle, who seems very young to be married to Mr. Chapelle, and sees an open, friendly face who leaves welcome space between them while Carrie becomes accustomed to even more strangers entering her life. Mr. Chapelle is more effusive, less aware of his effect on others. Having Mrs. Chapelle sit between them makes the conversation more comfortable for Carrie. They talk of changing linens and scrubbing floors, time off on Sundays for church and family, and a single room at the top of the stairs. When they leave, Frederick turns to his sister.

"What do you think?"

"I'd rather be here. But I like her a lot, and he's alright."

"Let's talk to Tante Retta."

Tante Retta approves of the relocation plan, as expected of a co-conspirator. Carrie stays two more nights in the Denzler brothers' apartment, then settles the contents of her bags into the tiny room by the top of the back stairs of the Chapelles' brownstone. When she peeks into the door across the hall, she finds a similar, slightly larger, occupied room. Someone else must work here, too.

She soon discovers that the someone else is Bridget, the senior housekeeper and cook for the small household. Bridget is twenty-two years old, born in New York of Irish parents, and has a gentleman caller she sees every Wednesday, her day off. Her broad face, topped with a mane of strawberry blond, matches the slight heft in her figure. She laughs as she greets Carrie, a twinkle glittering in her eye, and exclaims, "Thank goodness you are here! I can't do this job by myself for another day!" Carrie likes her immediately.

"Let's talk about the routine around here," Bridget says, getting right down to business. "Every morning, I will cook breakfast for the Chapelles while you make their beds and tidy their rooms. On Wednesdays, I'll leave rolls and coffee for you to serve before you tend to chores. I'll also leave dinner for you to reheat in the oven. You'll eat in the kitchen, whether I'm here or not, after you tend to them. I will answer the door to any visitors. You will scrub floors every day. I will dust the parlors and office, and we will tackle the silver together, every Friday before the Sabbath meal."

She goes on, but Carrie's gaze wanders to follow her thoughts. The floors go on for miles in this house. She knows she will have to be told specifics again later, but she understands the general idea. Her job is to be the assistant for everything in the house, like she was to her mother. But the job will take all day, every day, no breaks to run to the shop, or play, or even go to school. This life is no improvement over her old life, and she won't even see her brothers most days. Their presence is the point of her journey.

"You can call Mrs. Chapelle 'Miss Rosie' when the two of you are alone or when you are speaking with me, and Mrs. Chapelle around guests. Mr. Chapelle is always Mr. Chapelle, no matter what; he's kind of funny about that." Bridget has not taken a breath.

Carrie's eyes open wide at this strange information. She has never even been inside a house where every occupant has their own bedroom. And while her Mutti keeps a spotless home, she can't think of a single chore, other than washing up the dishes and mopping the kitchen floor, that they complete every single day. They have a shop to run, as well as a home.

"If we are finishing all these chores, what is Mrs. Chapelle — uh, Miss Rosie — doing all day?"

"Oh, she entertains her friends. They talk in the parlor, or embroider. If she's alone, she sometimes reads. And every Wednesday she goes to her club meeting, or does charity for the poor. Mr. Chapelle goes to The Office right after breakfast every day, and arrives back home in time for dinner."

This information is the strangest Carrie has ever received. She knows no one in Meldorf who lives this way. Families in her home village live on top of each other; they're in and out of home and work all day long. Talking to friends and charity for the poor are things the women in her family slip in between the house and the store or the farm; they are not a life in themselves.

Bridget goes on. "Miss Rosie will hire a nurse when the baby comes. The nurse will live in a room off the nursery." Bridget notices the wondering look on Carrie's face and laughs. "Yes, the rich are different."

"Everything is different," Carrie says. "Every single thing."

On the first Sunday of her employment, Carrie arises early, eager to meet her brothers at the Trinity German Lutheran Church on Kane Street. She clutches the map that Bridget draws for her, nearly trembling in anticipation of spending time with the beloved family she came all this way to be near. Her most recent year of Sunday mornings, divided from her brothers by an ocean, has been one of the loneliest times of her week. She looks forward to the familiar music and the prayers, to worshipping together. She aches for this time of uninterrupted togetherness, when she has missed her brothers most.

Carrie sets out on foot, navigating the gentle bumps and curves of the cobblestone streets so like the ones in Meldorf. She passes businesses of all kinds, the grocer, the barber, the tavern, the general mercantile, all sealed up tight for the day of rest. She rounds the corner onto Columbia Street, and stops at Maasen & Denzler Confections, where her brothers join her for the rest of the walk to the church. For the first time, Brooklyn feels a little bit familiar to her, as if she knows where to go and what to do. From the back doors of the buildings, others dressed in their Sunday best descend the stairs to the street, strangers joining her on the weekly journey.

"Hey, girlie!" Frederick arrives at her side. "I haven't seen you all week. Your new bosses must be working you hard!" She flings herself into his arms, ducking her head to wipe tears on his sleeve. August and Louis trail them. Henry is nowhere to be seen.

"Oh, Freddy — I have missed you more this week than I ever did in Meldorf. Knowing you are so close and still not seeing you is simply awful!"

"I'm right here. And now we'll see each other every single week."

"I know. But now that I have you back, I never want to let you out of my sight again!"

"Oh, Miss Carrie. You have become a woman, but you still have that sweet little girl heart. Come, now, dry your tears. I'm not going anywhere. Let us introduce you to your new church. Everyone is going to be excited that you have finally arrived."

After worship, the sole hour since her arrival to be delivered entirely in German, she feels a bit more settled, nestling into what could become familiar. She assumes they will return to the boys' apartment and make some lunch, visit awhile, maybe play some games as they would back home, but she soon discovers other plans.

"I promised Mutti to make sure you finish your confirmation instruction," Frederick says. "The class meets in this room across from the sanctuary, and the pastor knows you will be here."

"But—"

"We will see you at Tante Retta's for dinner tonight at 5:30. Do you know the way, or do you want to come back to the shop and walk with us."

"With you." Carrie is stunned into shocked silence. Sunday afternoons are for being together. How is it possible she will spend her day among strangers, and then alone, when she has family in town?

"Then everything is settled. We will see you at our place in time to walk to the Maasen's together." Frederick gives her a quick hug and turns toward home, while she joins the pastor and a dozen or so twelve- and thirteen-year-old strangers in the classroom. They first assembled in September, and she joins them in December. She suddenly and fiercely misses Meldorf. As least there she knows the cast of characters.

After confirmation class, Carrie wanders at a bit of a loss. She has four hours until she meets her brothers.

How will she spend that much time? On a typical Sunday afternoon in Meldorf, she might have walked to the shore. So before pausing for thought, she sets off in the direction of the river, lonely tears stinging her eyes as she walks. At home one road leads directly to the sea. Here, she thinks she has the direction right, but truthfully, she has no idea whether the street will take her where she wants to go. The shuttered shops and quiet alleys increase her isolation. The pealing bells echo in her lonely mind. She finds a cart vendor selling fresh bread, and rips off bites, chewing as she walks. The streets stretch out to the horizon on every side, never reaching water.

Finally, the river bank comes into sight, where the new Statue of Liberty rises to the sky. Funny, she felt freer among soldiers in the streets and parents overseeing every move at home. She felt freer with the drudgery of completing homework and accomplishing chores. She even felt freer receiving instruction on Mutti's expectations that she act like a lady. She felt freer then than she does now, in the home of the free. Because now, she feels the shackling emptiness of nowhere she needs to be, nothing she has to do, no one here to greet her. She feels lonely, not free.

Carrie turns away from the water and trudges back along the city streets. Maybe she needs to work on Sundays, as on every other day. Her brothers are living their own lives, which no longer revolve around their beloved little sister. The faces are all wrong at church. The promised leisure away from her employers turns into a crushing load of empty time.

By the time she reaches the festivities of Maasen family dinner, she finds herself unmoored in a room full of people to whom she has been connected her whole life. And as far as she can tell, her solemn presence goes unseen in a sea of friendly greetings. Even Henry, appearing as mysteriously as he disappears, fails to touch her soul.

The enormity of the changes imposed by this new life settle on Carrie, not all at once or in any one moment, but in a steady march through time. The lifestyle of her employers. The weekly glimpses of her brothers instead of daily enmeshment in their activities. The unpredictable schedule of Henry's visits. The joys of nature marred by a busyness never out of sight, or earshot, of the bustling city. Each item is only one on a long list of unexpected twists and turns that shock her, body and mind, about her new home in Brooklyn. Every day, some strange detail takes her a little further away from the bliss she somehow still believes awaits her.

Brooklyn, 1891

THANKFULLY, THERE IS BRIDGET. Carrie will never know how she knows, but she feels confident Bridget can be trusted. And Carrie needs a friend. A few weeks into their time working together, Carrie returns from her Sunday outing in tears. Running up the stairs, she throws herself on her bed, wailing. Bridget appears at her door.

"What on earth is wrong, my young friend? You sound as if somebody died."

"They may as well have done," Carrie wails. "I might as well not be here for all the attention they pay me."

"Rough day with the brothers, huh?"

"Ja! They show up at church, where I am, or maybe not; Henry's been there twice in all this time. And then they woo their sweethearts while I sit by, and wander off afterwards while I go to a class full of strangers. They spend all afternoon strolling with their girls and I finally see them again for dinner.

"Then after we eat, they hug me good-bye and head home early. 'Have to be ready for another work week bright and early in the morning,' they say. I am so sick of being invisible to them. I might as well have stayed in Meldorf for all the good being here does me. I came across the ocean because I missed my brothers. But my brothers no longer seem to want to pay me any attention at all!"

"You poor dear. So much disappointment all at once. How can I help?"

"Oh, I don't know. You and the Chapelles are so kind to me that I hate to complain. It's not your fault my life is falling apart."

"No. That's very true. But maybe I can help. What did you expect living in Brooklyn would be like?"

Carrie's wail fades to a sniffle. "I thought I would be living with my brothers and seeing them every day. I thought I would always tell them good morning and good night. I thought I would be working alongside them at the candy shop. I lose track of where they are from day to day, they have so many candy shops!

"And Henry! My very best friend, and he is not acting like my friend at all. It's as if they have all forgotten about me, but especially Henry. I never know when he's going to slip away and leave me all over again." Bridget waits, quiet.

"And I can't get away from this town! When I go to the river for a little peace and quiet, even on a Sunday afternoon, the whole city goes with me! I can't hear the water move. Noise is everywhere! I can't breathe. With all these buildings, there isn't any air!" Bridget remains silent.

"And I never wanted to keep house. Now it's not even my house that I'm keeping. I hate scrubbing and dusting and cooking and polishing silver. And I especially hate babies, and a little wailer will arrive any day now, needing to be the center of everyone's attention. Don't even try to tell me that the Chapelle's nurse is going to take care of everything, because I've seen babies come along, and they can't help themselves. They are the center of the world. Thank God my little cousins lived in their own house, and not in mine. I would have been driven to distraction if they had been underfoot all the time. No babies!"

Bridget's eyes smile wryly. "Anything else?"

"My brother bought my cooperation with ice cream." Carrie sulks openly now. "And now that he has what he wants, the ice cream completely disappears. I sound ridiculous, don't I?"

"You sound like someone who is adjusting to a new life, and it's difficult."

"I don't like this at all."

"I know."

"I thought I was miserable when my brothers started leaving. And I was devastated when Henry sailed. I accepted that they were not coming back, and dreamed of being with them. But now that I'm living in the same town again, my dream has turned into a nightmare. Nothing turned out the way it's supposed to be."

"You sound — normal."

"I do?"

"Sure. You sound completely unhinged and out of control, and that would be normal under the circumstances. What do you need?"

"I need everything to go back to normal, like in Meldorf, except here in Brooklyn where we are safe from the wars."

"Mmm."

"That's what I need."

"Let's start a little smaller. What if I sent you to the grocer on Tuesday instead of going myself? You could stop at Maasen & Denzler's and see Frederick, maybe talk him out of a scoop of that sweet stuff?"

"Oh, could I? I would love that!"

"Yes, you could. I'll talk to Miss Rosie. I think it would work fine for me to make you a list and send you along."

"Oh, Bridget." Her eyes threaten to overflow again.

"You're being too hard on your brothers, you know. They love you, but their lives have changed as much as yours, and they are no longer in the habit of putting you at the center. That's hard, but not impossible. We'll work on the problem together."

"Oh, Bridget."

"Stop 'oh Bridget-ing' me and dry those tears, little lady. We'll have you all sorted out in no time." Bridget is kind, and wiser than her years. And she may also be a little overly optimistic.

When the sun rises on Tuesday morning, Carrie jumps out of bed and into her clothes. Today is the day! She never thought she would be excited by the prospect of seeing one of her brothers twice a week instead of once. She hurries to finish her morning chores, all the bedclothes settled, all the floors swept.

Before she leaves, she stops by the kitchen to tear into the dark bread left over from last night's dinner and a stinky Limburger cheese. Better not be hungry at the grocer; she has a list to fill her cart, not an order to fill her stomach. Thus fortified, she grabs the huge basket from the kitchen table and the paper where she has written Bridget's order in her native German, so as not to confuse herself at the market.

Root vegetables are in plentiful supply at the grocery store, and Carrie picks up some early lettuce and peas from the peddler's cart outside. A whole chicken, a heady cheese, and hardy wheat flour quickly fill the enormous basket, leaving room for a bottle of milk and a dozen carefully placed eggs. She will need to put the milk into the ice box at home before it spoils, but even so, she has a few minutes to pop in to Maasen & Denzler's. Her steps are light as she rounds the corner.

"Carrie! What a nice surprise!" Frederick greets her enthusiastically.

"Bridget let me do the marketing this morning and I thought I'd stop by!"

"I can see that! Put that basket on the back counter, and come help us arrange the merchandise. New York is sweet on St Patrick's day, and we are creating some new designs for the occasion."

Carrie realizes then that the woman at the counter is Flora, not an ordinary customer, but the girl Frederick courts on Sunday afternoons. Instead of buying candies, she artfully arranges the pieces to show them off. Carrie's old job. Carrie's heart sinks, and her lips fall silent. All of the special places in her brother's life are taken. She leaves before he can even offer her ice cream.

79

Back at the Chapelles' brownstone, Carrie deposits the market basket back on the kitchen table. Bridget prepares lunch, and sets the peas from the basket in front of Carrie to shell.

"Did you see Frederick?" Bridget asks.

"*Ja*, I saw him," Carrie sulks. "And his girlfriend."

"Hmmm. And are they well?"

"They are." Tears sting Carrie's eyes. "And I am still invisible."

"Yes, competition against a girlfriend for attention is difficult, isn't it?"

"Why does everything have to change?"

"People grow up, Carrie. If you are smart, and I know you are, you will befriend that girl instead of competing for Frederick's attention. She may or may not be The One for your brother. But in case she is, you'd be wise to consider her your new sister instead of your enemy."

"I don't want a new sister. I want her to go away, and give me back my brother."

"I know. I also know that your brother may be getting to an age where he seeks the comfort of a wife. Do you really want to set aside what he needs?"

"I want him to need me."

"And you know you can't fill that spot in his life, don't you?"

"I don't know anything." And at that, Carrie flounces back to her chores, her early morning smile dimmed and her body sagging with the weight of her distress.

Carrie manages, and some days she even makes life happen without having to swallow despair. Bridget requires excellence at work, but she also supports Carrie. She wants her to grow and thrive and manage the turmoil of emotion that arrives as regularly as ships in the harbor. Conversation during kitchen chores becomes a standard feature of life.

"Are you enjoying your Confirmation class?" Bridget inquires one morning as they chop vegetables for soup.

"I guess. I miss my old class back in Meldorf. They were my friends. I saw the same people at church that I saw at school, and I'd known them forever."

"Being the new kid in class is tough."

"Being the new kid literally everywhere is way harder than I thought it would be. I miss school."

"For the friends?"

"Yes, but also the learning. I love to read and write stories. And these days I keep all the arithmetic in my head, nothing new that reminds me of puzzles, just sums at the grocer. So yes, also the friends. But mostly the learning. And the sense of being normal."

"You can find lots of places here to learn, you know, besides schools. Have you been to one of the public libraries yet? They are getting ready to build a big fancy one in Manhattan. Our former governor set out the vision in his will, of all places, and provided a large bequest for the project. That building won't be finished for ages. But the library at the Pratt Institute right here in Brooklyn has books on loan to the public. The libraries around here were built for the education of

81

boys, but the Pratt goes beyond that tradition and makes the books available for everyone."

Carrie's face shines rapt with interest. Something about breaking into territory that has so recently been closed to girls appeals to her. And the prospect of a collection of books she could borrow is simply amazing!

"I've never heard of a place like that. I've written stories since I've been here, and drawn pictures, too, but I didn't know I could borrow books. I want to go see this library!" She likes the feeling of looking forward to something.

Confirmation Sunday seems designed for joy, and Carrie tries to honor a feeling she cannot produce. Her classes, though interrupted by her trip across the wide waters, finally find completion in the festive Easter rites that confirm the baptismal vows of the faithful. She began with old friends in Meldorf, and now completes the journey with strangers.

Near the middle of the service, the twelve of them stand together on the chancel steps in the shadow of the resurrected Christ, at least in marble form. The young women in dazzling white dresses reflect the joyful light of stained class, and young men in their dark suits and narrow ties embody the solemnity of the promises they make. They quiver a bit as they face the congregation and answer the pastor's pointed questions about their intentions to renounce evil and follow Jesus.

Carrie knows beyond doubt the finality of her choice to renounce the evils against which her native Germany still struggles. She believes people deserve rights of faith and of conscience. She understands the

82

difference between following fear and folly, and living a life of intentional freedom. These vows are real to her, as real as running from encroaching soldiers and worrying over the safety of her brothers. She made the decision to come here, and stands by her decision as righteous. She understands that she made the choice out of longing rather than principle. But she also has come to embrace the core belief behind leaving her homeland.

Carrie wonders what the promises mean for the others. And she surely has little more idea than her peers, about what choices lie ahead, for good or for evil. They are making vows to last a lifetime at an age so tender they cannot know their own minds; they do not know what they do not know.

For a thirteen-year-old, living a new life in a new world provides no straightforward path. One thing she is sure of; the world is as lonely as ever. She thought she had renounced loneliness, too, as part of her decision to come to the United States, but that does not seem to be working out very well. She feels more attuned to Good Friday mourning than to Easter Sunday joy.

After the service, her brothers, and Tante Retta and her family, are all smiles and celebration. Even Bridget and the Chapelles join her mid-aisle to congratulate her. After cake and punch in the social hall, they all return to Retta's for Easter dinner. A pile of Confirmation cards and gifts holds down one end of the table, ham and potato salad the other.

The day full of promises unfolds with August and Minna showing off their bouncing baby boy, recently baptized in the same sanctuary in which Carrie is now confirmed. Bridget makes herself at home, visiting with all the characters whose names she has heard. Flora

83

flutters around Carrie as the rightful center of the family's attention on her special day, and begins to feel more like friend than competitor. But something remains askew, even in this close family circle, and Carrie feels the problem keenly.

"Where is Henry?" Carrie asks Frederick when she finally has a chance to question him.

"I don't know," answers Frederick. "I'm sorry he missed this occasion. Our rolling stone is not very reliable about special days."

"I can't believe he didn't come," says Carrie. "Well, I guess I can believe it. But on the one day I have the spotlight, you'd think he could show up for me."

"I'm sorry. I know his absence hurts. That's all I know to say. August and Louis barely find anything to say to him any more when he turns up. They are so reliable, and he—"

"—is so not." Carrie will not mince words. "Frederick, he was my heart, my very best friend in the world. And I've come all this way to find him missing."

"You sound much too old for thirteen."

Carrie shrugs. She has always been either too old or not old enough.

At the end of the day, the lilies and trumpet calls fade from memory. The excited hugs settle into quiet night and congratulations fall silent. The new white frock lands on the floor when Carrie crawls into bed, exhausted. Her mind wanders from the glad alleluias that seemed to bring others such joy, and settles into more somber thoughts. Grief is a burden better shared, even if silently and only with Jesus. A somber tune fills her ear as she slips into sleep.

> *What language shall I borrow*
> *to thank Thee, dearest friend,*
> *For this Thy dying sorrow,*
> *Thy pity without end?*
> *O make me Thine forever,*
> *and should I fainting be,*
> *Lord, let me never, never*
> *outlive my love to Thee.*

Meldorf, 1892

May 13, 1892
Dearest Carrie,

Congratulations on being a full-fledged voting member of the Trinity German Lutheran Church! Retta says the service was beautiful, and that you took the promises you made so seriously. I am very proud of you! I only wish I could have been there. Your father and I are putting money in the jar every week to get us to Brooklyn eventually, and your brothers add to that amount every month. Hopefully we can come soon. We want to share as many of your occasions as we can.

In the meantime, use your newly confessed faith to pray for Germany. Things are neither better nor worse, but generally miserable, and we are ready to leave as soon as we can. Formal charges are filed against Louis for avoiding military service, as they were also against your other brothers. But of course, they cannot make the charges stick or punish him, since the boys escaped safely to the United States. I hope you hear from Henry every now and then.

Vati is at the store, dreaming up confections to replace the Easter stock. I think he'll keep his pretty chocolate flowers and butterflies for a while. But people lose interest quickly in others, like the sugar eggs with tiny peepholes into miniature scenes of flowers and a tiny cross. We had few leftovers this year, so that's good.

Your teacher asked me to tell you hallo. She is even more disappointed than you are, I think, that you have not been able to go to school in the United States. She understands that your work allows no time for studies, but remembers how smart you are, and wishes you had the chance to continue. As do I. And as do you, I am certain.

I better go help Vati. Be good, my sweet girl. I love you always.

Love,
Mutti

Brooklyn, 1892

July 7, 1892
Dear Mutti and Vati,

I have made the most wonderful discovery! Bridget told me about a place in Brooklyn where I can borrow books to read!

I left Meldorf carrying only my Bible and prayer book, the book Frederick gave me for my birthday, and a few stories left over from when I was a little girl. More than anything else about school, I miss the books. Well, Bridget knows about a library at a school, full of books, that I can visit on Saturday afternoons! I can tell them which ones I want and they will let me bring books back to my room to read. Bridget is going to let me do the shopping on Saturdays so that I can stop by the library.

We stopped in today on our way back from the market, and I met Miss Annie Moore, the librarian. She went to school at Pratt (the place is called Pratt Institute) to learn how to be a librarian, and then she started a section of the library especially for children. She has lots of ideas about books I would like. I already love her so much! She has seven older brothers (can you imagine?) and is the little sister in her family, like me.

I'm getting to know Bridget better and better. Did you know that she grew up in a house called an Orphan Asylum? Her parents are Irish, and they love her very much, but when they came to the United States, they had a hard time finding jobs. People evidently would rather have the Germans working for them than the Irish. I don't know why; that seems unfair. Good for me, I guess, but sad for them.

Anyway, they were not making enough money to buy food, and Bridget was not getting enough to eat, so they took her to the orphanage to live for a while. She ended up staying until she moved here. The orphanage trained Bridget to be a housekeeper, and then helped her find a home that needed a helper. Almost like me, I guess. I didn't have a home here, either, and now I work for the Chapelles, too, except I didn't live at the orphan asylum. I lived with you, and then with my brothers. But I'm glad for the orphanage. I would hate to think of Bridget not having anyone to help her.

I love you. I miss you. When are you coming to Brooklyn?

Love,
Carrie

Meldorf, 1892

August 13, 1892
Dearest Carrie,

I hope we will come to Brooklyn very soon, maybe in a few months. We want to be there as much as you want us to come, truly! We have the money saved for the tickets; the savings grows much faster since the boys work in Brooklyn. They have been sending money back every month to help us.

Now we have to figure how to settle the business. We had hoped Amalia might run it, but she has not taken to the work as we had hoped. She lacks the attention to detail that makes the candy wonderful and the business successful. And, of course, the little cousins are – little – so we are looking for a buyer. I hope we can find one quickly.

Bridget sounds like a good friend. I'm delighted she has found a way for you to keep learning! You will have to show us the library when we get there. Maybe when we are all together, we can even find a way for you to go back to school. I know you would like that as much as we would.

Tell your brothers and Tante Retta hallo from us. Have you heard anything from Henry?

Love always,
Mutti

Brooklyn, 1893

S PRING IS HER FAVORITE season. Carrie finds her true home in New York in the greening and blossoming parks of the city. She never thinks about her connection to the seasons of the earth, she just enjoys what she loved as a child who spent more hours in the open air than indoors. She relishes fertile farmland on either side of the road to the sea, or phlox among the tomatoes in the garden beside the house.

Absent those pleasures, she finds havens to nourish her soul in the parks, even the cemeteries, of Brooklyn. She seeks out water, or more frequently green, as an antidote to her initial loneliness on Sunday afternoons. She makes her way to Lutheran Cemetery and settles on a blanket under a tree to devour one of her beloved books. Or she wanders a neighborhood park, listens to the ducks squawk in the pond, and idly draws tulips and irises in her sketchbook in ink, to be completed in rainbows of watercolor back in her room. The morning air, crisp and accented by the call of the sparrows, brings her back to herself.

When he manages the trip into Brooklyn for church, Henry walks with her, and they enjoy the quiet together, alternating conversation and silence.

"What is the biggest surprise of being in New York?" Henry questions her one Sunday afternoon.

"How little time I actually spend with my brothers," she answers promptly, "and how difficult I still find that reality, three years on."

"I am surprised at how much time I spend alone," he says.

"Our observations sound remarkably similar."

"And that surprises you?"

"Not a bit," says Carrie. "We've always been like one person living in two bodies. Having you across the ocean for a year sucked all the life out of me. And even now, with you only across the river, I still feel ripped apart. What happened to our pirate adventures and plotting against soldiers? I get so lonely when I remember those days, and feel them so far behind me."

"We grew up."

Carrie laughs. "Maybe I did. But you? The boys have choices forbidden to the girls, and I doubt you'll ever be a grown man." Henry freezes at her words, staring into her eyes.

"Why would you say that?" Henry stammers.

"Because I have to live all protected and safe, and you get to roam the world." The sharp edge of her tone radiates frustration. "I have to take care of the house, and you get to trim the sails. I have to be in church or people are aghast, but you go missing and they say, 'That's Henry.'" Henry nods in acknowledgment, but she forges ahead.

"I am supposed to look forward to buying the groceries and find fulfillment in scrubbing the floors. You get to go to the places where groceries grow, where the lumber falls to become chairs and floors. And I am supposed to like taking care of children. I don't. Not

August's boy. Not Rosie's twins or Tante Retta's gaggle of grandchildren. I don't even like being around them, but I'm expected to fawn over them, and to long for some of my own one day.

"You have no idea what it's like, wanting the seas and living in a box of perfectly packaged domesticity. What about what I want? No one ever thinks about that. But then, I wanted to come to Brooklyn, and that hasn't turned out anything like what I imagined."

"I think I can understand a little of what you're saying," Henry says. "I don't want to own a business, to be tied down to being in the same place in the same way every day. The others seem content as lambs to have a place to go to work day after day, and it makes me itch to think about living my life that way."

"Exactly! I spend my life itching, and you get to have all the adventures."

"What adventures would you like?"

Carrie turns quiet for a moment before she speaks.

"I want to see the world. I want to study the stars and the poets and the lives of the explorers. I want to turn my stories into books for people to read, and play the piano as if my soul were in the keys. I want to live."

Henry blinks, as if the problem is coming into focus.

"But the closest I will get is to wander the parks and read when I can. I wish for more, but it's something." Carrie sighs.

"What if I write you letters from all the places I go?"

She bolts upright. "Oh, Henry, I would love that!"

"I wish I knew of a way to give you your dreams, Carrie, but I can share how I am living them for both of us. I'll be sailing out of Hoboken to Barbados next week.

I will send the first letter from there. I'll describe every single thing for you, from the seasick sailors to the sugar plantations. If you can't be beside me, I'll give you the next best thing."

"Henry Denzler, you are the best brother a girl could ever hope to have! I will wait by the post box morning and afternoon!"

She lingers close to the front door, twice every day, for weeks. And the postman delivers one envelope for her in all that time, a letter from her mother, describing every detail of the neighbor baby's existence, from the cute little outfits to the contents of the dirty diapers. She rolls her eyes, and stops reading.

Later that month, a routine Sunday brings a seesaw of jolts, each landing a little harder than the last. When Carrie peeks around the corner of the enormous wooden doors that frame the church sanctuary, her forehead wrinkles as she realizes that Tante Retta's pew is empty. Carrie cannot remember a prior occurrence of this rare occasion.

Worried that Retta might be ill, Carrie seeks out each of her brothers in turn. She finds August attempting to aid his wife as she chases their three-year-old son in the wide space at the back of the sanctuary. Louis heads to his place in the pew, and Frederick is outside smiling at Flora. Just smiling. They each shake a head at Carrie's query; they know nothing of Retta's whereabouts.

Frowning, Carrie slips into the pew as the organ music begins. In a coincidence nearly as remarkable as Retta's absence, Henry joins her at the first word of the pastor's prayer and bows his head. Almost exactly one hour later, he and Carrie take off for their afternoon walk, Henry buzzing along the row of storefronts marked "closed" on the doors, Carrie slogging behind, sullen and out of sorts.

"What's wrong with you today, girlie?"

"I waited and waited for your letter to come from Barbados."

"Oh. I guess I forgot."

"'Oh! I guess I forgot!'" She mimics him with a knife of bitter anger on her tongue. "All these promises of 'every little detail' and 'good as being there,' and you can't even be bothered to lick a stamp! I don't understand you, Henry Denzler!"

"I'm sorry, Carrie."

"You are sorry, indeed—a sorry excuse for a brother. I counted on you! I opened my soul to you. And you let me down."

"Aw, now Carrie. It's just a letter. I'm here now, aren't I?"

"And you may end up wishing you weren't! I thought you understood what your willingness to share your adventure meant to me. I can't go anywhere! I can't do anything! You opened a chance to experience the adventure through your writing. And then you slammed it shut. I guess you're not willing to share, after all."

"I am more willing than you will ever know, Carrie. I would pack you in my sailing bag and stow you away on the boat, I'm so willing."

"Failing to put pen to paper says otherwise."

The conversation becomes more difficult as the afternoon slips by, and the siblings spend much of their time in silence, and not the comfortable, contented kind. At the appointed hour, and mostly out of habit, they land uneasily on Tante Retta's stoop.

When the door swings open, a young boy, perhaps ten years old, stands staring. He doesn't remember them, of course. His youth and their long absence leave them only vaguely familiar to each other, not immediately identifiable. Almost instantly, a more reliably familiar figure overtakes the boy in his post at the door: his mother, their aunt, the sister-in-law of their Vati, Timm. Carrie freezes. *That must mean . . . oh, no! Yes, she's here – her older cousin, Amalia! What . . .? And where are . . .?* Carrie wonders if this day could possibly get any worse.

"You have a greeting committee tonight, Carrie!" Tante Retta, who, despite being in the rear guard of faces from the past, leaps forward to be the first to greet her. She bustles around them to envelop Carrie's sinking body into a familiar hug. "Look who arrived at my doorstep this morning!"

"Well, I hardly even know what to say!" Carrie recovers quickly, at least outwardly. "*Hallo!* I had no idea you were coming!"

"My mother sent a letter, but I guess it was lost. The postal service loses more mail than it delivers," states Amalia. "The world can't be trusted. Nobody does what they are supposed to do."

"Yes. Well. *Willkommen!* Welcome!" Carrie struggles to overcome her speechless surprise. She looks around the room, behind and beyond her cousins, hoping against hope that her own mother and father have also arrived. The corners are empty of their presence. She closes her eyes for a moment, dizzy with the shock of the moment.

"Come on, let's get inside where we can visit," Henry says. "You must have plenty of stories to tell."

"Oh, we have lots of stories, but my mother will have to tell them," Amalia says. "I am far too upset to talk about it. The ship was awful. The men who were in charge of helping us were way too scary to trust, not to mention all those scruffy passengers. And then we finally got off and had no idea where we were and—"

"Amalia, come on in here, honey," her mother calls. Turning aside to Carrie and Henry, she adds, "We really had quite a pleasant journey. But you know Amalia. Flexibility and optimism are not part of her repertoire!"

"I remember," says Carrie. "I'm glad everything went smoothly. I rather enjoyed my journey across the sea, so I'm glad travel treated you well, too. Did the little ones enjoy the ship?"

"Oh, yes, now they all want to be sailors!" She laughs as she reaches behind her to bring a shy budding seaman from behind her skirts.

"That's my cousins!" says Henry. He leans down toward them and points his thumbs back at his chest. "Well, here you are, kiddos—a real sailor! Let me answer all your questions." The boy who met them at the door and two slightly younger children, a boy and a girl, soon flutter around Henry and his winsome tales. Carrie shakes her head and rolls her eyes. *More children. That's what I need.*

"Amalia and Carrie, can you come help me in the kitchen for a minute?" Tante Retta holds a cast iron skillet and wipes her brow. "I need some help getting dinner on the table." Retta continues her patter as Carrie and her cousin move through the crowd, "Carrie, if you could help me fry the potatoes, and Amalia, the silverware and napkins are on the sideboard. Would you please set the table?"

Good luck getting that done, Carrie thinks, and then immediately berates herself. *Amalia is grown now; surely she . . . well, we will see.*

The potatoes are already boiled, so Carrie can fry them up quickly. She has been helping Bridget more and more in the Chapelle's kitchen, becoming quite an accomplished cook. She reaches her wooden spoon toward Tante Retta's lips and receives a nod of approval in return. "Put them in that bowl and they're ready to go to the table," Retta says. "Thank you for helping me! I wasn't expecting this crowd!"

Carrie grabs that bowl and another full of green beans and heads to the table, where she finds the silverware and linens in a heap. Some things never change. Sighing, she hastily arranges them into place settings, then returns to the kitchen to fetch schnitzel and a loaf of dark rye bread. The chatter around the dinner table fades as she remembers a childhood conversation she overheard between Henry and her mother. The same cousins who sit around this table in Brooklyn had returned to their own home after having dinner with the Denzlers in Meldorf.

"It's really not fair that Amalia always gets out of her chores and Carrie has to do them," says Henry to his mother

after dinner. "I wouldn't like that either, if I were her." His earnest face brings a smile to Magda's voice.

"Maybe not," his mother answers. "But someone has to do the work around here. And Amalia is a guest in our home."

"But Carrie helps when we go to Amalia's house. And you expect her to. Why do you expect Carrie's help in both places and let Amalia squeeze out of either duty?"

"That, young man, is my business. Your younger sister is the apple of your eye, and I love that you take care of her. But your cousin has issues you do not understand, and I have to help take care of her. Can you trust me on this?" Henry nods slowly, but something about the way he moves expresses doubt. He shrugs.

"If I have to," he says. "But I still don't like unfairness one bit."

He always took her side then, reliable as the storms that blew in off the North Sea. Nothing changes because of his fierce protection, as confirmed again tonight six thousand miles from the home where Carrie first experienced Amalia's inequitable quirks. But Henry always watched after her, then. He always acted in the interest of what was fair for her. Where is that connection now? The gap, widening rather than closing, grows more profound by being closer together on the map.

She understands more now than she did as a child, of course. Amalia's troubled soul fails to find the good, leaving her at the mercy of her inner demons, disinclined to take responsibility for her own problems. In many ways she is younger and less able to care for herself than the young cousin who answered the door earlier that evening.

But Amalia is not the only cause, or even the primary one, for Carrie's angst right now. Amalia is a gnat, a mere irritation. And Amalia has worse problems than Carrie ever thought about. That side of the family converges on Brooklyn for a serious reason. Their mother's failing health leaves grave uncertainty about their future. No one knows how long she will last. But that sad news holds only secondary interest for Carrie at the moment, another piece of the chaos.

The others can wait; Carrie has her own concerns. She expected her Mutti and Vati any day, not this bundle of trouble. Where are they? And the brother whose soul is inextricably bound to hers ignores her, breaks his promises to her, fails to engage with her in any real way. What will she do about Henry?

Meldorf, 1893

May 24, 1893
Dearest Carrie,

I know you must be awfully surprised to see your cousins, and sad that they arrived in place of us. I want to explain. Your aunt is ill. She has been plagued by an array of symptoms that lead the doctor here to speak of cancer. He believes she might find treatment in New York's university-connected hospitals that she cannot obtain here in the Holstein region. We are too far away from the center of things in Germany, and to seek treatment here would leave her too weak to travel. So, we made the hard decision to give her our tickets so that she and the children could sail right away. Perhaps the move will make a difference for her, perhaps not. Only time will tell.

More important to our thinking, your father and I are not in a position to take on the children if their mother does not survive. We both are getting older, and Vati in particular is not nearly as spry as you remember him. Taking on a brood of young people at this point in our lives would be a disservice to them and would, frankly, be more than we could handle. You know that Amalia does not take care of herself, much less her siblings. And so, we decided to hasten their departure while her mother has strength enough to make the journey.

Unfortunately, the need for this choice comes at exactly the wrong time for all of us. The news from here may be even more serious than our delay in travel. I wanted you in front of me before I shared my worries about Vati, but I cannot keep the situation from you any longer. More and more, his hands shake so fiercely that he is unable to decorate the chocolates. He tires suddenly and deeply, and his balance is so unreliable that he has fallen twice at home.

I hoped we would be there by now so you and your brothers could see him and share your thoughts, but I can't put off telling you about him any longer. He reminds me of his brothers, and their symptoms before their sad and early deaths. Since he is already years older than they were, I hoped he might escape the cruel malady that brought them down. Alas, I see signs that he will not.

Please pray for all of us. I wish I had adequate words to voice my distress at still being so far from you. Perhaps one day soon we will arrive for a grand reunion. But at this moment, wishes are not yet reality. I'm sorry. I ache to have my baby girl back in my arms. We make the choices we have to make, but I find this decision particularly difficult.

Love always,
Mutti

Brooklyn, 1893

*C*OUNT ON AMALIA *to use up all available resources,* Carrie thinks, *and, not to be dramatic, but she has come from afar to interrupt my life, this time to separate me from my own parents!* Carrie sees herself as kind, not cruel; she feels awful for the impossible circumstances in her cousin's sphere. *But once again, the rest of us pay the price for their problems.* Carrie sputters and plots, but mostly in half-jesting frustration. She knows that revenge can hurt the avenger more than the target.

Carrie eventually resolves, for the thousandth time in her life, to make the best of this disappointing situation, a recurring theme that never becomes easier. In search of a way forward, she fires a barrage of questions at Bridget late that evening, as the two of them sit wrapped in dressing gowns over a pair of china tea cups that match the chintz curtains in Bridget's room.

"The world feels too weighty right now," Carrie says. "I've so much to prioritize and so little idea where to start. I have no notion where to begin even thinking about all the problems. Vati is clearly ill, and it's going to be bad. I was very young, but I remember the tears and the fears that invaded the house when each of his brothers died. Mutti and Vati are still far, far away, much too far, despite all our best planning.

Instead, I get Amalia, bringing her drama troupe along. I already say too much about that, so I'll spare you my laundry list of complaints. And of course, Henry never acts as I wish he would act. Not one word for months, and then we fight when he finally shows his face. The whole puzzle overwhelms me. What do I do?"

"Nothing."

"Nothing?"

"Well, you could ask your mother for more information about your father," Bridget says. "You could assist your aunt in securing further treatment, or caring for her children. But you aren't in a position to make any real difference in either situation. They've already made the decisions before you even became acquainted with the details. I think you start by addressing the situation you can most affect."

"That's not helpful. Everything has to be addressed, and time marches forward."

"In this case, I think your best chance of meaningful change resides in Henry."

"So, what do I do?"

"Nothing."

"How can you mean that? 'Nothing'? I have to do something! I came all this way to be close to him again, and he's nowhere to be found. And even when his body is present, his mind and his soul are still unreachable. What am I going to do?"

"Nothing," Bridget says again. "That's all there is."

"You don't understand. I have to do something. He's getting further and further away from me, and no matter how much I struggle, he won't go back to how it used to be."

"I do understand. And the more you pursue him, the faster he will run—away from you, not toward you."

"But how can that be? He is my Henry, the brother of my heart."

"I think your heart may be a bit much for him right now. He needs plenty of space to spread his wings, much like you do. When you pursue him, he responds by pulling away from you, to get the space he needs."

"But he needs to keep his promises!"

"I think it's more accurate to say that you need him to keep his promises. He no doubt means what he says when he vows to do better. He probably believes he will write you letters from all his exciting places. But your great need creates an impediment instead of an incentive. When he finds himself free to enjoy the adventure, he escapes your nagging by 'forgetting' to write."

"I am not nagging! You are not making even a little bit of sense, Bridget! Why doesn't he do what I need him to do? Why does he keep me out of his adventures?"

"All you can do is stay connected, and let him be himself. That's what you would want if the roles were reversed."

"What I want for myself is Henry! What can I do to get him back?"

"Nothing," Bridget says again. "You have to let him be, and leave the space open for him to come to you."

"You are no help at all!" Carrie expels an exasperated breath, turns on her heels, and bangs the door closed behind her.

The next morning, when Carrie's sheepish face appears at breakfast, she is more open to reason.

"I'm sorry, Bridget. You were trying to help. And maybe I am nagging. I don't know. I want a way of making him understand how much I need him."

"I know, Carrie. None of us have any real way of making anyone else do what we want. We can only control our own actions."

"Hmm. Maybe that's why Amalia bothers me so much. She doesn't want to take responsibility for herself."

"And you pick up the entire burden for everyone and everything. The conundrum is real. But you do it to yourself."

"I do not! If people would do what they're supposed to do, I wouldn't have all the weight on me. They make me take care of things."

"Carrie. They can't make you do anything. What will happen if you simply quit picking up the loose ends? What will happen if you leave the silverware and linens in the middle of the table that Amalia is supposed to set? What if you tell Henry how you feel, and then stop yapping? Make him carry the burden of staying connected to you. What if you take a curious stance instead of a controlling one? What's the worst that would happen?"

"I might lose him."

"So do you really have him now, doing things the way you are?"

"No. But if I did a better job—"

"No better job. Not your responsibility."

Carrie limits her frustration to a noisy sigh this time. Bridget sees her opening and continues.

"If I make everything right every time my young man messes up, I'm doing a disservice to both of us. I'm taking all of the work on myself, and I'm making him feel incompetent, so he's unlikely to try harder the next time. I need to be about improving myself, not improving him. Multiply that by the number of people I know, and a huge weight leaves my life. I really think the same is true for you, Carrie. You have to change your habit."

"Then I still do the work."

"Yes, but it's work you can do, that makes things better, instead of continuing an impossible task. Why don't you talk to him, but differently from before. Tell him how you feel, without telling him what he should do about the situation. Give him a chance to contribute to the solutions between you."

"Well, I don't see what difference that would make, but I guess I could try that approach. What do I have to lose?"

"You think about it. You can change only yourself. Bring the mantra to mind when irritations arise. See if you can look at the problem in a different way."

"Alright." Carrie sounds markedly unconvinced, but raised to be polite. "Thank you, Bridget. I don't see how it will work yet, but maybe I will see it later."

"That's all I can ask! You will conquer this problem in no time, my friend!"

Yes, overly optimistic.

Carrie holds out little hope, but she also knows that Bridget's instincts are reliable. She deliberately begins to prepare for the next occasion at which Henry appears. She can hardly think about him anymore, she notices, without inwardly rolling her eyes. Over and over again she tells herself, *Good never comes of trying to change him; I can change only myself.* Day after day she rehearses invitational words, polishing her speech until it sounds like conversation, editing out all phrases that sound like demands. By the time he finally comes around to see her, she is prepared.

"Henry, can we talk?" she asks as they walk away from the church toward the park. Seeing his wary glance, she hurries on. "No, I don't want a fight. I really want to talk. I think I have been expressing my thoughts to you very badly, and I'd like a chance to say some things that are important to me."

"You know, I'm not very good at keeping in touch. I'm very busy—"

"I know, Henry. And I'm very demanding. And between us, we're not doing a very good job at being friends. That's what you are to me, you know. My brother, yes, but even more, my friend. I'd like to talk to you like my friend."

"Oh. Alright. I guess we could do that."

"I love you, Henry."

"And I, you."

"I give you a harder time than I mean to because I love you, and want you as close as possible. But the fact is, you couldn't get any closer to me if you cut yourself up into little bitty pieces and pushed yourself in through my veins."

"I'll pass," Henry says, laughing.

"Good, because itty bits of Henry inside my veins would be too much adventure even for me! I want to be able to trust that you love me as much as I love you. I want to feel connected. That's what I'm trying to say when I fuss, but I'm not being fair. If you were to complain about me every time you were around, I would resent you so much. Fighting squanders our good time together. I want to say I'm sorry I have been wasting our time. I want to do better." Henry's eyes lose their strain and relax into puddles of blue.

"I want to do better, too," he says. "I think of you all the time when I'm away. I see things that would interest you, and want to tell you about them. I wonder about something, and want to ask you a question."

"You think of me? Oh Henry, that's exactly what I need to hear!"

"I do think of you. And the minute I try to write down my thoughts, my insides do flips and I get so nervous I can hardly think. I bet I have started a hundred letters to you from around the world, like I promise. But I get so jittery I never finish them."

"Thinking of me makes you feel bad?"

"Trying to write down my thoughts makes me aware of how far I fall short of giving you what you need."

"What if I work on needing something different?"

"What do you mean?"

"What if I work on accepting your love for me in the way that you give it, instead of the way I want to receive it?"

"I don't understand."

"I like hearing you say you think of me while you're away."

"But of course I do!"

"And I like hearing you say you will share your adventures by writing to me." She watches his face fall, but continues. "If writing a long letter makes you feel bad, then you are disappointed in yourself when you think of me. That's no good. I want you to enjoy thinking of me. I'd rather find a different way of connecting, that lets us both enjoy each other. I wonder—"

"I know!" He leaps up from his seat on the park bench and pulls her up in a hug.

"You know what?"

"I know what we can do. I can buy a little something in the country I visit, a trinket you can carry around in your apron pocket. When I return home, I can bring my gift to you, and you'll know I am thinking of you while I am away. I can tell you all about my trip, and we can share the adventure in person, instead of long distance."

"What a wonderful idea! I'd like that," Carrie responds. "And I will try to really trust your love, to trust that you are thinking of me even when you're not around to tell me so. A little something in my pocket might be the reminder that I need."

"I can't promise to do this thing perfectly," Henry declares.

"And neither can I," Carrie agrees. "But I do promise to love you with all that I am."

Henry nods. "Deal! And who knows, maybe I'll be inspired to write those letters after all."

Henry next travels to Puerto Rico, where he helps haul a shipment from one of the sugar plantations back to New York. He brings Carrie a postcard of boats waiting at the dock near the refinery, and tells her all about harvesting the cane, extracting the sugar, hefting the huge wooden barrels into the hold.

He returns to Barbados to move a shipment of whiskey and rum, and brings her a postcard of palm trees on the beach. He catches her fancy by telling tales of strange plants, dark faces, and open-air bars serving fruity drinks with fresh coconut.

When he travels again, he will bring another postcard, and another, and the postcards will cement a tradition between them. Carrie learns that ritual is the element they have been missing. She slips the postcards into her apron pocket, proof that he really does think of her every time he goes away.

Brooklyn, 1893

July 17, 1893
Dear Vati,

Mutti writes that your balance is off and your hands shake, maybe due to the family curse that contributed to your brothers' early deaths. I wish I could be there to throw my arms around you and then swirl the icing with a steady hand to help you cope. You always scooped me up when I was angry, and enveloped me in love when I was sad. (And I was angry and sad a lot, I know, which gives you some idea of how important you are to me!) You have forever been my silent buffer against difficult times, and I long to be the same to you. I hope you feel my prayers scooping and enveloping. Please come soon. Sometimes only a hug will do.

Love always,
Your Caroline

South America, 1894

September 5, 1894
Dear Carrie,

I'm writing from northern Colombia, where we are inspecting the farms which grow the coffee we will transport. Since this trip is my first experience in the coffee trade, I've had a lot to learn! I accompanied my boss into the countryside. Officials there showed us the big plantations that produced massive crops in the old days, the days when the Colombian economy ran on the backs of enslaved people. They compared coffee production in that era with the cotton, rice, and indigo plantations of the southern United States.

When slavery became illegal in Colombia in 1851, the coffee trade collapsed, no doubt disappointing our grandparents in Meldorf. Mutti always said that Opa loved a little coffee in his sugar, so now I've worked with both of his favorite crops!

The large acreage of the plantations has since been divided into smaller farms, again similar to the U.S. Our dealings here have involved several farmers who have abutting lands, all descending from the same plantation, but operated independently today. You would love the landscape, sort of like Germany, but boasting warmer temperatures and higher mountains. Lush, green foliage stretches for miles and miles on end. I'm sure the owners know where the *property lines fall, but no one else knows, giving the impression that the plantations are intact. They are, of course, actually being managed much differently than in those days.*

You will appreciate a story I heard about the beginning of coffee production in Colombia. Some say the crop arrived in the 1500s, others say not until the late 1700s. Whatever the date, the mythology persists that Jesuit missionaries introduced the plant. Many people tell the tale of a priest named Francisco Romero, who, after hearing confession in the village of Salazar de la Palmas, chose to forgo the typical gold and silver penance payments.

Instead, he ordered the villagers to plant a certain number of coffee plants on their property, and pay the indulgences in beans. I don't know whether the story is factual, but certainly it rings true — coffee is undeniably part of the fabric of the country at this point, both its culture and its economy.

While we are back in Cartagena, where the ship waits for us, we have a little time to play while we wait for the trucks to bring the shipment. I am fascinated by the fortress at the top of the hill, the Castillo de San Felipe. The Spaniards built the fortress in the seventeenth century, and to this day, no enemy has ever overtaken it. Tunnels underneath the entire fort are designed to reverberate and amplify sound in ways that allow even a footfall by the enemy to be heard and readily discovered. The design is genius.

But Getsemani would be your favorite spot here. No, not the garden in Jerusalem — the neighborhood in Cartagena! Something equally mundane and charming makes it delightful for an ordinary walk. After the grandeur of the old city and the impressive strength of the fortress, something settled me about wandering plain old gardens and shops, the same signs of life that you'd see in Brooklyn, a world away but like next door.

Well, the shipment will be ready for loading any time now. I'm surprised that I find this letter so easy to write. But I bought you a postcard of Getsemani anyway, and I'll bring it when I see you next. In the meantime, I'm going to find a stamp to post this letter in hopes that it will beat me home. I need to get back to work!

Love from your brother,
Henry

Brooklyn, 1894

CARRIE READS THE LENGTHY, long-awaited letter twice, then three times, weighing the scant heft of the thin envelope, breathing in the scent of faraway places wafting in with the paper, gazing at the exotic portrait of an unfamiliar stamp. She buzzes with excitement at this unexpected gesture from Henry, and she loves the details he shares. Her breath enters her nose and spreads all the way to her toes, satisfaction filling to the brim of her being. Smiling a grin wider than the distance between them has ever been, she reads a fourth time, then slips the letter in her pocket to share at Tante Retta's Sunday dinner.

By the time she arrives at Retta's door, however, a different conversation is already underway.

"Carrie, the wash smelled like mildew this week!" The complaints begin while the open door still frames Carrie's shadow. Carrie winces, then nods at the buzz of irritation around her. She made this mistake once, long ago. When mildew settles its stink into the wash, the clothes can't be worn, the linens can't be used, and the entire ritual of soaking, scrubbing, boiling, rinsing and wringing must start all over. The chore is a full-time job for at least one day of the week in every household in Brooklyn, and nobody has time for the wash to go wrong.

August's nose leads him to the discovery. The bundle on the ledge outside the kitchen window reeks of a tell-tale stench that attracts his attention. He and his wife now make a home not only for their son, but also for August's aunt and his four cousins. Now they will have to begin the onerous chore of washing afresh. But Carrie does not hear August's voice at this moment. The complaint comes from Amalia. Carrie's hands tremble and her face flushes.

"Whose responsibility is it to hang out the laundry, Amalia?" Carrie asks.

Amalia shrugs.

"Whose responsibility, Amalia?"

"You did the laundry."

"I left my own job to come teach you how to do the laundry. Did you finish the job?"

"I did everything you showed me how to do."

"Did you hang the clothes and the linens on the line outside?"

"You didn't show me how."

"You're right. I didn't show you how. I left you clear instructions and went back to my job. But you know how. You have watched people hang laundry all your life. Did you do it?"

By this time, August and his aunt, huddled together on the couch, alternate murmurs of 'it's okay, Amalia' and 'it's not such a big deal, Carrie' in voices little louder than whispers.

"I disagree," Carrie says. "Amalia's failure to do her part in this family is wrong, and a huge problem. The time has arrived for Amalia to learn to participate in the chores. And for the rest of this family to cease giving excuses, and expect Amalia to do her best."

"Now, Carrie, you know . . ." Amalia's mother tries to sooth Carrie's wrath, but Carrie is not in the mood. Rather than a reason to continue the excuses, illness is the reason to interrupt the excuses. The patient survived the surgery, but the prognosis excludes long-term survival, and Carrie knows they must press forward and prepare for the inevitable. She deliberately sets aside the taboo on dealing firmly with the ill, and continues to speak her mind.

"I know that this family is in the habit of doing everything we can to excuse Amalia's negative, childish, and irresponsible actions. That's what I know." By this time Amalia sobs, and her siblings erect a wall of glares to protect her from Carrie. "And I know that all the excuses only teach Amalia to offer more excuses. We cannot afford to do that any longer. We expect that she will care for her brothers and sister when their mother leaves this earth, and yet we do not even hold her accountable for hanging out the wash? How does that work?" All adult eyes fall to the carpet on the worn wooden floor.

Carrie presses on. "Right, ignoring the challenge will not get the job done. So, I am stepping up to change my behavior right this minute. I am no longer in charge of Amalia's laundry. Nor the table she is to set, the food she is to prepare, or any other chore that belongs to Amalia. I suggest you all make the same decision."

Carrie leaves that night without eating. She would rather be on her own, back in the Chapelle's quiet kitchen. Even Tante Retta cannot smooth things over, and Carrie secretly relishes that failure. If no one acts on his behalf, August will have four extra children to corral without extra help. Carrie cannot keep the injustice of that predicament to herself. Someone has to talk about the problem. Someone has to jolt them all into addressing the situation. And as the most irritated, it might as well be her.

"I have a newly revised job description," Carrie announces as she and Bridget share cold chicken and green salad later that evening in the Chapelle's kitchen. "I now limit what I do in the Denzler family to things that are my own job, not someone else's business. And you are the one who convinced me that the change that temporarily raises my hackles will also lighten my load!"

"Good for you," Bridget says. "I knew you could change the dynamic. But it does take a lot of fortitude to rearrange the pieces and reassign the parts everyone else wants you to play, doesn't it? I am really proud of you!"

"Thanks. Standing up hurts more than I thought it would, but I let my anger work for me, like you said. I'm uneasy about letting the pieces fall and how everyone will feel about that. But I'll survive."

"And in the nick of time, too. Because I have some news."

"News?"

"Yes. Are you ready?"

"Yes." But Carrie wonders.

"I'm getting married on Thanksgiving weekend!"

119

"Oh, Bridget! I am so happy for you. You have been waiting for that proposal for as long as I've known you. That beau of yours finally made up his mind, *ja*?"

"Yes. And I want you to be my bridesmaid. Will you? Please?"

"Of course I will! You are the closest thing I have to a sister, after all these brothers! Flora is getting closer, but not quite. And goodness knows, Amalia doesn't fit the part!" They laugh in unison.

"You'll need relief from the way the Denzler family drama siphons off your time, I think. I need to give the Chapelles my notice, and then I'm willing to bet you will have a new job description around here, too. I predict they will move you into my position and hire you some help. You will be great at the job!"

"Thank you! And all the more reason for me to rid myself of the work at August's house, if I'm to have more to do here."

"You will accept the job, won't you?"

"I will, if they offer it. You're forgetting the decision is theirs, not yours, to make!

"Well, yes, I suppose."

"And I should say, I have one condition. As long as they continue to hire a nurse, I'd love to take your position. These babies are coming too fast around here for me to keep up!"

"As if you want to!"

"You know me too well! Now, about that wedding . . ."

They chatter on into the evening, planning simple touches to transform Bridget's occasion at her parent's humble home into a very special day.

The wedding goes beautifully. The Chapelles offer Carrie the job. The family somehow survives when she holds firm. While love still floats in the air and the snow begins to fly, Carrie ripens for the next adventure to come. Life settles into a pleasant hum, agreeable enough, but hardly exciting. Basic news dominates these days.

"How is Bridget?" Frederick asks, on a Sunday evening as Christmas nears.

"She is well," Carrie says. "I'm not sure she likes living in her mother-in-law's home as well as she liked being on her own, but she's adjusting."

"And you are enjoying your new job?"

"Enjoying? It's fine, I guess. Not all that different from my usual week, except I do more bossing and less being bossed. The new girl works hard. The children sure can leave a mess in their wake, but I'm staying out of their way. Life is still housework." She shrugs. "One thing I really do like, though. I really like having someone to meet at the wurst vendor's cart for Sunday lunch! As much as I miss Bridget, her departure does give me a friend outside the house."

Their brother and sister work-weary bodies melt into sturdy oak chairs opposite each other across a dining table dressed in muslin. They sit, bemused as a sulky Amalia actually extracts flatware from the buffet and arranges the pieces into place settings around the table's edges.

Between August and Retta, Amalia progresses toward becoming a semi-competent, if still unwilling, helper around the house. The occasional mildew still creeps into the laundry. And even when they are clean, the linens are never folded as neatly as Carrie would require. Still, they are on their way to coping, and Carrie leaves any problems to the others. Not that they don't occasionally try to pull her into their arguments, and sometimes she bites. But not often, not anymore. They are all a little afraid to cross the new Carrie, and she secretly enjoys the power she wields.

"Do you hear anything from Henry?" Carrie asks, moving to a topic that leaves her feeling vulnerable.

"You haven't had any more letters? He makes regular runs on the high seas, two more trips to South America since Colombia."

"Neither a word nor a visit. He entertained royally, sharing postcards and live commentary after each trip, for a while. Then he produced that one bright flash of writing, and faded against the sunset."

"I'm sorry. He really does stay busy, you know."

"I'm sure he does. But he doesn't share any of that busy-ness with me. And he promised. I thought we had reached an understanding." Tears creep into her voice.

"Oh, Little Carrie. Not so little any more, but still carrying such tender affection. I wish I could either change him or rid you of him, but then you would no doubt be even sadder. At least now there is hope that life will move in your favor."

"Hope fades too fast," she replies. "And setting free what I long to grasp close is a deeper discipline than I typically practice. But I try. I try to let hope lead me."

Carrie acts on another piece of Bridget's wisdom in the service of hope. She begins to use her spare moments to do things she enjoys, rather than wasting her time worrying over Henry. She spends more time at the library, browsing among the books and periodicals, following world events more closely than before, finding new authors and subjects to explore. She even heads across the alley to the Astral Tenement House, a Pratt Institute project, to participate with the residents in English lessons to improve both her reading and speaking skills. Hope rises as she puts her effort into improving herself.

Between mundane events and splashes of ordinary feeling, the rule that death comes in sets of three punctuates the lives of the Denzlers with sharp pains and dull aches.

First, Amalia's mother takes leave of this ordinary world. She goes quickly and quietly. August takes her to the doctor the day after Christmas, before they even remove the candles from the tree. She becomes so weak that the doctor admits her to Brooklyn Lutheran for monitoring overnight.

A night turns into another, then another. Amalia visits each day and comes home complaining about the nursing staff and the stench of disinfectants, hardly saying a word about the patient. On the eve of New Year's Day, as fireworks light up the sky, Amalia makes the stony announcement that her mother's light has been extinguished. She is gone. Amalia then retreats into a place where no one else can reach her.

And second, on the evening of the very same day, Magda posts five letters from Meldorf. Knowing she might not have words in the moment, she prepares notes a few days ahead of time on her best stationery and slips them into a kitchen drawer among the towels and household bills.

On that evening, unknown to the family already grieving in Brooklyn, she retrieves the sealed envelopes, attaches a stamp to each, and pens the date on the back flap. December 31, 1894. She walks the familiar cobblestone lane and drops the envelopes in the postbox. Just after the start to the new year, each of her children receives an ivory envelope, the card inside informing her offspring that their Vati is dead. She plans to sail on the next ship from Hamburg.

The Denzler world waits, in silence that doesn't quite catch a complete breath, for the third death to complete the cycle.

Brooklyn, 1895

CARRIE BRAVES A winter storm to make her way to Tante Retta's dinner on the third Sunday in February. Why would anyone come from the sunny south to New York during its most brutal month? But regardless of the timing, Catrina is in town from Charleston. Catrina stayed with the Maasens on her arrival to the New World, and bonded tightly with Retta in a time of transition for both of them. Retta naturally insists that Carrie meet her.

For anyone else, Carrie would have remained bundled up in front of the fire reading a book, where she had been since early morning. But for Retta, she attempts the miserable feat. For the fifth day in a row, temperatures fail to rise above eight degrees, and the buildings near the river form a wind tunnel through the streets.

Braced against the winter storm, Carrie's image against the gray afternoon is at once both colorful and anonymous. Her face buried in multiple scarves, her fingers unmoving in two pairs of gloves, whether from bulk or from cold temperatures makes no difference. She fights for every step, gaining slow progress against a wall of wind and snow. When she finally reaches the landing and the door bangs open, family and friends already surround the table. Now that she's here, she will be glad to meet Catrina.

Slipping into her usual chair, Carrie looks around the table, her eyes scanning the occupant of each chair. Sitting to the left of her, both August and his wife emit a hazy golden glow since the announcement of another little Denzler on the way, nearly five years after their first bundle of joy. Then Flora, joining Frederick again today, perhaps a sign of permanence to come? Swarthy Louis sits dutifully alongside his fair brothers. He and Frederick have temporary charge of Amalia's siblings, their mother now two months gone. The children are in the living room using footstools as makeshift tables, out of sight, out of mind. Then Amalia herself, her face frozen in time, unable to move or think beyond nodding a head or passing a dish on request. She alone speaks to no one else.

No Henry today, no surprise. But Retta's children are here, the parents of the youth who eat at the kitchen table. And Retta herself sits in the center of this family, clearly the matriarch, presiding at the crowded table.

Carrie's own matriarch, her darling Mutti, sits quietly in the shadow of her lifelong friend, absorbing the human extravaganza of Sunday night at the Maasens. Newly arrived from German shores, Mutti slips into the landscape of Brooklyn as if she were there all along, demanding little, happy to be on the same side of the ocean as her offspring. Carrie's work, whirling around the holidays and the arrival of yet another little Chapelle, has prevented her from much more than these few Sunday dinners with Mutti. But a break is coming, and she will spend it properly catching up with her mother.

On the other side of Retta sits a woman Carrie doesn't know. She must be Catrina, the daughter of

Retta's old friend from Hanover. Carrie has always known her name, but never seen her face. Next to Catrina sits her husband Diedrich, to whom she was introduced at this very table.

And completing the circle, closest to Carrie, sits a young man. She searches her memory. Did Retta say something about a son? Ah, Witt. Now she remembers. Retta quickly introduces him amid the chaos. Hmm. This man could be the real reason Retta requires Carrie's presence at the table today. She suspects that Retta's insistence on this dinner invitation is more about Catrina's offspring than his mother. Young men have appeared at their dinner table before, as if by magic.

"How are you enjoying our lovely weather?" The stranger seems nice enough, but Carrie chooses a safe, polite topic when she speaks. "It's very tempting to curl up and resolve never to leave the house again!"

He laughs. "Yes, we have those days, too. But we would stay inside for a different six months of the year, seeking cool in the heat of summer, if it were left to us."

The niceties continue. They both turn to Retta's excellent dumplings and chicken, German style, and proclaim them delicious.

Later, more casually, Witt approaches Carrie again.

"Do you like Brooklyn?" he asks. "Everything seems awfully busy, but then, Charleston is a very small city compared to this one. I fear I would be lost in the hustle and bustle."

"I came from a very small town, just a village, really," Carrie says. "At first, I scanned constantly for trees among the concrete and sky between the buildings. Now that I can find those things in the parks and along the river, Brooklyn and I get along fine. Do you like Charleston?"

"I wouldn't live anywhere else. I enjoy having just the right mix of city mouse and country mouse, especially living on the farm as we do."

"I can understand that mix of desires. Sometimes I long for an easy way to return to the uninterrupted nature I enjoyed as a child." *This conversation is going nowhere fast,* she thinks.

"I've never lived anywhere except Charleston, so I hesitate to make comparisons." He pauses. "You say you long for the outdoors of your childhood. What else do you long for?"

She turns her head sharply to look him square in the eye. "I long for adventure and learning."

"Where would you go and what would you do?" He doesn't even blink.

"I'd travel to every continent and learn all their languages. I'd make art as casually as Retta makes dinner. I'd read every book ever written. I'd learn the farm by working on the farm and the ballet by dancing. I'd go back to the schooling I left behind at twelve. I'd travel to places my brother Henry has never been, and tell him about the world. I'd connect my life to his through my own experiences, and not depend on him to share his."

"Yes, I believe you would." And that's all he needs to say. Dinner conversation shifts in that moment from mundane to monumental. Carrie glances around the table again, wondering if anyone else notices that her breath catches, that she dares to believe that someone in this world might take her dreams seriously. The house chatters on around her, but she hears no words. All she can hear is the pounding in her chest.

After dinner, Carrie and Witt stake a claim on one corner of the kitchen table, away from the crowded living room. They enter each other's lives in earnest over tea and *apfelkuchen*, the favorite dessert of both their mothers. Cinnamon perfumes the room to provide the perfect aura for their beginning. Apples baked into the top of rich, brown-sugar cake fresh out of the oven give them a common heritage from which to start. Brooklyn adds a scoop of ice cream that breaks from German tradition. Carrie floats home on warm bubbles the frigid weather cannot pop, on the arm of the man who will join her in her next adventure. Before tonight, no one has ever thought to walk her home from Sunday dinner.

Not since her small childhood rebellions has Carrie slipped away from her duties so often. Thoughts of Witt occupy her mind to distraction, and she feels like her five-year-old self slipping out to play pirates with Henry. She cleans the kitchen and retrieves the post, but although her hands remain at Miss Rosie's command, her mind wafts completely beyond the house. In an almost unseemly way, she floats through the days that follow. Her mind drifts to the dusky moment when she has finished washing the dinner dishes and stoking the fire.

At the time when she would usually retire to her room, tonight she bundles up in her wool coat and muffler to slip out the back door. The man she thinks she loves waits in the sleepy street to see her. They walk arm in arm past the empty storefronts, bracing each other against the wind.

"What did you do today?" Carrie chooses the obvious question.

"I thought of you!" His smile accompanies the reply. "Also, I learned to shovel snow. And I mastered the art of scattering ice cream salt to make icy steps safe for humanity. I put on my warm clothes and took them off again about fifty times as I ran papers and sweet treats back and forth between the shop and the warmly ensconced Retta upstairs. Oh, and your mama and my mama and pop."

"Wow—Tante Retta puts you to good use!"

"I think everyone who lives here is just tired of doing the winter chores, so she's taking advantage of new blood," he laughs. "I don't mind. What did you do?"

"I thought of you, too! While I put meals on the table, and wood on the fire, and washed and boiled and beat and wrung and hung every last piece of household fabric. But I stayed warm and cozy while I worked. Not a step outside until now. I even took inventory of the kitchen and rearranged the menu so I could skip a day at the market."

"You are one smart woman! Saving all your chilly moments for me, I assume."

"Naturally. Someone has to pay proper attention to our guests." *And snuggle up to keep you warm,* she adds in her head. They stop in the street to look at each other, the wind whirling around their flushed cheeks as the blush of new love whirls between them.

"Do you believe in love at first sight?" Carrie asks.

"I didn't before, but I'm becoming convinced," Witt answers.

"I like the concept," she says, "and also the reality, which I didn't expect. The unpredictability is part of the charm. It feels very much like adventure."

The conversation drifts, until the moment can no longer be delayed when everyone returns to their own beds, each with a rubber bottle of scalding water to warm the sheets.

The next day passes roughly the same, Carrie folding the clean laundry and returning clothes to their cupboards, and Witt alternately tending the snow and reading the gleam in his mother's eye and the circumspect way his father wonders aloud. Witt worried, when he agreed to this journey, that the days would creep slowly. Carrie had not given time a thought, as accustomed as she is to another routine dinner at Retta's table, until the gentleman charmed her. Now, they both find themselves wondering where hours go when they fly. Too quickly, the time for parting arrives.

Carrie accompanies Witt and his parents to the train station three days after they meet, not knowing when she will see them again. But she entertains no doubt of another meeting in their future. Witt most certainly figures into her next big adventure. For a long while, they will have to exist together entirely on paper. Charleston and Brooklyn are a world apart. Even further than Meldorf, because she has never been to South Carolina, and has no pictures in her mind to make the place real. Her only image of his world is in his eyes, as she bids him farewell. They each check at least three times to be sure they have the other's mailing address. They each have three more things to say. Finally, Carrie has to wave good-bye to Witt, framed in the train window, his parents' faces dimly reflected behind him. *My daddy would have loved you*, she thinks, the thought surprising her. *He would have trusted you to protect my heart.*

Curiously, for a woman whose newfound love chugs away on an iron path, Carrie continues to think of her father as she winds her way back to the Chapelles' house. She forgets sometimes that her father is gone. The six years in Brooklyn without him reduce him in some ways to a blur in her mind, a dim figure far away from her life.

In other ways, her memories are pure and clear and present. She remembers his strength as he holds her when Frederick boards the ship, and his laughter as he restrains her from walloping Henry. She remembers his quiet serenity as he waits for the sound of her voice when she retreats into silence. She remembers his acknowledgment of her sixth sense, the one that tells her what no one else will speak aloud. She remembers his kiss on her brow as they arrive at the port in Rotterdam, his gentle voice as he utters the last words she ever heard from his lips: "My Caroline."

Yes, her Vati would have liked this man she resolves to call her own. She feels sure, and reassured. Her Mutti will find Witt acceptable, solely because the family line stretches from Mutti through Retta to Catrina. He is already family.

The challengers will be her brothers. They will question her haste in rushing to love him. They will claim she lacks adequate experience to handle a man trying to woo her. They will wonder about the man's honor in light of his sudden appearance, whether the love is real since the excitement blossomed so quickly. They will take her aside and warn her, question her, seek to protect her. And she is ready for their objections.

She will admit to appearing impetuous. She also will remind them of what they have forgotten, that her experience of men is rooted in these four brothers. They are the men who helped raise her, who molded her taste and understanding. They taught her how a man who cares about her should behave. And maybe, just maybe, she will say she is being true to her nature, for she knows what she wants, what nourishes her spirit. But the best evidence she can think of is the unshakeable certainty that fills her breath in this moment. She knows, beyond any reservation, that her Vati would have loved Witt Gruening. And she knows beyond knowing that she loves him, too.

Brooklyn, 1895

CARRIE ENJOYS HAVING her Mutti in town. She enjoys finally having the privilege of seeing first-hand her long friendship with Retta. Magda has aged rapidly over the six years since Carrie left Meldorf, the inevitable result of fretting over the state of her homeland, her husband's poor health, and her children growing up at a vast distance.

Carrie is grateful for the gift of time. As winter turns to spring, the Chapelles wend their way abroad to introduce the children to their French grandparents. Carrie maintains daily tasks in their home, but, for the first time since her arrival, she also enjoys plenty of open time to pursue her own interests. She makes a list of things to show Mutti, and Retta joins them to make vigorous work of checking off their activities.

They spend an afternoon wandering from store to store in the now vast enterprise of Maasen & Denzler Confections, seeing what the boys have accomplished in a little over a decade in town, listening to Retta chat about the decisions they've made and the work they've accomplished. They worship at the Trinity German Lutheran Church, giving Mutti an hour of uninterrupted mother tongue in her new English-speaking world. They visit the wurst seller's cart after services, and Mutti meets the famous Bridget, with her hefty evidence of rapidly approaching motherhood.

They wander the hillside homes of departed Denzler and Maasen relatives as the first blossoms of spring warm the chilly air at Lutheran Cemetery. Since her Mutti arrived in Brooklyn, Carrie's life has been a whirlwind of work and winter. She welcomes the chance to share the core of her life with her mother, and her mother's dearest friend. She also enjoys the uninterrupted return to her native tongue in their presence.

"You have done so well here, Carrie," Magda says. "In just a few years, you have made this city as much home for you as your ancestral village will always be for me. I'm proud of you."

"Thank you, Mutti. I wish Vati could have come here, too."

"Yes, my dear, I know. Please believe me when I say that he knew beyond sight that you were whole and well. Your Vati embodied the very picture of faith."

"Mutti, did he suffer much after I left?"

"I'm afraid that to answer truthfully, I must say yes, he did. Not from your absence, but from the illness he rejoiced you did not have to see. You left in the autumn, and we began to see signs by Christmas that he would join the fate of his brothers. Perhaps mercifully, the eternal creep of the disease also meant weakened organs and bodily systems. In the end, a short struggle against the flu finally ended his life. I am at peace, knowing that the suffering stopped at his death.

"And Carrie," her mother goes on, "you remained his light in those dark days in a way you cannot imagine. He spoke of you every day, wondered what you were doing and how you were getting on in the United States. Every day he wondered aloud what we

135

would see when we all were reunited. Every day he chuckled at some memory, bright and alive in his being, of your antics, your arguments, your striving to outpace your brothers. Every day his satisfied sigh signaled another memory of his Caroline. You were with him, Carrie. Every day."

Carrie dabs the corner of her eye with a freshly pressed handkerchief.

"Thank you, Mutti. I needed to hear exactly that!"

Just before the Chapelles arrive home, Carrie reserves one entire Tuesday for a very special tour. She wants to show her mother the Pratt Institute, especially the library that sustains her where school is impossible. Retta has been there on her own, but she has never seen the place through Carrie's eyes.

"Can you believe the wonder of this place?" Carrie begins the tour almost giggling. "I come here most days just to read the newspaper, over here." The sweep of her hand indicates the racks over which various newspapers are draped.

"And over there are the reference books, like dictionaries and encyclopedias, that I use when I have a specific question. Or, I can go to the desk and ask for any subject or story I can think of or imagine, and they will find a book to match my request. A book about whales, maybe, or tomatoes, or clothing styles of the 1750s. Or just a good story, or a collection of poetry. Anything. I have my own number on a card, and the librarians let me take the books home to read!"

"Oh, my dear, you sound as excited as you were about your adventures as a child," her mother says. "But

Carrie, Brooklyn didn't invent this phenomenon. Don't you remember the library in Meldorf?"

"I haven't thought about that place in years!" Retta says. "Wasn't it up the hill, around the corner from the church?" Magda nods.

"I don't remember that," Carrie says, "but I do remember we had a library at school. I used to put books back on the shelf for the librarian on Thursday afternoons. But Mutti, since I don't go to school here, I didn't know for a long time that I still had a library, and I missed reading so much. When Bridget brought me to this one, I just about burst open!"

"I can hear that." Her amused mother's eyes smile. "Your father and I often used the public library in Meldorf. I didn't realize you wouldn't know to look for one here, but I guess it makes sense that you would have connected the library with school."

"I would still rather speak in German," Carrie says, "but I have become very, very good at reading in English, and can learn anything I can imagine to ask. Now, come out here and let me show you."

The three women round the corner into a broad hallway to see tall wooden doors spaced evenly on either side. A narrow open window between the hallway and the classroom tops each door. A slight breeze crosses the hallway from the open windows inside the rooms. They hear voices coming from the rooms behind those doors, and Magda and Retta realize immediately that Carrie intends to show them the school to which the library belongs. They creep down the hallway to an open doorway at the far end.

"Shhh. Look." Carrie points through the doorway. A dozen or so young men and women, a little younger

137

than Carrie's eighteen years, surround three black-topped tables. The white clapboard walls stretch nearly a story and a half to a ceiling of dark wooden planks. Near the top, the outer wall melds into a row of windows. Shaded lamps hang above the students' heads on long cords connected to the ceiling, and colorful charts and photographs adorn the lower sections of the walls.

A man of about thirty-five years, dressed in a black suit, tie, and buttoned waistcoat, carefully pours liquid from one glass beaker to another. The liquid gives off a coiling smoky wisp. He instructs the students to don their goggles and gloves, and then observes them as they carefully duplicate his actions. Their murmured questions entirely consume their concentration; no one even notices the three quiet figures in the doorway. Carrie turns away and gestures for the others to follow. On re-entering the library, Carrie speaks quietly, urgently.

"He does things like that every single day, Mutti! And a woman reads poetry and explains all the symbols, and another has her students write on the blackboard when they solve problems. I think they do mathematics. I sometimes sit in the hall and listen. I am disappointed when the girls have to take cooking classes while the boys build airplanes, but mostly they learn wonderful things together. I wish I could come to school here, too!"

"Oh, my darling," Mutti says, "that's exactly what we wanted for you. But plans don't always work out as we'd like, do they?"

Carrie's face falls in a rare wistful moment, but she quickly returns to her tour guide role.

"Now we will go to meet Miss Annie. Do you know her, Retta?"

"I've heard you speak of her," Retta says, "but I don't think I've ever met her."

"Well," Carrie continues, "Mrs. Plummer, who is in charge of the whole library, taught Miss Annie at the school for librarians at the college. I would love to be a librarian. A library isn't life on the sea, but the very next best thing—I would have such an adventure!"

Magda has difficulty absorbing all of Carrie's monologue, and Retta feels as if she is meeting a whole new person. Both women listen carefully. Their eyes meet in silence. *This young woman would have made a fine librarian, if things were different,* they each read the thought of the other. They hear a woman laugh as Carrie hugs her, then see her turn toward them.

"Mutti, Retta, this is Miss Annie. Miss Annie, my mother, and my Tante Retta."

Anne Carroll Moore extends her hand.

"I am pleased at long last to meet you both. Mrs. Denzler, your daughter is quite the fixture around here, and I am delighted to meet you! And Mrs. Maasen, I have heard such wonderful things about you."

"And I, you," Retta replies gracefully.

"Hallo," says Magda. "I am quite happy to meet the famous Miss Annie, too. You are a well-known figure at our dinner table."

"I understand," says Annie, "our families have quite a lot in common. I think I remember correctly that Carrie has four older brothers. I grew up as the baby sister to seven strapping lads. I was a bit spoiled, but growing up that way buoyed my confidence and strengthened my zeal!"

"Oh, yes. My girl spent her childhood as the shining star of the universe! But she seems to have turned out just fine. A little doting never hurts."

"A girl does need to feel loved, doesn't she?" Retta says.

"I've always adored children," Annie says, "which Carrie and I see very differently." They all laugh, and Annie goes on. "But when we met, really just beyond her own childhood, she eagerly devoured everything I recommended from the children's library. We have always gotten along famously, haven't we, dear?"

Annie smiles fondly at the young woman, then turns back to her mother. "Carrie borrows her reading almost entirely from the adult sections now, but she still comes back to visit me."

"You have been very important to her," Magda replies. "I so appreciate both you and Retta for the attention you've shown my daughter during a time I've been so far away."

"Getting to know Carrie has been entirely my pleasure." Miss Annie smiles broadly, and Retta nods. "I'm glad I could help fill the gap. She feels like a success story to me. Sometimes I think Carrie single-handedly transformed me into a children's librarian, with all the advice she asked me to dispense!"

"She can do that," Retta says. "Carrie is a wonder."

"And she's always loved her teachers," Magda says, nodding at the other women.

"Have you seen the school yet? Or the museum upstairs? Or Astral House?" Annie asks. "The current

Mr. Pratt—all the directors here have been one Mr. Pratt or another—is dedicated to the quest of making a big tenement work for the residents rather than against them. You must visit Astral House."

"Our tour guide has taken us through the library itself, one hallway of the high school, and now the children's library," Magda says. "I have a feeling we have a lot more to see!"

"We do, Mutti! Let's go upstairs!" Carrie fails to play the role of a grown-up very well. She is too excited about showing off her favorite indoor venue to worry about appearing sophisticated. Returning to the hallway, they climb four short sets of stairs that turn back on each other to reach another broad hallway, this time stretching both ways from the windowed stairwell. More of the doors stand open on this level than below, and the others shadow Carrie in peeking around doorframes.

Up here, the walls are dark and the ceilings white, the opposite of downstairs. But bright light from a similar bank of windows keeps the feeling airy. Classes in academic subjects fill the classrooms at one end, art classes focused on drawing, painting, and clothing design near the stairwell, and instruction in some of the more practical skills at the other end of the hall. A sewing class is mostly girls, and a metal-working class mostly boys. But the woodworking class at the very end of the hall is a mix of both.

"I can see why you like this school," Magda says to her daughter. "You always have wanted boys and girls to do the same things together."

Carrie shrugs. "I just think you should be able to do what interests you. No one should be bored in this

141

world. There are too many things to learn and do." Her mother and Retta nod their heads in a twin gesture of agreement.

They return to the stairwell to climb again, to a huge open space completely lined with bookshelves reaching all the way to a high ceiling made of large glass panes in wooden frames. Wooden ladders on wheels provide access to the volumes stored here. The vast space, uninterrupted shelving and glass ceiling create a heavenward sweep that precludes any sense of limits.

Half of the room is populated with additional bookshelves and sturdy chairs around large wooden tables with green-shaded lamps. The other half of the space boasts display cases constructed of wood and glass and placed at regular intervals. The cases are full of pottery. Tiny placards indicate that some of the bowls and vases are student work, and others part of the museum's historical collection. The walls of books pull the divergent spaces into one.

"Isn't this place wonderful?" Carrie's voice and eyes shine in equal measures of awe.

"These rooms are full of magic," Retta concedes. "I understand why you love it."

"And they don't limit the library to families who can afford to send their children here to school," Carrie says. "Everything is open to me, and also to people who have even more modest means, like at Astral House. Come on, I'll show you."

The women descend the stairs the same way they had come up, the older lagging somewhat behind the younger at times. Back at the street, they walk a block or so, turn into an alley, and enter a very tall brick building from the back. A gymnasium occupies that end of the ground floor of the apartment complex.

"The high school students come across the alley to use the basketball court," Carrie says, "or to play other games."

Today, however, a kindergarten class sits cross-legged on the floor alongside two adult teachers, rolling a ball from one to the other across the circle. The action pauses briefly while one of the teachers speaks, and then restarts. This time, the students stand, and the ball bounces between them. When a student releases the ball, they take half a step backward, so that the circle becomes larger and larger.

"I've seen this game before," Carrie says. "Once, many years ago, I saw every kindergarten teacher in Brooklyn in this room. They were sitting cross legged in a circle on the floor, just like today, but gathering their long skirts up short to let them move." Carrie giggles at the memory of all those women and their ridiculous positions. "Now I understand what they were prac-ticing. The teachers, like the little children, learn by doing.

"Miss Annie says that other teachers, who depend on more traditional methods — learning things by heart, reading from a book, repeating information over and over again — have to work hard to change their mindset to implement a true kindergarten program."

Carrie is not so much interested in the children as in the way activity infuses the entire Pratt curriculum. She readily comprehends the connection between kindergarten play and active learning for older students. Her pride radiates in the fact that German immigrants just like her originated these programs. The fact that the kindergarten has its own library in the Astral tenement, supplemented by books of interest to their parents, captures her fascination.

"Can you imagine having a library in the same place where you live?" Carrie asks. "The residents can just run downstairs when they finish one book and want to begin another. They don't even have to leave the house if they want to answer a question. I can't imagine living anywhere quite so grand."

Magda smiles at Retta. What a curious viewpoint her daughter holds. Even as a recent arrival, Magda has been in the city long enough to understand that tenements are not always nice places. The tall buildings, hurriedly erected to accommodate a burgeoning population, can be unpleasant and downright dangerous. Rapid construction with subpar materials, and lack of insight into safety concerns like emergency exits, make the units death traps in a fire.

The apartments are tiny and lack basic amenities such as running water and cooking facilities. Cramped and overcrowded, living on top of each other too often exacerbates the effects of hot tempers on even hotter summer nights into a different kind of conflagration. Anyone who is able would rather make their home above a local business, like the Maasens and Denzlers.

Only their Carrie would think of a tenement as a life of luxury, because of the library a forward-thinking social worker thought to install in the basement. Only Carrie, boasting a mere elementary education, could so casually evaluate the methods of a prestigious educational institution. Only Carrie, thrust into adulthood early, could return so readily to her childhood, all her excitement born of curiosity.

Brooklyn, 1896

HER GIGGLES AND innocence sometimes represent her as girlish, but Carrie carries herself as a woman. Her maturity shows most clearly in the care with which she nourishes her relationship with Witt. Her passionate lifelong quest for meaning and truth blends into a newer thread of acceptance and deep listening to foster a growing relationship of mutual respect between them.

May 8, 1896
Dear Witt,

Your comment that our immigration experiences make us very different people is very perceptive. The ways of the old country inform your upbringing. My upbringing happened in the old country. Many people would not understand that distinction. Moving between cultures probably shapes my place in the world more deeply than any other single factor. If I were to return to Germany, I think I would fit in even less comfortably than I did in my childhood!

Because I have experienced the American spirit, I can never go back to being just German. (Well, I suppose my parents might say I lacked a completely traditional German sentiment anyway, and I cannot argue!) If I returned, I would always be German, but not completely. My spirit of adventure has been nurtured by my experiences in New York in a way I never would have known had I remained in Germany. I would always be pushing forward in a culture that begs me to go back.

On the other hand, I may always feel a little of the 'new kid in town' pressure to fit into my life here, too. Being in the United States does not erase the first dozen years of my life. I bring those years in Meldorf alongside me: the pressures that accompany lack of opportunity, the authoritarianism oozing into every corner of daily life, the separation from people I love no matter which side of the ocean I call home.

I lived in the middle of a tough time in my birth country. My family had to make some decisions and take some stands that were uncomfortable and even dangerous. Because of that experience, I take some things very seriously that North Americans ignore. And I look at some things that North Americans take seriously and wonder why they are so worried about that, of all things. I see more than someone born here. Even you.

I'm also never quite at home, no matter where I live. I have to make home where I find myself. I like your way of listening to me and attempting to embrace all of me, the part that I can't quite leave behind, and the part that I can't quite fully enter, the part that's a little odd. You let me be where I am, and who I am, and I am deeply grateful.

Lovingly,
Carrie

January 17, 1897
Dearest Witt,

I so long to have you beside me in person, not just in ink! I think a thousand thoughts I would share if you were here,

146

and my pen is not quick enough to gather them on paper. If I could see you, I could simply speak them, and you would understand.

I've been thinking about when my brothers left me, and when I left my parents. How different the distance between us feels than at those earlier times in my life. Of course, I long for you, as I did for them. But we connect across the miles in ways my brothers and I never managed.

Then, I felt I could not find the right place to settle. While in Meldorf, I couldn't reach far enough to touch Frederick; I could only long for his return. When Henry left, I could only long to join him. In Brooklyn, even though the letters crossed the ocean with great regularity, I wanted to be there or to have my parents here. My location never felt comfortable, or satisfying.

Now, I am more settled, more content. I am where I am, and you are where you are, and we are connected across the distance. Our relationship grows while we are apart. We are not just straining toward some return to normal. Rather, writing letters is our way of being. For now, it is our normal. We are deepening our knowledge and understanding of each other. We have the feel of waiting until the right time.

Do you know what I'm trying to say?

Lovingly,

Carrie

May 20, 1897

Dearest Witt,

I received a postcard from Cuba this morning. Henry beat the card back to New York. I saw him on Sunday, so I already knew that he escaped the ship that mysteriously exploded in the Havana harbor yesterday. He missed being in danger by only a few days. He could have died on that boat. I

147

shudder to think that his postcard about plunging sugar prices came so close to being his unspoken goodbye to me.

Gratefully,
Carrie

November 20, 1897
Dearest Witt,

I am so very sad to hear of your father's death. As I read your words of admiration, I can see clearly how he lives on in you. All the traits for which you express gratitude – his connection with the land, his devotion to your mother, his often-expressed affection and pride in your accomplishments – in all these words I hear both his strengths and yours. You are so ready to step into his shoes, to run the farm, care for your mother, take leadership roles in the community. But you can never be ready, I think, for a parent to die. The loss is personal, a shift of your position in the world.

How are you adjusting to life in his absence? So often, in the first days, you can do nothing but sob. I wonder, sometimes, how I have survived all the losses in my relatively short life so far. That old saying of Job's often strikes me as the story of my life: "The Lord giveth and the Lord taketh away; blessed be the name of the Lord." Somehow blessing is never the first place I land in the face of grief! And I'm not sure I really believe God is testing me through losses, but certainly grief has molded me as a person. I understand more about life because I have wrestled in the face of death. None of that makes losing your father any easier, of course, but it does remind us to look for the points of celebration, which you have so admirably articulated.

Do you ever feel like you wish all the hard things in your life would just stop? Sometimes I find myself thinking 'I'm tired. I'm worn down. I have nothing else to give and no more resilience to bring forth. I just need it all to stop.' I don't mean that in the way that I would rather not be alive or that I have any thought of harming myself, although I guess some people would hear my words that way. Amalia, for one example, sometimes says the world would be better off without her. I don't see myself that way. I just want a moment of peace in the middle of the chaos when all the changes are happening at once. I can imagine you feel that way, but my thoughts are just a guess. Only you can say how this moment feels to you.

Please give my love to your mother. In my experience, grief never goes away, but it does change, and the whole of life grows to accommodate the changes grief brings. You both will get through this hard transition. I'm glad you have each other to lean on.

Lovingly,
Carrie

December 11, 1898
My dear Witt,

Both of my mothers have now joined my father, slipping away so quietly among the others in this vast season of death. Mutti survived Retta by only a few months, yielding to illness as Retta yielded to old age. I'm glad they were together here for a time, and sad that they are both gone.

As I sit here on a dreary, wet morning and contemplate their lives, I take comfort from the gray of the skies and the drip of the rain. The rest of the world is still asleep, but I am awake, my ear attuned to every drop. Days like today make me happy to live in the attic, where I'm close to the rain, and can hear my soul washed clean. The tears of sweet grief rid me of all that I no longer need, washing my excess away.

I think back to the day that the three of us went to Pratt Library. They were so delightful to be with, and so delighted at the glimpse into my life. I think I would be selfish to want more than delight, which they gave and received in abundance. Yes, a funeral will follow, but my mourning cries out in the rain, and sets my time free for a new adventure. Somehow their absence clarifies that I enter the adult world with their passing.

Carrie

May 16, 1898
Dearest Witt,

I am grateful today for your strength. I doubt you will ever pour out your feelings like I do, but neither do you withdraw behind an emotionless mask. You feel things, and that takes real courage. You leave people free to be who they are, whereas I struggle against them so they will do what I think is right. (Don't tell me you haven't already discovered this about me!) You are rooted in serenity where I am tossed in a restless sea. You are a steady counterweight to my search for rollicking escapades, real and imagined. I would give you too much responsibility for my peace to say that you are my anchor. But I find my anchor by being yours.

Thank you,
Carrie

Brooklyn, 1899

S HE IS HERE, but not present," Carrie tries to explain to Bridget. The topics of conversation this Sunday afternoon are weightier than the menu of shared sausages with mustard in the park suggest. Nearly a year has passed since the deaths of Amalia's mother and Carrie's father. More recently, Witt buried his father in the family plot in Charleston, and Carrie saw Tante Retta, and then her own mother, join the ancestors in Brooklyn's Lutheran Cemetery. As this season of loss grips the next generation with the weight of departures, the survivors trudge through life together in the absence of their forebears. Amalia remains a focus of concern.

"She moves through the world as if she can prevent her mother's death from touching her. And as far as I can tell, she meets that goal. Amalia acts as if her mother kidnapped her soul, and just left her body behind to fill up empty space. I've never seen anyone so — vacant. I don't know quite how to express what I see, much less to understand it. She sits, staring into blank air, entirely devoid of expression. She will move if you tell her to, from one place to another, not to actually do anything. But if no one tells her to move, I'm pretty sure she would stay right where she sits until the day she dies. I'm so glad her little sister and the boys are living with Frederick and Louis. I may not be enamored of children, but even I know they need someone's attention. I don't think Amalia even knows they are in the room." She shivers. "So strange."

"Are you concerned she might hurt herself?"

"I think she dare not feel the grief, for fear it might kill her. I felt that way, when Henry left Meldorf before me. I didn't want to die; I just didn't want to live without him. But I never withdrew as severely as Amalia. I fell silent, but I worked to gather energy for action. She completely lacks vitality. I came out of the silence ready to fight the separation for all I was worth, until my mother finally let me follow him. Amalia seems to have given in to the powers of lifelessness."

"You poor dear," Bridget says. You were way too young to endure those feelings. And God knows she is, too."

"Yes, but I had the love of my parents and brothers to keep me grounded in the world. I had something to live for, in spite of the loss. I don't know that Amalia has ever let anyone's love enter her orbit that way. Well, except maybe her mother's hovering affection. But that relationship crippled her, more than supporting her. I think she doesn't know her way out of the deep hole that has swallowed her. She doesn't have the skills to find the world again."

"What do you think would help?"

"Honestly? I have no idea."

"Not knowing leaves you in a tough spot."

"Not as tough as hers, but yes. I'm at a loss."

152

Brief bursts of conversation spill out between choosing ears of corn and juicy watermelons at the bustling morning market. They tick off food items alongside an emotional grocery list.

"How is Amalia doing? Any change?" Bridget asks.

"Yes," Carrie says. "She at least seems to acknowledge that her mother is gone. She alternates between that ghostly presence and bouts of endless crying. And now, for a week or so, she seems quieter, more at peace. She actually interacts with her siblings, tells them she loves them."

"Sounds like she's coming out of the worst of the grief. That's a good thing."

"Yes . . . I'm not so worried about her anymore."

"Have you heard from Henry?"

"Not a word."

"That's too bad."

"*Schade*. Pity. I know. Breaks my heart."

"And Witt?"

"A letter every week since he left!"

"You're a very lucky girl."

"I am. And I know how lucky I am!" They return to their respective shopping baskets, and then back to their homes.

By afternoon, the morning's peace shatters. Louis arrives unannounced at the Chapelle's home, a unique event in the tenure of her work there. Carrie answers the knock at the door as if the day is like any other, but immediately recognizes that any assumption of normalcy is false. She pulls the heavy door inward and

153

takes in the sight of her brother, weighing down the steps as if his shoes are full of stones.

Louis trembles slightly and raises his hand to remove his hat. She knows in an instant that she is completely unprepared for what he has arrived to say. Upending even the normal chaos of children and chores, Louis holds his hat in hand and quietly answers the question he reads on Carrie's face.

"It's Amalia. Frederick is with the children, and August waits at home for the police to come."

"Come in." They close the door to the outside world, and stand in her employer's front hallway to talk. She glances around. Satisfied that they are alone in the busy house, she goes on. "Amalia's being arrested? But what . . . ?"

"No. August went upstairs for lunch and found her there. The wash fluttered outside the window. A plate of cheese and rye were on the table, covered by a towel. Her head and shoulders were in the oven, one knee propped on the door, the other foot stretched out to touch the floor." He shudders. "Limp and lifeless, peacefully dead."

"But . . . .. she seemed so much better!"

"Yes, well, looks can deceive."

"Dead? Amalia?"

"Yes. Where she always tried to tell us she would be better off."

Carrie sinks to her knees. She cannot feel, she cannot think. The walls spin around her, and she closes her eyes. Louis sinks to the floor beside her, his arms around her as she leans into his body.

"But . . ."

"I know. Her eyes almost smiled toward the end."

"But . . ."

The eternal quality of the moment steals her breath. The reality cannot penetrate her awareness. A person is alive and breathing, and then gone, never to return. *But remember,* Carrie thinks, *Amalia is different from everyone else, perfectly capable of doing anything to pull attention away from chores required and yet undone. Perhaps she is bluffing, again, and will somehow wiggle beyond the moment to plead her breathless case.* Carrie feels a searing blast of anger. And then, nothing. Louis holds her.

At the moment Carrie goes silent, the Chapelle's nanny chases a lone wayward child through the hallway, reminding the pair they are not alone. She stops cold at the sight of the brother and sister, then rushes to bring Rosie Chapelle, who sends her to fetch hot coffee, wheat crackers, a blanket.

Still wrapped in the wool blanket Rosie tucks around her, Carrie makes her way in a daze to August's home, where she waits alongside her brothers for police to finish their duties. She cannot touch the world from inside her body. She cannot see future, only past. And she cannot think, or speak. The whole world has gone cold with shock.

Carrie's belly carries the frigid weight of unbelieving through an entire week, the conversation with Amalia's younger siblings, the solemn procession down the long aisle of Trinity German Lutheran Church, the dull skittering of earth on wood at the Lutheran Cemetery. The shock begins to melt at the funeral dinner, hosted by Tante Retta's children, where

155

stories about Amalia flow like a balm of sweet hot tea across the lips of the guests. Carrie returns home to dreamless sleep for the first time since Louis knocked at the Chapelle's front door.

She wakes in a panic, and all her unrelenting thoughts roll in a fury. *Why would Amalia do such an awful thing? Why, when she finally began to return to herself in the shadow of her mother's death, would she suddenly join her in the ground? Did Amalia really begin to adjust to her mother's absence, or did she feel better because she resolved to reunite with her? Did the thought of her own death bring her to peace?*

None of Carrie's questions lead her to serenity, but instead to endless spinning through the unanswered and unanswerable morass. And when she finally breaks through the cycle, she does not find resolution or freedom in her mind, but flies into another twisting storm of thoughts.

Why had Carrie been so impatient at Amalia's neglect of duty? Couldn't everyone see that Amalia coped as well as she could manage? When Carrie groused about a neglected table, she ignored Amalia's broken soul. Carrie encouraged Amalia to acquire the skills for living without her mother, the one thing Amalia genuinely could not do. Carrie mistook Amalia's upswing in mood for growth, for independence, for courage to go on even in her mother's absence. But she could not go on. What had Carrie been thinking?

And what had she done? She had forced the family's hand, and made them urge Amalia toward independence. She had refused to take any more responsibility for Amalia's chores. She had, in fact, taken a stand that led Amalia directly

156

to her death, demanding that Amalia be held responsible for her actions, or lack of actions, and stand on her own power to be part of the family.

Amalia finally, for perhaps the first time in her life, took independent action. And plunged them all into the twisted quagmire of her ugly death. Carrie has ruined not just Amalia, but the rest of the family. Her lack of empathy and judgmental expectations forced Amalia into a situation where she could never be successful. Carrie caused this tragedy, had forced Amalia into action. How could she survive that lapse in judgment, the shame of destroying her family?

Once more, Carrie finds Bridget by her side, arriving to answer the door and sweep the floor when Carrie forgets what she is supposed to be doing. To prepare the meals that keep the Chapelle household fed. To force Carrie to the market and manage the million tiny tasks that sustain a family's humming. And to swat away the thoughts, as if they were a thousand gnats converging on her sanity.

"You are not responsible for an illness that swallows a person whole and attacks their will to live, Carrie. That sickness wormed its way into Amalia's entire being from childhood. You know that."

"I know that I killed her."

"You do not have that kind of power."

"I know that I killed her."

"You have too much grace in your heart to do anyone harm."

"I made the family abandon her. She couldn't take the pressure."

"You encouraged the family to be their best, including Amalia."

"The fault for her death is at my feet."

"Carrie Denzler. Laying out the silverware and hanging out the wash cannot kill a person. You did call on her to live out her responsibilities. You may even have successfully empowered her for action in ways she had never been able to grasp before. Those traits are good traits, meant to nourish Amalia and help her."

"But I—"

Bridget pushes on, past Carrie's objections.

"Your determination to equip Amalia and teach your family to support her in productive ways can never be portrayed as selfishness or evil. You summoned a great deal of strength and courage to make her life, and the lives of your family members, better. Please don't be confused about that. You acted for her good. And Amalia, well, Amalia used her new strength to accomplish exactly what she wanted to do. We disagree with how she used her power, of course we do. But you allowed her to do what she always dreamed of doing. You delivered her from anguish to peace."

"Even if that's true, I sent the rest of us directly to hell on earth," Carrie says.

"For now, I know that's how you feel. You are hurting. Your brothers are hurting, and their families. Her siblings are hurting most of all. But they are also relieved. They no longer bear the responsibility of keeping Amalia alive. They are now free to grow into their own lives."

"I feel neither relief nor freedom."

"I know you don't—for now. But you will find truth as the months go on, and you will embrace the freedom it brings. All of you will. Not one of you is haunted by the inner demons that drove Amalia to her decision. All of you already have the strength and optimism she lacked, and will live past the deep hurt into joy."

"Oh, Bridget."

"I know. But I am right. You'll see."

In the months that follow, Carrie slips a small diary into her bag when she leaves the house on Sunday mornings. She sets aside her drawing and her reading, and turns almost entirely to writing on those Sunday afternoons. As she wanders flowery paths and listens to the blast of steamship whistles, she pours out her myriad imaginations as real pen-and-ink words, moving them outside her head and placing them at the very feet of God. Slowly, slowly, clarity emerges in the pages.

. . . I am sorry that I caused Amalia so much pain. But I cannot regret the changes I encouraged in the family at large. They are all recovering from her death so much faster than I am. They profess to have no qualms about her abrupt departure, and act surprised when I say I believe I contributed to her unhappiness.

Instead, they express their own peace in the fact that she finally rests. Even her brothers and sister feel . . . lighter somehow. They are free, without her brokenness weighing on their every move. I did not realize how heavily they felt the burden of Amalia's illness. They know they could not help her, and relieved of trying, they can throw themselves into joyful living . . .

159

. . . *August finally talked to me about the horror of finding her in the kitchen. He says that for months, he saw her ghost every time he walked into that room. He worried over his own baby, that the tragedy during his infancy would somehow seep into his little being. But the child smiles on, unfailingly happy, as if the baby holds the peace all of us needed on his arrival . . .*

. . . *I think being at a distance from these events must be harder than being present and experiencing them first hand. Henry still has not had much to say about Amalia's death. I keep my counsel and, for once, don't expect him to talk. If I have learned anything, I have learned the danger of pushing too much responsibility for my happiness onto another person.*

I have been so focused all my life on getting Henry to listen to me, on getting Henry to respond to me, on getting Henry to make me happy, that I have neglected my own happiness. I shudder to think how much pressure I placed on him, without even remotely taking responsibility for my own joy. He seems to think he has nothing to forgive, but I am so sorry for the expectations I have put upon him. I hope in the future to accept what he offers as love, and demand nothing more . . .

. . . *Amalia, in her own way, taught all of us so much. I never would have admitted such a thing in the moment, of course, but the great gift of witnessing her life taught me something important. I would not want my pleasures or even my pains to be lost in the madness as they were in her life. Living that way must have been pure hell.*

Yet I came dangerously close to reenacting exactly those qualities. I tied up all my worth and all my dreams in Henry, and blamed him for my unhappiness, exactly like she tried to live through her mother, and blamed everyone else for her missteps. I held Henry responsible for meeting my need for adventure. His life is his. My life is mine. We can't enjoy and love each other unless we can each be exactly who we are . . .

. . . Frederick and Louis are doing such a good job supporting Amalia's siblings. Bless them, to grow up without their father, and then lose their mother and their older sister in such quick succession is such a shock, but they are resilient beyond words. I suppose the years of being Amalia's siblings make her actions seem more normal to them than to the rest of us.

Now that the cousins are nearing an age to be on their own, maybe Frederick and Flora will finally marry and Louis will be free to pursue his dream of owning a bar. I am so grateful for the way they all stepped up to care for these children. I wish their actions hadn't been required, of course, but I so admire them putting their lives on hold for a while to support others.

I should not be surprised at their generosity. After all, these are the same people who welcomed me to Brooklyn and helped me get started when my parents were so far away. I can't believe I actually accused Frederick of bribing me with ice cream. How silly it all seems now . . .

. . . I still cannot find peace over the fact of Amalia's death. No one in the family seems to feel I did anything wrong. Both Bridget and my brothers try regularly to talk me out of

my guilty morass. Even Witt tries to talk me out of my shame in almost every letter.

I feel selfish for having called Amalia to account, and now I hesitate to let my thoughts be known, for fear I will drive someone else to desperate action through my thoughtless demand. The problem is not precisely that I'm wrong to speak up, it's that I cannot tell how the other person will absorb my words. I can't help thinking that Amalia might have heard me denigrating her worth because she didn't do her part. I just meant she needed to grow up, like the rest of us. I'm afraid my attitude made the world more dangerous for her. I hope I've learned to make love my highest aim, to examine every word for the effects it carries . . .

She fills one thick notebook, and then another. And as she scratches her winding inky path to clarity, she wonders whether her mother, or Retta, could have helped her sort out her confusion. She wonders whether Witt's outstretched arms could have soothed her undulating soul. She feels their absence deeply in the wake of this devastation. Would she write if they sat next to her and heard her words?

Yes, she believes she would write even if they all could hear her speaking. Something about opening her veins on paper meets a need deep. Loss gives her a reason, an outpouring of her desire to write. Loss meets longing that extends beyond the grieving. *And*, she thinks, *I hope my need is thoroughly met, for I cannot bear another day of mourning.*

Brooklyn, 1901

March 8, 1901
Dearest Witt,

Thank you for reading all of my ramblings during these months since Amalia's death. A full year already — it's unbelievable! My days since then have been full of guilt and distress more than sorrow. Of course, it's sad when anyone so young dies, especially at their own hand, so sorrow is part of it. I felt no special affection for her, as you know; irritation more than kinship formed our bond.

And yet, her demise rattles my core, even a year later. The shock of unexpected death forms but a narrow slice of the picture. We all experienced the sensation of crashing into a rapidly moving train, and then freezing in time as the days rolled on without us. We all experienced that second point of bombardment when feeling returned after the blessed relief of shock, the frequent retreat into denial when emotion threatened to upend us.

We all felt that. But my guilt almost overwhelmed my good judgment, still does, some days. Knowing that she believed I punished her for being sick, expected more of her than she could give, makes me shudder in regret. On the days when I have not been able to distinguish truth from fiction, when the guilt pulled me into places better avoided, the most profound of changes have worked their way through my soul.

Today, I'm thinking about the fact that she left all the chores done for the first time in her life. That last day, she finished the washing and hung the wrung-out clothes to flap from the window. She made August's lunch and left it under a neatly-placed towel. And suddenly, I realize I never asked more of her than she could give. I never demanded actions she could not perform. I brought out the best in her. I let her show what she could do, how she could cope in a world that overwhelmed and threatened her. That's what my family could see when I could not. She really could do what I demanded. They don't blame me for treating her badly. They praise me for bringing forward the good in her. After a full year, I'm finally beginning to hear them.

The problem is, she could not trust her best to be enough. She truly believed she would not survive after her mother died. She readily accepted that she had no power in this world, that her whole life happened beyond her control and outside her responsibility. She could not cope with being capable, and useful to her family, and responsible for her own life. She did not cut off her life as more terrible than she thought. She discovered her life to be more wonderful than she thought, and being wrong was harder than the truth.

This year has given me a chance to face my failings, too, and I want to do some things differently from Amalia. I want to admit my failure and lost time. I want to reach out to people who love me and let them help me, even when I don't think I need any help. I want to try and fail and try and do better. I want to change things in myself that give me grief. The real adventures in life are not sailing the seas and staring into the stars. I'll always want those things, you know I will. But the world gives even more. The truest adventures are living fully and completely right where we are. The real excitement happens inside our souls, not outside our bodies, the conscious embrace of growing in maturity and faith.

I am at the edge of a new adventure. I can feel it. I don't know where life will lead, what I will do, who I will be. But I can feel the winds of change moving. The world lands at my feet and no fear can chase it away. Something inside me shifts, and I know I will be whole.

My love,
Carrie

Brooklyn, 1901

THEIR LETTERS CROSS in the mail. But oh, how happy she is at his news!

Dearest Carrie,

Just a brief note today. My mother and I are coming to Brooklyn! Peter Maasen will know our arrival time. We will be there the last week in March, and will stay in Retta's unoccupied apartment. My heartbeat nearly stops at the very thought of having you next to me again!

Until then, my love,
Witt

They slip into town on a moonless Saturday evening, the last train of the day. Their tiny, weary procession winds its way through quiet streets to the door that used to swing open to Retta's laughter. Catrina bends under the advancement of her aging body. Her eyes still weigh heavy with tears after the death of the man she had met in this very house, and the woman who presided over it, all those years ago.

Witt stretches tall, his neck arching with spirit, his long strides in lively contrast to his mother's well-traveled shoes. His lanky frame rattles down the sidewalk and up the stairs, his step full of energy even after a full day of travel. He is ready to arrive, ready to make his claim.

Carrie sleeps soundly in her small bed nestled under the eaves across town.

In the morning, they awaken in rooms separated by a narrow slice of Brooklyn, to the warble of the sparrows, the flutter of chimes in the breeze, the glint of dew on the grass. As she makes her way to the Trinity German Lutheran Church on Kane Street, the air becomes electric. Long months, well over two years, have passed since the last time they were in the same room. Masks gradually dissolve into truthfulness, as if stripped from them through the very art of letter-writing. Politely at first, then increasingly deepening their revelations, they share their souls. Will the people they discovered on paper translate into the same people who sit side by side?

When Carrie finally stands framed in the door of the church, she knows where to look. Retta's vacated pew, midway down the left-hand side, filling with next generation Maasens and Denzlers. One head to Peter's right she spies Catrina, and finally, Witt. Carrie lifts a foot to move into the aisle, floating to the pew in the glow of stained glass. She slows to slip behind the massive stone column and between the polished wood of the pews. She is standing beside him, and his smile breaks her open into shards of sunshine, tinted in blues and golden reds. She knows in that moment, she has come home.

God has a difficult job that morning, competing for the attention of young lovers. Their hands are restless, hers grasping a German prayer book and his shuffling between his knees and the hard wooden seat of the pew.

167

Their eyes shift, lighting as expected on the pastor, the bread, the cup, yet pulled like faithful gravity each toward the other. Carrie catches his eye every now and again, but misses Catrina's knowing smile, the one that says she knows her son. The pensive tilt of Catrina's head says she expects to see Witt back in church very soon, exchanging vows with this lovely girl.

Retta's apartment stands empty of personal effects prepared for a new family to make it their home. Church bells still echo as the place that has been home for all of them flings wide its doors for one last Sunday gathering. Her children and their families, the Denzler brothers and theirs, even Henry in a rare appearance, arrive to bid the old place farewell. They beat a leisurely path to overstuff the tiny second floor living room. No one is in any hurry, and yet Carrie and Witt still lag far behind the others, forgetting to walk as they speak directly, face to face for the first time since the visit when they met. As they approach the house, they detour into the park. Carrie invites Witt to the bench where she spends many a Sunday pouring her heart onto paper, slipping the words into an envelope that bears his name under the stamp.

They sit side by side, keeping watch over the ducks in the pond between the azaleas and the buttercups. The words that have passed between them on paper all compete for air time at once. And then, silence. So much more to be said that they cannot decide what comes next. Then they both speak at once, the young woman lifting her finger toward the red head of the woodpecker that brings noise into the silence, the young man reaching into his pocket and dirtying the knees of his

168

trousers in the place by the bench where grass refuses to grow. Then they sit for a while, exchange a gentle kiss, and rise to share the news with their families.

On their walk between the sweetly accented quiet of the park and the raucous Maasen homeplace, Carrie and Witt become a couple. Surrounded by the warmth and laughter of all the relatives, they enjoy the celebration of their love.

"So those letters have been working their magic, *ja?*" Henry sidles up to Carrie in the middle of the chaos.

"Oh, yes, my brother. Letters can work miracles when they're written and posted!" Her voice is excited, warm, but Henry catches the steely glint of hardness.

"Touché!" He is always in trouble.

"I'm sorry, Henry. I don't mean to give you such a hard time. You can see, though, that distance really can be made small by spilling ink on a page. We have just never managed to perfect the art."

"Ah, yes. And now you will no doubt be moving far away, on the trail of adventure once again."

"I will. And I'm excited at the prospect."

"I will miss you."

"Henry Denzler, how can you even . . . ugh! How can you possibly miss me? I've been right under your nose for the last decade, and we're not even half an inch closer than we were when I lived in Meldorf and you lived in . . . wherever you have been all this time!"

The light in Henry's eyes dims as he struggles to speak.

"I'm sorry, my Carrie. I know I have disappointed you."

"Sometimes expectations don't pay. They too often lead to hurt."

"Well, I'm happy that this fellow brings color to your cheeks. I want the best for you, even if I never tell you."

"Going away feels like finally giving you up, Henry. Releasing something I never really had, but still. Somehow losing the dream feels even more depressing than letting go of something I had a chance to enjoy. I will miss you, too, Henry, but that is nothing new."

They board the train within the week, the three of them, Witt and Catrina returning home, and Carrie with them on a new course of adventure. They speak of another long wait, but Bridget steps up to fill the gap at work, all the brothers give their blessing, and they have no need for delay. As they sit shoulder to shoulder, mile after mile, Carrie and Witt watch the leaves change shape and the bark change color, like a retrospective of life itself.

Along the way, as well, Catrina instructs Carrie in the ways of being Charlestonian:

"Charleston presents a culture shock no matter how many different places you've lived," Catrina begins. "Meldorf is a mere village, where people know your grandparents and your great-grandparents and love you from the womb no matter what. Brooklyn is a grand portion of an even grander metropolis, where nobody knows you and comfort comes from anonymity.

170

Charleston, on the other hand, is a mid-sized city where people talk like they think they know you, but the better part of you hides beneath gracious convention."

"My, how daunting." Carrie is not really worried, but perhaps she does not know what to be worried about.

"Social conventions can be intimidating, especially if you do not know the rules," Catrina affirms, "but the population includes many German transplants, so in some ways all the differences blend into a very familiar setting."

"Where can I get myself into trouble?" If she is truthful, Carrie cannot say whether she seeks to avoid trouble or make more of it. She has never been much of one for convention, after all, particularly in the context of the playbook of womanhood.

"Women in the South keep the secrets of their men. To acknowledge the secrets that are in plain sight puts too much weight on the code of silence. Speaking too forthrightly alienates the neighbors."

"And the whole culture reeks of the customs of slavery," Witt says.

"We will not have slaves, will we?" Carrie asks, frowning. She shudders; she can barely grasp the possibility.

"Oh, no," Catrina hastens to say. "Slavery ended with the war, before you and Witt were even born, before Diedrich and I moved here. But attitudes born of that long era still firmly hold sway, and laws enforce white superiority over other colors, as if being forced into servitude makes one less than a person."

"What does that look like?"

"Separate public facilities, like restrooms and water fountains and train cars," Catrina says. "Not merely eating in the kitchen like you did, but requiring separate dishes in white households, as if darkness might be contagious. And although they are stuck by law letting Black men vote, they seem to spend all of their waking hours dreaming up ways to prevent them from actually getting to the polls. A tax we can afford and they cannot. A literacy test, when even owning a pencil or touching a book could get a slave killed. And silly "grandfather" laws, saying that if your grandfather voted, you are eligible, too. Guess whose grandfather wins that lottery!"

"All of this sounds like a whole lot of effort," Carrie says.

"Life would indeed be a lot simpler without the silliness," Witt says. "And I guess we see the burden so plainly because we are the paler version of the outsiders excluded by the customs."

"And then, of course, there are the ladylike rules," Catrina goes on.

Carrie rolls her eyes.

"I'm going to love this!" Witt says, sending a guffaw all the way down to his toes.

"Thank-you notes for everything," Catrina continues. "Never correct a man, show yourself smarter, or, God forbid, win a competition against him. All skin covered by clothing at all times, with the possible exception of the hand and the face. Eyes downward, never the challenging eye contact of an equal. Food should be whatever the man prefers, served when the man wants to eat. And close your eyes and think of England, or the north of Germany, as the case may be."

Witt rolls with laughter as he imagines Carrie trying to meet all of these demands. "Please don't worry, darling. The people who make those rules don't live at our house. You will be fine."

"She sounds like she has been studying the natives in a far-off land," Carrie remarks, nodding toward his mother.

"You're not wrong, my girl," Catrina answers. "Charleston will be different from anywhere you've ever lived before. But these are good people, and a pleasant enough place to live." Carrie laughs. She has already moved halfway around the world; the thought of another new place feels exhilarating, not frightening.

Carrie realizes they are almost to Charleston when the thick pine forests meld into stately oaks and squat palmettos, the shorter cousins of palm trees. She has never seen them before, but recognizes them from Henry's description; palms are abundant on his journeys through Miami to the islands and South America. He describes them as "towering," but these are low bushes by comparison. Sure enough, as the train slows to a screeching brake, Witt begins gathering their things and preparing to depart the train.

Thirty minutes later, the family's travel bags, plus every one of Carrie's possessions, perch precariously on the back of a carriage guided by one of Witt's employees from the farm. The same horses that tomorrow will pull the plough to prepare the soil for planting now draw them toward home. Almost immediately across the bridge from the city, the roads turn from cobblestone to dirt, washed out in places by rising water and disappearing into muddy marsh.

"How do they ever keep the roads usable?" she asks, as a wheel dips into a rut and bounces the carriage. "The uneven surfaces must be awfully hard on vehicles."

"Oh, yes," Witt answers. "Every year we replace at least one axle, usually more. And we travel this road every week during harvest, to bring potatoes into town for market. The drive can be quite the challenge."

On they go, negotiating the treacherous pathway with great care. Witt points out the area where the first English colonists came ashore more than two hundred years before. He directs her gaze out over the land to a plantation house arising over fields now parceled out to various farmers like themselves. Compared to the farmland she remembers from outside Meldorf, these fields are frighteningly immense.

"How do they farm such massive plots of land?" Carrie asks. "This landscape dwarfs the land between the North Sea and the Baltic in our area of Germany, where hundreds of farmers plant their crops. How could one family possibly farm all of this land?"

"Slave labor," Witt answers. "The owners skipped the physical labor and left the backbreaking work to the slaves. Often, the slave traders went specifically to areas in Africa where indigo or rice were grown, taking knowledgeable people away from their own farms to set up operations here. Without slavery, you are correct, what you see is not possible. The big plantations have been divided into smaller farms, more like what you remember from your childhood."

He points off to the left. "The farmers who plant over here own the land, especially where former slaves took ownership over on the islands. But over there, closer to the city, many of the families of the original owners retain the land and lease it to farmers like me, either for a flat fee or for a percentage of the crop yield. If the fields look bigger than you are used to seeing, it's because instead of farmhouses every few miles, you'll see one large plantation house that no longer functions as the center of the farm."

"I can understand why this place fascinates you," she says, turning to Catrina. "I don't really understand the business of farming, both because we weren't farmers, and because I moved to Brooklyn so young. But I do remember enough to notice some real differences."

"Diedrich and I both grew up on farms," Catrina says, "So we set up our business according to what we knew, and the operation is a mere fraction of even the smallest plantation."

"We don't believe bigger is necessarily better," Witt adds, "but seeing the livelihoods they fought so hard to preserve gives you a glimpse into why they valued the lifestyle. We see the means as morally corrupt, but the properties they were protecting are quite impressive."

"Be careful, though," Catrina says. "The Low Country royalty still believe the United States robbed them of their culture, and they don't take kindly to hearing what we are telling you."

"I will remember," Carrie responds, slowly nodding. "I will remember."

Carrie joins in the work from the day she arrives. A week later, she and Witt return on that risky road to

Charleston to worship among the good people of St. Matthew's German Lutheran Church on King Street. Before they return to the farm to manage the next day's planting, they stop by the church rectory and quietly make their vows. The day is April 7, 1901, Easter Sunday. They return to the farm the same afternoon. He is twenty-seven years old. She is twenty-one.

Charleston, 1901

AT FIRST, CARRIE awakens stiff and achy every single morning, discovering new muscles through the pain. The work itself is not very different from what she did in Brooklyn; domestic work results in long hours and physical exertion. Through her years working for the Chapelles, she grew from taking orders to giving them, from having the tasks organized for her to organizing them herself. She finds the work of household management intimately familiar. But she finds the relationship of wife different from any other. And the farm is an entirely new world of challenge after both the village and the city. Time passes differently in the country.

"What are you doing in here?" Witt tucks his head around the edge of the hen house door.

"She doesn't want me to take her eggs," Carrie says. "You'd think she's protecting a half-grown baby! When I reach up under her, she flutters wildly and threatens to peck my hand off."

"In and out quickly and calmly," he says, reaching under the unhappy mama. "Don't give her time to figure out what you're after." He stops for a minute to watch her work. "Yes, that's right. You're getting the idea." The eggs are for their own use; the farming operation supports potato crops for sale to others.

"Are we having lunch today?"

"Are you already back for lunch? What time is it?"

"Noon. The crew and I went out at 6 a.m."

"You must be starving! I'll leave this until later and get you something to eat."

"These chores take quite a while to learn, don't they? Let's find my mama—I bet she already has something on the stove."

Sure enough, Catrina's inner clock reads the situation better than Carrie's. Lunch awaits them, plates steaming hot and laden with fuel.

"I'm so sorry," Carrie says to Catrina. "I left you cooking on your own. Those pesky chickens—well, I don't even begin to understand how to gather the eggs and cook the lunch at the same time."

"You'll be managing everything in no time," Catrina assures her. "And I've been doing the job on my own all these years; I certainly don't mind putting food on the table without making you work for it. Calm yourself, and sit down."

Witt's bowed head signals readiness, as did his father's for many years before him. "Bless, oh Lord, these gifts which we to receive from your bounty, and bless us to your service. Amen." Then, the bowls move like a steady train around the table, dispensing generous mounds of mashed potatoes, fresh sliced tomatoes, fresh-baked biscuits, fried okra, and collard greens boiled in pork lard. Catrina places the roasted hen, snatched just that morning from Carrie's chicken coop, in the middle of the table like a centerpiece of fine roses.

Silence reigns in the shadow of hunger as the three of them refuel. The women clear the table and wash the dishes; Witt returns to the fields. The day will be long and require a second dinner as the sun starts to fade. Planting won't wait if they want to keep eating these feasts. And still, Carrie must gather the final eggs from the nests. The work never ends.

As she settles into the pace, Carrie's body gradually adjusts, and within a couple of years she, too, begins to tell time by the angle of the sun. The months roll by like sea grass in the breeze, and the rhythms of the tides feed her knowledge of day and night. Almost three years after her arrival in Charleston, her brother Frederick calls her back to Brooklyn.

Brooklyn, 1904

January 6, 1904
Dear Carrie,

Flora and I have made you an auntie for the second time, and you have yet to meet these children of ours. Will you visit Brooklyn in April, to hold little Charlotte for her baptism and act as godmother? Henry will stand as godfather for young Fred, Jr. August and Minna want you to stay at their house with their boys and Louis, who still basks in his status as the newest Denzler to become a citizen of the U. S. of A. (Besides, you know Retta will haunt you from the other side if you're not here for dinner after the service!) Please say you'll come . . .

The rest of the letter combines teething and toilet training with baby diet and diapers, which she skims and quickly dismisses. But she keeps coming back to the opening paragraph, and wondering about the possibility.

"Of course we will go!" Witt has fewer qualms than Carrie expresses. The immediacy of planting season does not seem to faze him at all. He had been the one, after all, who had interrupted planting three years earlier for a trip to claim his bride!

"We will figure out the planting," he says, "and you don't need to worry about it at all. We'll be gone, what, a week? I can hire an extra hand for that amount of time if we need the help."

"Go, Carrie," Catrina urges.

They buy tickets, and pack to board the train.

Before daylight on Tuesday morning, the day they board the train, she awakens with a stiff and achy body for the first time in a year. The soreness passes, both from her body and from her mind, as they go happily on their way.

When Carrie and Witt enter the sanctuary, the usual family pews, halfway up and beside the column on the left side, are empty. Instead, family members occupy the seats at the very front, possibly in a spot from which another family is temporarily evicted. They are a formidable crowd. all decked out in their best suits and dresses. They fill an entire section of four pews, where all of them can see the faces of the baptized and their sponsors. Retta, God rest her soul, is of course notably absent, but her children represent her. Her parents, too, are present only in spirit.

Little Fred, Jr., is very much there in body as he darts to bait and switch, dodging his harried father at the back of the room. Frederick buries Carrie in a hug as soon as he spies her. The child does not know this woman, and proves more reticent, almost suspicious in his greeting. She stoops down on one knee on cool stone, eye-level with the little boy, but preserving a little distance for his benefit. The child, deciding to accept her, finally raises his hand.

"Ahoy, mate!" He intones his blessing, and her delighted laughter floats above the organ prelude.

"Well, I guess that one is related to me," she laughs. And she rises again to greet Henry as he arrives, throwing herself into his arms as if they are still children. Witt, one step behind, gazes at her fondly and greets her relatives as his own.

At Frederick's signal, they join baby Charlotte and her mother in the front pew, and amid greeting the others, share introductions. They seem unconscious of the congregants gathering behind them with indulgent smiles and murmurs. The pastor, already robed and ready, speaks briefly to the parents and godparents, then moves into place as the organ announces the first hymn and the choir starts up the aisle. A festive day for the family, and also for the church.

When the time comes, Carrie and her favorite brother answer questions that echo their own confirmation services, promising to love and teach this new generation of Denzlers to make faith their own. The pastor dips his hand three times into water, blessing the baby in the name of the triune God. The whole congregation adds their cheerful and heartfelt promises of support as the faithful who gather week after week in this place.

As she stands in the church of her confirmation, Carrie reflects on the church of her childhood, its interior of brick and dark wood. She thinks also of the church of her married life, its whitewashed walls and colorful glass. How different the buildings are, and yet how alike, as well. The soaring arched ceilings reach toward the heavens and hard floors give a solid place to stand on earth. Sturdy columns allow the newer sanctuaries to spread wider in their footprint. But all of them soar to ancient heights, touch points with holiness. She is glad to be here.

On the Monday morning after the baptism, Carrie's breasts are sore on waking. She puzzles briefly over the unfamiliar ache, but easily forgets as she eagerly bounds down the steps from apartment to candy shop to greet Henry. He waits at street level holding a picnic lunch, ready to share in the park for old times' sake. A good long talk at her brother's initiation and decent German deli food — surely life does not get any better than this!

"Talk to me about playing farmer's wife." Henry chooses the topic.

"Well, life is no playground, that's for sure!" Carrie says. "I have all the same housekeeping duties I did at the Chapelle's, and the additional load of tending to the chickens, cows, and goats. All the men work from sunup to sundown every single day in spring and fall, and their bodies adjust to the time. All of their clocks are internal, so unless you follow the movement of the sun and the moon, you have no idea when they want dinner. After a year, I finally figured out the schedule. After nearly three, the aching in my bones has ceased." She pauses thoughtfully, then continues. "I've never worked so hard in my life. But I have to confess, I enjoy farming. If I can't sail the seas, it's a pretty good substitute."

"Witt is good to you?"

"The best. Every time I get a letter from Bridget, I'm grateful all over again. Her husband has turned out to be such an unhappy soul, boasting his high expectations and exacting standards. Illusions of excellence, I call them. I saw her on Friday and nothing has changed.

Witt is very much the opposite. He spoils me terribly, happy for me to have and to do what I want. More than flowers and chocolates and outward things, he really wants to see me happy. I work hard, but I play hard, too. I have plenty of time for my reading and writing, for getting out and seeing new things, because he makes sure I do."

"He seems like a good man. He'd better be. I will come after anyone who makes my little sister unhappy!'

"Yeah, like you are around to do that. Where have you been lately?"

"South America during the winter. Summer there, of course. Argentina, Uruguay, Peru. Sheep-shearing season in the southern climes. I still deal mostly with sugar and coffee, sometimes oil or liquor. But so many people are working the import-export trades right now, my season is pretty slow on the usual fronts. I'm taking a detour into the fabrics market, private business, and luxury items. Brooks Brothers wants to expand their buying power into South America where the prices are lower and the hills are covered in sheep, alpaca, goats, vicuña, guanaco, and other wool-producers. For myself, I still hope the job will eventually take me to their usual markets in New Zealand and Australia, places I've never seen."

"Yes, you would be more interested in location than product!"

"You'd better believe I have my priorities in order! I have little use for a Brooks Brothers suit, but I have lots of use for their steamship journeys!"

"I'd still like to see those places, though I probably never will. I never thought I'd work with animals, either. But I do feel better adding something to my expertise more than keeping houses clean."

"I'm glad. You seem more settled, less angsty, than you did up here."

"I am. I still miss you, though. I get my news through August and Minna or Frederick and Flora, now that Retta's gone. Evidently in this family you have to have a woman around to get any information."

Henry laughs. "That may be true. Not going to happen here, that's for sure. No woman would tolerate my life!"

They unwrap Henry's bundled lunch to find beautiful meats and fragrant cheeses, dark brown bread and a heady mustard. Carrie nibbles on a bit of mild cheese while Henry assembles a sandwich thicker than his teeth can clear. Giggles ensue as he attempts to consume his monstrous creation.

"You're not hungry?" Henry says. "You've hardly eaten anything."

"I think the travel, and all the excitement, are affecting my appetite. Nothing smells good to me, and you know that's not like me!" Carrie answers.

"Well, there is plenty here if you want it." Henry says. Carrie nods.

"What's your next adventure?" Henry asks. "Frederick's little ones were awfully cute at the center of the universe yesterday. When are you going to give me a little niece or nephew?"

"Ha! Never, if I can avoid it! You know I've never had much use for children."

"Yes, I know. But I've seen a lot of women get broody about your age. I thought maybe taking up with the hens might—"

"Henry Denzler, you stop that!" She hits him a bit more than playfully on the arm. "Don't you go wishing things on me that I don't want! The last thing I need is a bunch of snot-nosed ragamuffins to distract me from living!"

"Hey, hey, I'm just asking!"

"Well, stop!"

"Yes, ma'am. So sorry."

"You certainly are. And nobody knows that better than I do!"

"You make me tired."

"I just want you to toss me a word every now and then. That doesn't seem too much to ask."

A child-free life, however, is too much to ask, at least in 1904. Still sparring with her brother in her mind as she returns home to Charleston, Carrie wakes up sore for the third time in as many weeks, not even wanting to move. Catrina watches her during breakfast, and casually asks, "What hurts, honey?"

"Everything. But it's weird. My bosoms are really painful. I've had cramping at my monthlies for as long as I can remember, but always at belly level. My breasts have never been sore before."

"Your monthly is due?"

"I'm running late. Maybe that's why I feel different. I'm always right on time, but I'm at maybe five, even six, weeks."

"Hmmm. Have you vomited recently? Or had any unusual reactions to food?"

"No. Well, I had no appetite for most of the time we were in New York. I felt fine, not hungry, but not sick . . . Oh! You don't think . . . ?"

"Time will tell, but I hear a strong possibility that you are going to make me a grandmother."

Carrie's silence lasts the rest of the morning and into the afternoon.

And then, absent all ceremony, she dashes out the back door and throws up into the flowers.

Charleston, 1904

BUT I DON'T ACTUALLY want to be a mother. I don't want her talking to me about the subject."

"Carrie, please be kind to my mother. Yes, we are her sole chance to become a grandmother. But she's not trying to force you into anything. She's merely naming what she thinks your body is telling you."

"But I don't want to hear what she's saying."

"I know. I hear that objection loud and clear. The news is a shock to your system. You hope it's not true. But please don't be mean to my mother because she brings the signs to your attention."

"But what if she's right?"

"We will take each thing in life one at a time, and together. You know that's how we do things. Calm down."

"Don't tell me to calm down! I cannot be calm in the face of a life-long commitment that I don't want to make. Agitated is the appropriate way for me to feel."

"Alright. Okay. I'm sorry. Let's wait and see whether you have anything to be upset about before we dive off the deep end."

"I have every reason to be upset even if we only think I might be pregnant."

"Carrie. I won't argue with you. I will wait with you. And we shall see."

Partly mollified, Carrie at least quiets herself in the moment. Her fear could come to nothing, or she could have the longest nine months in the history of pregnancy in front of her. And an even longer life after that.

The weeks do indeed pass at the speed of molasses flowing from a chilled measuring cup, but her monthlies do not resume and new flesh begins to fill out her dresses. At every new sign that her body cradles life, she furiously rejects the implication. Then come the days when she rails at the obvious.

At four months, she despairs at a no longer deniable bump in her belly. She finally allows Catrina to call the doctor, and to dress her in pregnancy frocks instead of continuing to squeeze her tall, expanding frame into her usual skinny garb.

At five months, she complains endlessly of her elephantine stature, her constantly active bladder, the need already for a new size of dress, the swelling in her feet, the bitterness in her mouth. Catrina shakes her head, as if secretly wondering if any of them will survive her.

At six months, they receive news of August's death, interrupting her litany of complaints. Carrie cannot absorb even the possibility of death for her forty-two-year-old brother, and now he is gone, felled by a short-lived but virulent illness. The doctor will not let her travel to join her family for funeral services, so she drops to her knees at the altar of the Saint Matthews German Lutheran Church to remember him in prayer. She needs Witt's help to pull herself back to her feet.

At seven months, Carrie begins to bleed. She catches Witt's shudder at the shadow behind Catrina's frightened eyes. Every bit of the terror that gripped Carrie in her first moments of womanhood, back on that ship in the middle of the Atlantic, rushes back into her soul. She tries to breathe, and fails. Her body tosses her out of control, adding piercing pain to the flow of blood. She grasps the chain around her neck and pulls hard, screaming, "I never wanted to be a woman! I am an explorer! Why does God think making me have children is adventurous?"

The tiny, timeless silver charm of womanly solidarity with Frau Schlech pings on the floor board below her bed. And then, a mere hour later, two miniature bodies, tiny fingers and toes perfectly formed, emerge from her womb to be stealthily removed from the room.

Neither draws the shadow of a breath.

The doctor sedates the hysterical mother. The father weeps to watch, knowing that she despairs, not with him over the babies' death, but alone, over their very existence.

As Carrie emerges from the drug-induced stupor of her postpartum hours, her exhausted body aches, but will heal in time. Her soul disintegrates into a million tiny particles. She has killed her babies; she is sure of that truth. Drifting in and out of consciousness, she alternates her terrors. She calls for Witt, frantic for him to rescue her sons from the tightening grasp of her nightmare-guided hands. She stirs to scream, to demand their return into her arms. She drifts back into troubled sleep, and dreams of tiny bodies submerged in a barrel of water that breaches not a single bubble of air. She half awakens, to begin all over again.

Witt sits beside her, every time, holding her hand, gathering her into his arms when she will permit his touch, waiting and watching, tears flowing down his cheeks when she will not consent. And, thoroughly spent, she settles into a morose trial and conviction for rejecting the flesh she has borne.

At first, the whole proceeding takes place internally. As long as she traps the angst inside, she continues to toss and turn through the night, awaken exhausted, numb her pain to get through the day, and cycle back to another night. Finally, in desperation, she takes up her pen.

If I could control one portion of my life, childbearing would be the part I would choose to manage. I didn't want babies, and now I don't have them. But since my body removed the very problem I fought so fiercely, all I can do is cry. Those tiny beings were mine to take care of, to cherish, and I resisted. I had no choice but to nourish their bodies as far as I could; the whole world watching sees to that function. But I certainly failed to meet their small needs.

Did my insistence on avoiding motherhood put them to death? Did I exercise control I failed to know existed? My body expelled them, and I don't know whether to feel aggrieved or relieved that they are no longer mine to carry through their tiny lives.

Mutti trained me almost from birth to take care of a house and the children who were born there. All the women in and near the family have written every detail of babyhood, as if I should be interested. Frau Schlech explained the changes in my body solely based on the function of bringing children into the world. They all make it seem like my body, like those of my mother and grandmother and all women everywhere, is here for procreation. I don't believe it, but I have heard this role rehearsed for my entire life. Not one of them ever mentioned the delight I have discovered in my husband's arms.

Now, I feel guilty, instead of only rebellious. I'm not sure that's progress. I'm almost convinced that the only way to show progress would be to embrace the essence of womanhood as they present it to me. Am I an evil woman to have no interest, and in fact a great objection, to this part of my fate? Perhaps I am. Perhaps I have finally found the unforgivable sin, the one thing in me that God will not be able to love.

I have nothing to offer in the inner world of women, the receptive nature of creatures who are meant to be soft and nurturing, a receptacle to the lives of others. I have always known myself as the pirate. The initiator, the swashbuckler, the daring enjoyer of escapades, like Henry and I used to play when we were children. That time of imagination made me feel most real, the most content in my life. Everything since has been outside of my true character. Everything else has been forced instead of natural.

When I came to Charleston to marry Witt, I thought I had finally found my adventure. Indeed, the years with him overflow into learning and growing and brand-new ventures to risk. But now, beyond the boundary of curiosity, I cannot find my way back to the center. Even Witt, who has always taken me exactly for who I am, must be disappointed in my failure to thrive in the womanly art of bearing life into the world.

Carrie shakes her head as she puts down the pen. She feels no better for having committed her heresy to paper. But she sleeps through that night and the next, undisturbed by nightmares. And on the third day, she greets the sun with a lilt in her step that she has not experienced since New York, since before her breasts were sore, then engorged, and settled again.

So, she takes up the pen once more.

> *I don't imagine Witt will ever forgive me for my failure to bring his sons to life. He doesn't think I noticed, but he took into himself all the cries the babies never uttered. He held my hand and sobbed when he thought I slept. He reached to embrace me and bawled when I received his offering. He turned his head and wept in utter defeat when I would not accept his caress. He acted like a man in grief. I acted like a madwoman, unreachable and inconsolable, not that my babies were gone, but at the impossible expectation that I bring them into our lives. What must he think of me?*

> *And his mother, what does she see when she looks at me? Catrina's heartbreaking confusion at my unhappiness with being pregnant fills me with dread. I want choices that she does not understand. She has one much-loved son, and hope for continuation of a family line she and Diedrich began together. But as deeply as I have come to love her, I cannot commit my body in order to please her. I would not lend my body to this endeavor at all, were it not an inevitable consequence of my love for Witt.*

As she writes the words, the world begins to loosen its chokehold. She draws a shaky breath, one which takes air into her whole body, and exhales slowly to expel a tiny ounce of grief. She holds her pen firmly but lightly aside the embodiment of her emotion. She counts this day as the one on which the sun begins to dawn around the edges of her dark clouds, the one on which her thinking begins to change around the subject of

193

children. The inevitable consequences of her love for Witt.

In that morning's post, a card arrives bearing a New York postmark. On one side, a colorized photograph of the New York Public Library. On the other, her name and address, and scrawled almost illegibly:

> *My Carrie,*
> *I am so, so sad to hear your news.*
> *Love from your brother,*
> *Henry*

Carrie sits up so startled that she thinks for a moment the card must have come from someone else, someone signing Henry's name as a cruel joke. Henry's cards are chatty and interesting, but never explicitly emotional. When she pulls the card out of her pocket and reads again, the handwriting still belongs to Henry. She sits with the message in her lap and weeps genuine tears, huge and uncomplaining, for all she has lost in her life — for all the damaged dreams and false starts, for the terrifying thought that she might share the genes of her cousin's madness, for the pain she has caused herself and others in her utter refusal to change what she can, instead of trying to control what she cannot change.

Brooklyn, 1905

HENRY DASHES OFF a quick postcard to Carrie over his morning coffee. He chooses one of the picture cards he brought home from Puerto Rico. The card will be postmarked Brooklyn, but he still maintains his travel theme.

> *Off to Puerto Rico again next week.*
> *The army needs sweetening, so sugar this time.*
> *Back in a month or so.*
> *Hope to pick up decent coffee for Louis.*
> *Love from,*
> *Henry*

He has an appointment with his brother at the new restaurant at 10 a.m., over in Manhattan. He won't make the appointment on time. First, he has to figure out how to post bail. A wild time around his apartment last night leaves his brain foggy and his progress slow this morning, but he thinks he can remember.

Around 2 a.m., he hears screams, both a man and a woman, from a house across the street. Sirens follow a few minutes later; someone else is awake to call in the emergency. Pulling on his dressing gown, he pads on slippered feet down the stairs and out to the street. None of his four boarders join him. The restlessness built into his nature since childhood often makes him a light sleeper. He wonders now if he thought he would miss something by sleeping deeply.

Henry would gladly miss this wee hours incident in favor of more sleep. The young woman across the street apparently has slain her aged father in the bloodiest of ways. He sighs in relief to have only noises, without images, to relay to the police. He approaches an officer who grimaces when Henry asks about the incident. The officer takes his name and address, but no statement. In this moment, the Brooklyn Police Department focuses on physical evidence inside the residence.

In these later hours of the morning, he will almost certainly be late to meet his brother, even though he rises early to stop by the precinct station as requested. They are a beehive of activity. Still, the captain offers coffee as they make their way to a quiet room amid the chaos. Henry answers the questions truthfully, but he knows very little to tell.

"What did you hear?" The captain begins a long series of questions.

"Yelling. A woman screamed—no words, but a long, high scream as if she had been attacked. And a deeper voice bellowed, 'No! No, Agnes! Put that down!' His voice went quickly silent at the thud of gunfire, but she continued her screechy keening off and on for another ten minutes. The silence sounded eerier than the noise. I wondered about her location and action, but the void held no clues."

"Anything else?"

"When the police arrived, I went outside and joined a group of neighbors. They were, of course, chattering about the events."

"What did they say?"

196

"One of them knew the people involved. She said the woman suffers from hallucinations and visited the emergency department earlier that evening. But they sent her home—said they weren't equipped to help her, so they gave her a sedative and shuffled her back to her father and a taxi before she could fall asleep."

"Anything else?"

"A man said he saw the taxi arrive outside the building. The father evidently had a terrible time rousing his sleeping daughter to take her inside."

"Do you know any of the neighbors?"

"I don't know either of the people who seemed to know something about the situation. My neighbor in the apartment next door came down, but he seemed as ignorant as I. Our bedrooms each face the street, so the noise wakened both of us. My roommates said this morning they slept through the incident in the back bedrooms."

"Still, leave me his name and apartment number, will you? Maybe he's thought of something else he heard or saw. What do you do for work, Mr. Denzler?"

"Supply shipping," Henry answers. "I go out of the docks in Hoboken whenever I'm needed." He checks his watch. "I'm supposed to be talking to my brother right now about a bartending job. I do odd jobs when I'm in port, and he has the idea that I would have steadier opportunities if we begin working as a team at his restaurant and bar."

"When are you next due to sail?" Henry misses the cues. The captain worries that Henry will be out to sea when the court date comes up, and he must retain the few available witnesses.

"I'm leaving next week for Puerto Rico on the *Luchenbach*." The captain nods. Then he walks to the door and sticks his head into the hall.

"Ludwig, can you come in here a minute?" When Ludwig arrives, Henry's mouth drops open at the conversation. The captain says, "Please file a complaint against Mr. Denzler, Ludwig. If he posts bail, he won't be inclined to go offshore until the hearings are done."

"Wait—what?! I didn't do anything!"

"I can't afford to lose even a single witness in this case," the captain declares. "I can't keep this woman off the street if I don't have the witnesses to hold her. Let your ship's captain know you will be available in a month to six weeks to sail again. They'll have to make this next trip without your help."

"But—but . . ."

"I'm sorry, son."

"I have no reason not to cooperate, sir. I wish always to do my civic duty. But ..."

"The detective can show you where to post bail. You are free to work, but you can't leave the city."

One hundred dollars later, his pockets empty with no work in sight, Henry resigns himself to the fact that he'd better hustle to see his brother if he wants to eat for the rest of the month.

Louis happy as a cozy clam.
Boys & Minna settling well.
Lucky family.
Havana next on the schedule.
Love from your brother,
Henry

Across town, Louis rises early with much to accomplish before he catches the train to his Wall Street bar. He is a lucky man. He inhales the scent of strong coffee from Minna's kitchen, and knows he will emerge from his shave to scrambled eggs and brown toast on the table. He still cannot believe his good fortune. On his own, he probably would have lived out his life as the old maid brother.

When they lost his oldest brother, August, to a quick and early death, Louis was crushed at the demise of his closest ally in a tumble of boys. The one person even more upended by August's death was Minna. Her two half-grown boys needed a father more than ever, and instead suddenly were thrust into caring for their mother.

When Louis steps into the gap, he provides both a model for manhood and a sheltering tree for the widow. They all settle nicely into his tender affections, and eventually into his home, as he assumes the biblical role of care for his brother's widow. The fact that coffee and breakfast now appear on his old bachelor table every morning is still a miracle to him. This accidental family is his brother's greatest gift.

Saw Frederick last week.
Candy business thriving.
Kids growing like weeds.
Off to Buenos Aires.
Love from your brother,
Henry

In a different second-story apartment in Brooklyn, Frederick is up in the night tending to his three-year-old

199

son. Flora finishes three days and three nights of baby duty nearly crazy with fatigue, but little Duncan is still fretful from illness. Frederick cannot not settle him, either, but holds him through much of the night so Flora can sleep. Ever since the death of Fred, Jr., Frederick can never sleep through the cries of an ailing child.

Fortunately, five-year-old Charlotte always defies the odds to get a good night's sleep. But Frederick rises weary to face a full shift of work at the candy store. Some days he wishes he had followed August and Louis into the liquor trade instead of continuing in the family business. Contrary to popular belief, smelling too much chocolate and tasting too much sugar in repetitive twelve-hour stints gets old. He can make chocolates in his sleep. Which, especially today, is fortunate.

Frederick sets up the molds for the candies of the day, the shapes of hearts and flowers, tiny love letters on which he will paint a rose seal of icing, and little bitty cupids on which he will add a tiny daisy at the tip of the bow. Valentine's Day is almost here, the busiest day of the year in their shops. Maasen & Denzler Confections has the best selection in town, but their reputation will never weather the grief of irritated customers if they run out of candies on the big day. Hopefully, after he fills a red-ribboned box to take home to Flora on Valentine's night, they will have few extra pieces to sell off at half price the next morning.

Opposites now working together,
Louis & Henry as a team.
Wish me luck!
Love from your brother,
Henry

Savoring eggs and toast, Louis turns his thoughts to business. Unlike the rest of the family, who still weave in and out of each other's lives in the confectionary business, Louis turned to the liquor trade, starting as a bartender and working his way up to ownership. An hour at his desk will give him time to balance the books and set his mind on solid ground regarding invoices for the month.

His recent purchase of the restaurant next to his bar exponentially increases the headaches of cash flow. He means the new part of his business to be a sideline, a convenient, easy opportunity. The complexity quickly accelerates the restaurant into the main event. The liquor distributorship both simplifies operations and adds to the overall business dealings. His sanity depends on that hour of silence at his desk.

Buying the restaurant creates a need for additional staffing, which unexpectedly makes a way for reconnection with his little brother. Henry accepts Louis' offer of a bartending job between his stints at sea, and the arrangement works well for both of them. Henry gains a steady side gig when he is in New York, and Louis goes home early when Henry remains to close the bar.

Louis finds, to his surprise, that he enjoys working alongside his little brother. The restless Henry will always be "little" in Louis' mind, unready to take on a truly adult lifestyle of steady work, investment, and family at home. But Louis discovers Henry's humorous side, and decides to enjoy the ride. All the years they spend trying to get Henry to settle down come to nothing. Henry is still their rolling stone. Frederick is

201

just Frederick, honest and true. Louis stands for honor and duty. And August, of course, is no more.

In Charleston, Carrie suffers from a distance that extends beyond the miles. But she learns to read their lives between the scant lines that Henry pens.

Charleston, after 1906

THE LOVE KEEPS flowing between Carrie and Witt, nurtured by nights spooned together under the quilts. The babies continue to arrive, another every couple of years until two boys and then a girl stand in stair-step formation for every family photo. Witt and his mother supply the over-the-top excitement for each birth, when Carrie busies herself fretting. And Carrie gradually acquires knowledge and motivation adequate to keeping babies alive and cared for. The others fill in where her skills lag behind. The infant days are the greatest mystery for her. She breathes a sigh of relief at each new stage of independence. But even new freedom is fraught with ambivalence, for both mother and child.

"Richie, where were you this morning?"

"I went over to the Geddes farm, Mama, and watched the workers build the new barn."

"I worry about you. I didn't know where you were."

"I'm sorry, Mama. I must have forgotten to tell you.

"Sorry won't do, son. I need to know where you are."

"I stay safe, Mama. I only watched, from far away."

"I need you to do exactly as I tell you, and always, every time, tell me where you are going."

"But I—" He is eight years old. All his friends have been wandering into the work sites of their elders for years without ill effects.

"No buts, young man."

"But—"

"No buts."

"Yes, Mama."

When had she crept so far away from her own childhood, when she and Henry claimed a building site as their own and used it for their pirate ship? Their parents neither knew nor expressed any interest in knowing about their third-story leaps from one beam to another. Now her paranoia robs her child of the freedom to nurture his imagination. But she can't help herself. He is hers to keep safe, and she doesn't know how, and so in the absence of a better idea, she insists on knowing everything, as if that will help.

A good day for Carrie is a day she has honed a skill, read a book, come upon a good idea. She has little patience for the status quo, and a natural affinity for learning. Unfortunately, this thirst for excellence can have unconscious repercussions for others, including Richie.

"Did you finish reading the book your teacher gave you?"

"I don't like that book, Mama. I don't understand the words. I want a book with easier words."

"You are a very smart boy, Richie. If you can do those hard math problems, you should be able to read the books you are assigned. We will read together before you go to bed." Richie sighs, knowing that the evening will be tense.

"See, you put the letters together and they turn into words. And the words become sentences. And they tell you all about the subject of the book. Now, try this one." She would be able to figure it out, so he can, too. Richie gives the first sentence a good try.

"They think the games are nothing ..."

"No, no! This word right here is not 'nothing.' Look again! That word does not have the 'th' letters. What are the sounds?"

"Nuns ..."

"No, not nuns! Look again."

"N ... O ... S ... Nose ..."

"No, Richie! 'N ... O ... N ... sense.' That word is 'nonsense!' 'They think the games are nonsense.' What is hard about that? You can read that word."

"I'm sorry, Mama. I didn't know."

"Well, look carefully and think hard! I spend so much time doing things for you that I don't have any time left to do what I want to do!"

"But Mama, what do you want to do?" She sputters and noisily dismisses his question.

"What do you want me to do?" His voice is a whisper. The child thrives on pleasing his mother, but how do you please someone who so often does not articulate what she wants? Nonsense, indeed.

Meanwhile, Onkel Henry does his part to help her cling to dreams of something more, something closer to her full talents. He sends a postcard from every destination, reminding her in a handful of words that adventure still thrives beyond the confines of cradle and hearth, if not always within them.

Henry also challenges Carrie's fears. He sends cards to each of her children from afar. They love getting their own mail from their uncle

> *Dear Richie,*
> *I'm in Rhode Island this week.*
> *Not far from New York, but new things to see.*
> *Have you started school yet?*
> *I want to hear what you are learning.*
> *Love,*
> *Onkel Henry*

Whenever Richie and Witt go further than the city of Charleston to conduct farm business, Richie always wants to send a postcard home, no doubt his Onkel Henry's influence. Even if they go only as far as Winnsboro to pick up a new axle for the wagon, or to Abbeville to meet a supplier who promises a hardier batch of seed potatoes, Richie insists on sending a card. County Court House cards are his favorites; Carrie and the younger children possess quite a collection from Carolina cities. She wonders at the cost of postage, but Witt sees the purchases as an investment in their son. The father and son almost always make their way home before the cards arrive.

As he grows up, Richie remains the one who often accompanies his father on business. He also enjoys the puttering, the projects that life on the farm presents. He's like his father that way, and Carrie will not be at all surprised if he is the one to take over the farm when Witt retires. Not, of course, that such a day is near.

Richie has a keen mind for projects. He sees what needs to happen and plans accordingly. At eleven, he builds a storage shed to keep the farm implements dry and organized. At fourteen, the year his father suffers from spring pneumonia, he supervises the planting on his own. By the time he is sixteen, he keeps the weekly books of crops sold and profit gained. He seems to understand the work as puzzles to be solved, and she admires his acumen.

She admires him, but she often fails to understand him. He reminds her of her brother Louis—dutiful to a fault, but too often joyless. *Does any remedy exist for your child reminding you of your least favorite sibling?* she often wonders. *Can a child make you overflow with magic, when he harbors such strange reasons for applause?* He's a good boy, but overzealous in his solicitation of her approval.

"Mama, look what I made!" At ten, he rushes in from the barn one day dragging a contraption made of rope, sticks, and worn-out tires. She has no idea what the thing could possibly be.

"Aren't you a clever boy? How will you use it?" Carrie sidesteps her ignorance for the sake of encouragement. She is learning.

"If you put the bag of seed potatoes here," he says as he points, "and tie the mouth closed here, you can drag the seeds along beside the plow and keep everything together.

"Well, so you can!" He runs back out into the yard, trailing black Charleston dust behind him, while she shakes her head and wonders at his excitement. She would never name the thing miraculous, but he has his own ways.

Richie is the first of my children that I had the chance to get to know, she writes in her now omnipresent journal. *The twins, of course, were gone before they could be known. In many ways, I could say the same about my brother August. The years between us practically assured we had little in common. Always two steps ahead of me in life, he was interested in adult affairs while I remained a child. He crossed the sea before I developed any interest in his pursuits. He had a wife when I got off the ship. He started raising children, in short, before I quit being one. And then died before I had the chance to return to Brooklyn as an adult. All along, completely mistimed events prevented me from truly knowing him. Sadly, that fact also applied to the twins' brief lives. The time passed too quickly to know them, too.*

But Louis, I knew Louis. I always found him mildly irritating, far too rule-bound to enjoy. I never knew how to handle him. As a sort of wild child, I simply could not relate to living within the confines of that sense of obligation. He was more foreign to me than an immigrant to a new country. I simply could not fathom his inner workings.

Richie is my little Louis. I try to be patient and kind, but I have no confidence that I receive him as he intends, nor that he does the same for me. He has his father's head for business, but not Witt's ease in dealing with people. I am supposed to be the adult, the self-assured one.

But the truth is, Richie unnerves me. I don't know how to reach him. Nothing easy exists between us. The barrier is not lack of trust, exactly; he is highly principled in his behavior, and I am nothing if not loyal. But that day to day feeling of give and take, the sense of connection that doesn't need words, the understanding I saw in Catrina's eyes when she looked at Witt – that feeling that says 'I know my son.' I wish I could have that look in my eyes for Richie.

By the time Richie grows into Rich, he trades all the sweet German Lutheran playmates in his mother's church for a sweetheart from the Catholic parish across town. He lives at home to finish two years of college, then goes to work for Standard Oil Company in Charleston. In the city directory, it's his brother Walt who now lists himself as farmer, a strange turn of events from what Carrie envisioned. She is not completely at ease with the twist in what she predicted, but at least both young men still live with them. She often doubts their desire to do so.

When Rich transforms into a grown-up Richard, the change is complete, abrupt, and baffling to Carrie. He transplants himself from Charleston to New York, where he accepts a management position in the oil business. He couches the news as a return to family that has become distant in the passing of years. And technically, his claim is true; one of Retta Maasen's grandchildren alerts him to the job opening, and he stays with Frederick's son until he settles on his own. He lives at the center of all the Brooklyn addresses occupied by Denzlers in the previous generation.

But in his explanations, Carrie hears disloyalty, to their little family of five, to their home in Charleston, to southern sensibilities. The piece of her mind she gives him references "moving up North among those stinking Yankees" and rips a hole in the fabric of their relationship that cannot be rewoven. He takes his Charleston bride to Brooklyn to marry. And when they move his recently widowed New-York-born mother-in-law into their home, the tear in the fabric of his relationship with his mother is complete.

Carrie mutters some harsh words about Yankees stealing her son, forgetting that she herself traces her arc of home through a borough a few blocks from his house. Two granddaughters from this union visit Charleston a time or two. Their little-girl pictures from an Easter Sunday in Hampton Park occupy the mantle in their grandmother's living room. But more and more frequently, they appear in her life as little more than disembodied voices on the telephone on this Christmas Day, that Mother's Day, Carrie's annual birthday call. She feels cheated, a familiar state now reaching its tentacles into a new generation.

I think he has completely abandoned us. I don't understand how he can establish himself at such a distance from us, and then take his widowed mother-in-law all the way up there. I would think he would move back closer to us, if she needs them as well. They could join her in her home, or live near her, and be near us as well. Then I would not have to listen to that pompous woman brag about granddaughters I don't really know. Shopping for uniforms for school, making first communion, cheering one on in the grade school program and taking pictures of the other at her piano recital, knowing everything about their lives. All her little hidden messages remind me what I'm missing. I don't like it one bit.

Charleton, after 1908

CARRIE NAMES HER youngest son, Henry Walter, after her youngest brother, Henry Gustav, each a happy wanderer. She never knows where Walter roams, and she probably never will. He is the baby who can dismantle pieces of furniture right under her nose, simply by quietly working his mischief. From the time he can talk, he has an easy story ready to distract her. By the time he is eight, she puzzles over her seemingly willing lack of awareness, harboring uneasy suspicions that her failure to know her child's whereabouts is problematic.

"Mr. Walt, where were you this morning?" He deftly sidesteps conflict with his mother by delivering a smiling lie. She participated in many dubious activities as a child, but she never lied outright when caught. Why can't he speak honestly to her?

"Helping Papa in the fields," he says. And she nods, when she knows very well that Witt will tell her that he hasn't seen their younger son all morning, if she asks. But she doesn't ask. She accepts the answer, because she lacks the courage to do anything else. She sees Henry in him at every juncture. She pours all the love that she saved for her absent brother out on this son of hers. But she can't seem to practice what she has learned from her brother to connect with her son. She acts on his terms, but not in his best interest. She learns part but not the whole of the lesson. She recognizes potential consequences to this approach, in a way. Her fear for this child is that one day he really will go missing, and she won't even know where to look. But she fears alienating him even more.

Walt is left free to retreat unchallenged into secret places, to embrace whatever dreams he chooses, to take whatever actions he deems appropriate. She never questions his absence, whether away from her physical supervision or into daydreams to which she is not privy. If she's learned anything about avoiding the mistakes she made on the way to a peaceful place with his uncle, she's learned how to make all the opposite mistakes.

Henry does nothing at all to discourage his nephew's habit of meandering. Instead, he feeds the dreams by sending little Walt an album to collect the postcards Henry sends from all over the world. Walter wants to collect as many different countries as possible.

> *Hallo, Walter,*
> *You like adventures, don't you?*
> *I am on an adventure in Cuba. Very interesting.*
> *Maybe you will come here one day. I hope so.*
> *Love,*
> *Onkel Henry*

And of course, she does understand the hungers of a wanderer. She has lived them, and still does most days. A woman does not leave girlhood behind so thoroughly that the old wishes and rebellions disappear; instead, they settle into something more palatable to the world she occupies. Those who don't find a way to cope go miserable, or mad. But in spite of missing what she cannot have, she becomes absolutely clear about her longing. She protested vigorously when the rules kept her caged in tradition. Henry did not need to scream so loudly, but always knew himself meant for the sea. Walt seems less purposeful in his approach; she doesn't really know what captures his ardor.

When they are nearing adulthood, and Rich leaves the farm for the oil company, Walt attempts to take up farming. Carrie has to resist breaking into laughter when he announces his intention. She never notices him enjoying freshly plowed fields or hauling truckloads of potatoes to market. She never sees him display any intention of duty to his father, whose load increases exponentially with Richard's departure. She cannot imagine what drives Walt to display the moniker "Farmer" after his name.

"I'm surprised that farming attracts you," she says to her younger son. "I'm glad to see you working alongside your father, but I'm curious. What do you like about the job?"

Walt shifts his weight from foot to foot.

"I guess I thought I'd try something new."

"You don't have to take on the farm, you know. Your dad has very reliable help. So dependable that he could walk away tomorrow and the work would go right on."

"I know."

"So, what motivates you to make this shift? I assumed you would want to finish school and then find your own line of work."

"I'll finish school."

"I'm not doubting that. I just wonder what you are thinking."

213

"I don't know. Why are you asking me all these questions?"

"I'm curious where your life leads you. A mother has the job of caring about things like that."

"Oh."

Carrie harbors a leaden cold in her belly that perhaps the conversation is exactly what it will turn out to be, too little, too late.

She may not know his intentions, but her instincts are correct. Farming sustains Walter for about six months, and when the crops are in, he is done. His appellation in the next year's city directory is "Mariner" instead of "Farmer." Instead of daily chores on the farm, he hops onto a trolley to the Navy Yard and wanders the docks. Between the ships and the sailors, he must find some unnamed element that draws him in. He whistles as he does his share of household chores, and conceals whatever drives him behind a cheerful face. Carrie does her best to express interest in what happens in his life, but he is always hiding.

When he gravitates to the merchant marines, all Carrie can grasp is that he leaves her bereft and unanchored, abandoning her like her brother Henry, all those years ago. Like Richard, more recently. He is so young (but still six years older than Henry when he disappeared off the ship into Hoboken). And indeed, against her tearful protest, Walter leaves their home in Charleston for a boarding house in Manhattan. Carrie cannot tell whether he has joined his brother in the city, or roamed off on his own. A dark cloud covers his departure.

He promises to write, but he will break his promises. He flashes his "aw, shucks" grin and says he is still her loving son, reminding her of Henry's earlier protestations of loving brotherhood. Any inch of progress she has struggled to gain will disappear the moment he finds his sea legs. He has finally done the thing to which she cannot close her eyes, because she knows all too well the cost of adventure that goes unshared.

All of my fears are reasonable, she tells herself, trying to hold her heart inside her body. *Every mother fears for her children.* But she suspects that not every mother is willing to alternate between dogged pursuit of a compliant child and willful ignorance of a winsome renegade's folly. She feels the inconsistency, and the helplessness of a missing middle way to connect to her own sons.

The way she forges does not satisfy her longing. She loves them dearly, flesh of her flesh. But in one case, her demands outweigh her capability for unconditional love. Her need to control outcome far outpaces her capacity for allowing her children to grow into their fullest selves. And in the other case, her benign neglect replaces good sense. She leaves the child lacking a tether, and the mother missing a firm idea of his story.

Carrie is healing her relationship with her youngest brother, but her sons replace him on her hapless agenda. The boys fall prey to her old habits, and although their physical needs are met, connections falter on her watch. She cannot tell them she is proud of their adventurous spark, and so they find their assurance elsewhere. She cannot encourage them to take risks, and so their spirits either die on the vine or outgrow the tiny pot in which

215

they are planted. And in these choices, conscious or not, she forfeits the right for her cautions to make any difference in their young lives.

For some time now, no one knows where Walter has landed, if Walter has landed. Each time the post contains a cherished postcard from Henry, Carrie wonders if Walter might also visit the port of that postmark. Postcards from Onkel Henry become her only way of holding on to the both of them, one requiring skill in reading between the lines, the other existing entirely in the shadow of familial imagination.

Charleston, 1910

Y OU SEEM MUCH MORE relaxed during this pregnancy," he says. Witt recognizes the difference in her attitude at almost exactly the same moment he sees the tell-tale changes in her body.

She shrugs. "I feel more relaxed. I have none of that cold dread that usually invades my stomach at the first sign of pregnancy." In truth, by the time they prepare for their last baby to join the family, Carrie actually feels excited.

"Any idea why you feel different this time?" Not that he has any argument with the change.

"Not really. Maybe I am finally becoming an expert on this baby-making thing. I know what I'm doing at this stage, even if I still don't always know what to do after they arrive!" But she can feel the difference. She dares to hope that her relationship with the pending arrival will be different, more bonded, healthier.

"I hope you will enjoy this child as much as I have enjoyed the others," Witt says, and pauses before going on. "Thank you, Carrie. I don't thank you often enough for giving me these children. If you are my sun, they are my moon. And I know your idea of a perfect occupation does not include birthing babies."

"No, you're right about that," she laughs. "And that's very mild language for the predicament of my pregnancies! But I'm not sorry we have them. Parenthood is its own sort of adventure, even if I don't naturally embrace the idea."

"I'm proud of you," Witt says as he draws her to him. "If I could have made having babies better for you, I would have."

"I know." Carrie closes her eyes. "Do you think I am awful for feeling the way I do?"

"Excited to be having a baby? I think not!" His eyes glitter with joy at teasing her.

"No. Not that. I kind of like that, for a change." Her inside smile shows on the outside. "No, I'm talking about my utter hopelessness knowing how to love a child after arrival."

"I actually think your hesitation makes perfect sense." He hugs her close. "All of your experience prompts wariness. Your brothers left, quite beyond your control, when you were still a child, and you had little means of staying connected to them. So, you held on tighter and tighter, hoping you could restore them in your life by sheer persistence. That's a powerful lesson in dealing with distance. Why wouldn't you try to hold on to your own children in the same way, even when doing so leaves all of you unhappy?

"And then your Mutti, your Vati, Retta, August, they all departed this world about the time our children began entering the scene. My father died before they came, and even my mother left us soon after they were born. Why wouldn't you begin to have some resentment about that changing of the guard? You were not done securing your deepest connections when they were all replaced by new obligations in the form of tiny squirmy snot wads.

"So no," he concludes. "I don't think you are awful. I do wish the experience were happier for all of you! I long so deeply for you to relax and let each other grow into who you are, without the angst and irritation."

"My mind gets muddled, and then I mire myself in blame. I'm thankful you see me so clearly and can explain me to myself, Witt." She sighs, though whether in contentment or frustration, anyone would find hard to discern.

Lena arrives into the world heralded by an uneventful pregnancy and an easy delivery. Carrie notes the apt full-circle of Lena's position as the fifth child and only daughter of the family, mirroring Carrie's own family configuration. Mostly, however, she enjoys this baby girl, as if she knows what to do for this child in ways she didn't grasp for her baby boys. Pinafores and dollies become part of her daily existence. She never writes letters full of the teething and diapers, like the ones she received as a younger woman (who would she send them to?), but she relishes the ruffles and bows. She feels like she's playing when she cares for the child. She sees Witt watching ecstatically as Carrie's interactions with Lena bloom in obvious joy.

"You like having a girl, don't you?"

"I do. She feels like she's mine in a way none of the boys felt when they were born. I wonder why."

"I doubt it's the ribbons and lace. You've never cared for fancy dress for yourself."

"No, I haven't. And maybe she won't either, when she's older. That's fine. As a child, my Sunday clothes always got in the way of whatever expedition Henry and I cooked up. I had to be able to keep pace in his world, and would rather be allowed sturdy trousers and a cotton shirt, like he wore! But her girly things do make her look awfully cute, don't they?"

"Oh, yes. And as pretty as her Mama."

"Her Daddy is a sweet-talker, now, isn't he?"

"Depends. Is it working for me?"

"Mm-hm!" She pauses to return his kiss, and then goes on. "I have the sense that I already know her, because her little life mirrors my own. The sole girl joining four big brothers. Of course, her life will be different, since she never knew the twins. But I feel a kinship, not so much mother-and-daughter as daughter-and-daughter. Her little being feels familiar."

Witt smiles as she calms the child's fussing.

"Maybe I'm finally getting the hang of mothering after all."

> *You finally have your baby girl!*
> *Bet she will be a pirate!*
> *Love from your brother,*
> *Henry*

A tiny one in arms makes the big brothers look huge. From that new perspective, Carrie becomes able to trust Richie one step further in monitoring his own activities. She manages to lead with curiosity rather than suspicion when she asks Walt about his interests. The parents and children, in short, become more nearly family under this newer version of Mama. Life is better. Until it's not. They all enjoy new ways. Until they don't. Parents do the best they can do in the moment, but they are also human. And sometimes the mistakes they make cannot be ironed out.

Sometimes a wrinkle becomes a permanent crease in the fabric.

Carrie has some vague understanding that the real difference in mothering this last child is that Lena stays home. As much as she reflects her mother, she does the opposite of going halfway around the world at the age of twelve, or up the coast the minute she turns twenty-one. She goes and comes. She leaves Charleston for an interval, but never for long.

Lena never accompanies her father on business, as the boys do. When they are away, the mother and daughter have "girl time," whether out on the farm or at the house in town. They bake cookies and go for picnics on the beach. They search the marshes for signs of wildlife, or the storefronts near the church and the library downtown for special "girls only" treats. And then they go home together.

Lena joins the newly founded Girl Scouts at ten, the first possible moment she can. She loves the excitement of exploration and skill-making this new organization offers. At the time of her birth, scouting exists exclusively for boys, but the rapid expansion of the Girl Scouts in her first ten years of life creates an adventurous avenue for girls. Lena streams with thousands of little girls in eager pilgrimages to organizational headquarters, down the coast in Savannah. She enjoys outings to the local history and art museums, the city park and the county hiking trails. She swims and boats and camps with her troop all over the Southeastern United States. She even attends scouting conventions as an older youth, first in Savannah, then in Atlanta, and then all the way down in Miami on a moored cruise ship. Each and every time she completes an adventurous trek, Lena comes home.

She joins the high school track team and travels to hone her skills on competition. She finishes a college degree that Carrie considers a sojourn in a foreign country — early childhood education, of all things! She spends college summers as a counselor for Girl Scout camp a state away. But every fall, she comes home to work in Mrs. Buncombe's kindergarten and study at the local college.

After graduation, she finds a job at home, working for the Girl Scouts in whom she finds her greatest adventures. She meets a local boy, Conrad, an automobile mechanic who holds aspirations of teaching at the high school where he graduated. They embark on the adventure of marriage, and make a home in their own house, halfway between the farm house and the city house, right in the center of home territory.

Summer schedules always differ from the winter months. The heat in Charleston threatens life itself, melting the tar and sliding it right off the roads. Everyone who has the means or an excuse leaves the city during the summer. The farmers, of course, must work the land during the growing season, so Witt and Carrie remain in the sprawling farm house. Lena and Conrad leave the heat behind to drive up to Durham so Conrad can spend the summer studying at Duke University, living in tiny rooms, where baby Lynn sleeps in a dresser drawer. The year the baby turns five, he completes his graduation with induction into the Phi Beta Kappa honor fraternity.

The next day, the Japanese hit Pearl Harbor and the United States enters the conflict that their generation would forever remember as The War. The War Between the States always held that status for their most recent forebears, but Lena and Conrad relocate that moniker to the world arena. He goes around to the recruitment office to enlist the following week.

After basic training, Lena and little Lynn join him for a year of travel, first to Atlanta and then up the eastern seaboard wherever the Army sends him. Some posts last for months at a time, and others for mere days. They move their way up the coast until they end up in her mother's former home in New York. At the end of the second summer on the road, Conrad ships out for North Africa to keep Army vehicles in top working order. Lena and Lynn bundle all their worldly possessions into the Army green Chevrolet, and they return home.

Lena returns to Mrs. Buncombe's kindergarten, and Lynn, having outgrown such juvenile pursuits, moves on to the neighborhood 'big school' to begin first grade. The rhythm of summers continues with treks off to camp, Lena on staff and Lynn as a camper. And every fall, they return home to their third-floor rental on Ashley Avenue. There they await the postman's buzz that signals a letter from Africa or France, a missive from Conrad. Carrie is finally content to let a child of hers have adventures, secure as she is in the knowledge that Lena will always come home.

Brooklyn, 1921

THE YEAR IS 1921. Richie is fifteen years old. Walter is thirteen, Lena eleven. And Carrie has the opportunity of a lifetime, to go back home. Not to Meldorf, always too far to travel, too hostile to affect a safe return, and eventually too empty of connections to want to go there. But to Brooklyn, which brings a different promise of a return to her roots. In the twenty years since her marriage in Charleston, she has returned to Brooklyn exactly once, the joyful occasion of baptism for her niece, at about the time her less happy journey to children began. Since then, she has never been out of Charleston. The endless restriction to home, she now thinks, is exactly the curtailing of adventure she had feared.

Carrie has a full life, but a restless marrow remains buried within her. For their twentieth wedding anniversary, Witt gives her the perfect gift. He corrals the children and delivers them to school in the mornings and returns them home in the afternoon. He raids the grocer for the easy-fix provisions that keep them eating three meals a day. And before first light on Wednesday morning, he puts her on a train to New York. Alone.

She is thrilled. And she is terrified. Facing into the prospect of returning to her people fills her belly with excitement, and no small measure of dread. What will she find, in this place she left so long ago? As the visit turns out, she recovers a piece of her soul.

Bridget meets her at Penn Station long past sunset.

"Let's get sausage with mustard for dinner, like in the old days," Bridget suggests after a huge *hallo* hug. They stop at the cart, place their orders, and continue their walk to Bridget's rooms, chattering non-stop to fill in the missing years.

"Oh! Your apartment building looks like a school. I love all of the paper flowers hanging in the windows."

"I live in a school now. I think the last time I wrote a real letter, I still lived at my son's house. I moved there after his father died, and I loved being there. He has a very sweet wife, and, of course, I love them and their babies to pieces!"

"You always liked the babies," Carrie says, giving in to an eye roll.

"Well, yes, and when they are your grandchildren, I think you can't help but be crazy about them. It's part of being a grandparent."

"We'll see. I have learned to love my children very deeply, after all. Anyway, you live at a school?"

"Yes, I do. I moved here about six months ago. I always felt very welcome in my son's home, and would have stayed there forever. But his mother-in-law moved in with us after his father-in-law died. Oooooooh, let me tell you. That arrangement did not work at all. Not at all. She got to me far more than Amalia ever irritated you."

"I find that claim extremely difficult to believe. But you've never lied to me, so I suppose I must take your word for it." Carrie laughs. "We spent a lot of air talking about that one, *ja*?"

"You can trust me on this. That mother-in-law's tongue could slice a spirit into jagged quarters. I felt bad leaving the kids with her, but I had no choice. I couldn't have you coming up here to visit me in jail for committing murder! And I've always wanted to repay the orphanage for their generosity to me, so I thought to myself, 'Bridget, this is your chance!' And so here I am."

"Good. Murder leaves a tough reputation to overcome. Where are we?"

"St. Joe's Orphan Asylum. I am a teacher for the girls here."

"I would not have thought you would ever want to be anywhere near an orphanage again. I mean, I know they took care of you, but that time of your life does not hold the happiest memories."

"Oh, but I had the best teacher in those days," Bridget says. She loved me like an older sister, and taught me much more than books and sums. Didn't I ever tell you about her? She taught me about life."

"I don't think so, but I do think I understand. I know someone like that. That's how I would describe you."

"You are very sweet to say so. I love the thought that I might have given you what she gave me."

"You gave the best advice," Carrie says. "I still lean on it, all that wisdom about being honest about what you need, and speaking up for yourself, and living your own life while avoiding the temptation to live someone else's life for them. I don't think I would have survived if you had not taught me."

"I know I wouldn't have lived through the orphanage without her," Bridget says. "I learned so much, but I took so little of my own advice. I failed so spectacularly in choosing a father for my son that I spent all of my parenting years protecting my dearie from that man. And keeping the peace to keep us safe."

"You drew a bad lot on that one," Carrie says. "You are so sensible, I was surprised when a situation you chose went so wrong."

"Well, like I always tell you," and Carrie joined to chant in unison, "The only one you can change is yourself." They dissolved into laughter. "In this case, I couldn't change him, and I couldn't get rid of him."

"You gave it your best effort. And that man, frankly, did you a favor by dying young. Hmm. Now, let's talk of pleasant things. I want to hear about your life here at St. Joe's . . ."

The two friends talk until late in the night, until they finally surrender to sleep in Bridget's tiny room, Carrie in the narrow bed and Bridget on a thick pallet of quilts on the floor. At forty-three and fifty-two, they still know how to have a slumber party! The next morning, they rise at first light to get Bridget to her classroom, a space jammed full of joy. Carrie remains until the lunch break, gives Bridget a quick kiss, and dashes around the corner and up Fifth Avenue, eager to find her brother.

Her breath catches at the sight of the famous lions she has heard so much about. Enormous and majestic, carved from marble barely tinged the palest pink, they fit the shrine she has looked forward to seeing for years. Finally, after all the years of hoping and dreaming, she stands before the New York Public Library in Manhattan.

"There's my best girl!" Henry's voice greets her as she rounds the corner base of the marble stairs. They meet outside the main entry on Fifth Avenue. He leans against a white column to one side of a famous marble cat. He opens his arms. She turns, laughs, and skips up the steps into them.

"You are really here," she says. "I half-believed you would leave me standing on the steps alone. Maybe that's why I chose a place I really wanted to see. I could keep the trip to the city interesting, so I would not waste the time if you didn't materialize."

"Of course I am here. Where else would I be?"

"Oh, sailing the high seas in search of adventure." But laughter underlines her words, not a trace of resentment.

"I had that option. They scheduled me for Argentina for three weeks, but I had to decline."

She blinks. "You canceled a sailing to be here to meet me?"

"No, not the sailing; I don't have that kind of power. I canceled my participation, and told them they needed to find a different quarter-master for this trip. I have to see my sister!"

Carrie realizes in that moment that she finally has what she wants, a close and steady bond with her favorite brother. One in which he commits to taking action to bring them together. One in which he pays attention to what she needs and meets her halfway. She sighs deeply. A husband at home and a brother here, double love colliding on the same day, bathes her heart in joy.

"Thank you, Henry."

"I couldn't have you here for the first time in two decades and be gone. A long time ago, that might have suited me fine, but no longer. I guess I've mellowed in my dotage."

"I guess you have!" They turn back toward the steps and begin the climb from Fifth Avenue to the front door.

"I've heard," Henry says, "that the first director of the library sketched the original building plan on the back of a postcard, way back when you still lived here. I suppose he showed off his new workplace by bragging to a friend."

"Too bad you can't acquire that card to send me sometime over the years," Carrie says. "That piece of cardboard would certainly be worth a fortune by now. Or at least, far more than the Henry Denzler Album of Collected Penny Postcards my younger son maintains at home in your honor!"

"Indeed. Most collections are more prestigious than my contributions."

"More prestigious, perhaps, but never more precious," Carrie says. "Oh, Henry. Look!" She inhales audibly as they enter the library, but lowers her voice instinctively to a whisper. "They must have used most of the marble in the world to build this room!"

"Looks like a world full, doesn't it?" Henry produces a low whistle as his head lifts of its own volition to find the top of the room. They make their way to one of the staircases and begin their ascent. The space that Carrie holds as sacred as any cathedral does not disappoint them. The cavernous entrance hall would be the smallest room they visit that day. On the third floor, they pause, breathless, at the entrance to Room 315. Then they enter the largest room in the country, constructed entirely without columns or domes. The reading room of the New York Public Library.

"Oh, my." Carrie closes her eyes for a moment. When she reopens them, her body floats to the very center of the room. She would guess the expanse goes on for miles to either side, but she would be exaggerating; the true measurement is under three hundred feet. The ceiling stretches up several stories of any ordinary building, dressed in sky-like artwork that takes the room directly to the clouds. Stretched from one end all the way to the other, amid three stories of books reaching upward, people sit grouped in wooden chairs at twelve-foot wooden tables, reading. The sight is more like heaven than anything she can imagine.

With reverent footsteps, she approaches the shelves. Dictionaries. Encyclopedias. Every sort of reference material imaginable, like the Pratt Institute library, multiplied by untold numbers. Carrie is not one to swoon, but she comes pretty close. She selects one volume at random and lugs the heavy tome to a seat at one of the mammoth tables. She looks. She holds the "G" volume of the latest edition of Collier's Encyclopedia, printed anew that very year. Placing the tome near a lamp to supplement the daylight from high windows, she opens the volume directly to the article on Goethe. She breathes in the smell of the page, and begins to read.

An hour later, at the bend in the staircase halfway between floors on their descent, Henry pauses on the marble landing and places his hand on the wall.

"Here's something that will make you jealous," he says. "On the mezzanine level, maybe even right behind this wall, the library director lives in an apartment with his family. I remember reading in The Times that his wife birthed a daughter here among the books. She's a little younger than Lena, if I remember correctly."

"You're right; I am envious. I could get used to living in a library. On the other hand, the housecleaning in this spacious abode would take an edge off the privilege. Can you imagine emptying trash bins in a place like this? Or dusting?"

Henry laughs a little too loudly, clapping his hand over his mouth to bring him back to library volume. They continue to the basement level this time, back to earth. In this windowless space, the employees operate a cooperative general store, boasting everything from brown sugar to silk stockings as merchandise. They snag a pair of Coca-Colas, exit through the 42nd Street door, and cross over to walk through Bryant Park.

"I could have been a librarian, you know," Carrie says. "Miss Annie tried to get me to apply for a seat at the library science school in Brooklyn."

"Miss Annie?"

"The children's librarian at Pratt Institute."

"Ah, I remember. You were there every chance you got when you lived here in Brooklyn."

"I was. I would count that library as my second home, except I think maybe I valued it way more than the Chapelle's bedsit!"

"So why didn't you?"

"Why didn't I what?"

"Why didn't you go to library school?"

"I had missed so much of high school by then, and graduation was a requirement for admission. And then shortly after she and I talked about the possibility and what we might do about my missing credentials, Witt arrived to woo me south."

"The world lost a good librarian when you missed that opportunity," Henry says. "And you would have been able to travel the world from your desk!"

"Yes, I think I would have loved to study, and to work at the library. But life is good. I'm gradually learning motherhood, even without a school to teach me."

"The children are doing well?"

"I think so. I know Lena's fine. Who can ever tell about the boys?"

"What interests them these days?"

"Lena spends every minute lobbying to go to Girl Scouts. You do know about Girl Scouts?"

"Oh, yes. We've already established that I read The Times."

"She loves every minute of scouting. Last week the girls took a field trip to the beach and you would think they had gone to the moon! She's also crazy smart, good in school. She's a wonder."

"Good for her. I can tell she takes after her mother. What about the boys?"

"Rich loves the farm, and he's a genuine help to his dad. I expect he will be running the place on his own one day. He really has a knack for the job. He's Witt's child."

"And Walter? Who does Walter belong to?"

"Himself, mostly. And you. He reminds me so much of you. And I have no more idea how to live with him than I had with you in earlier days. His mind is always active, roving around the universe. I expect that one day his body will follow. Maybe he'll be a mariner like his Onkel Henry."

"He could do worse."

"He could. But he doesn't communicate any better than you ever did, and that's hard. I don't seem to have learned a single thing from you that helps me parent him."

"Give him his freedom, Carrie. He'll find his way back to you."

"I hope you're right."

"Hey, I'm surviving to live to the proverbial ripe old age, whatever number that might be. He will be fine."

At the appointed hour of 5 p.m. Henry and Carrie arrive at Louis' Wall Street restaurant and bar. The ferries from Jersey City and Brooklyn both dock close by, so the brothers will head easily in opposite directions from their gathering.

Louis, his dark hair now tinged with silver, gives his sister a bear hug. "I got here early," he says, "to meet with the manager of this fine establishment. Now that I'm the owner but not the manager, I have so much less work to do. I list myself on every piece of paper as retired, but I can't help myself. I have to be involved!" The restaurant and bar do very well, and have outlived most of the competition in a way restaurants seldom experience. The location is perfect, right in the Financial District. The bar suffers from the newly imposed Eighteenth Amendment to the Constitution, but not much. New York tends not to pay much attention to Prohibition.

"Having Henry join me in this venture is a blessing," Louis says. "He pushes us to risk more, and I pull his ideas back into reality. We are like we have always been, at our best and at our worst!"

"*Ja*, I'm a pain in the neck, but I still do the old boy good," Henry says, a grin accompanying his rejoinder. Carrie knows Louis' conscientious nature keeps him involved even when all would be fine without him.

Frederick arrives and the four of them take up residence around the men's usual backroom table. They make the tacit decision to actually drink coffee this afternoon in deference to the lady in attendance, not that Carrie considers herself much of a lady, even now. Two brothers pull pictures of their children out of their wallets. All of the faces would be completely unrecognizable to Carrie if not for the pictures the brothers had sent occasionally over the years.

"My eldest son," Louis says, "works as an accountant. His baby is now five, and his wife even prettier than this picture shows." He passes a posed family shot to Carrie, who nods appreciatively.

"Will I get to meet that little rascal?" Carrie inquires.

"Oh, yes," Frederick cuts in. "Everyone is coming for dinner tomorrow night. Flora says we cannot possibly have everyone in town and not gather the crowd. Retta and Mutti would haunt us for sure!" They chuckle, but know Frederick speaks a serious truth.

"And this handsome child lives at home with his mother and me," Louis says, handing her another photo. "He's a shy young man, not all gregarious like his brother. But he's a good boy. He repairs tires for the car service station down the street from the house. The marriage bug has not caught him, but he has plenty of time."

"August would be proud of these boys," Carrie says, thinking that August would also be grateful to Louis for loving his whole family so well.

"And what about you and Minna? How is retirement for you?"

"Truthfully, I think she'd rather I were out from under her feet a little more often. And I probably will make the staff around here a little crazy in my advancing years, too. I'm used to being a producer, not a bother." Carrie notes a restlessness in Louis that she has never seen before. She suspects his retirement does not quite suit him, and that he will end up finding another job before long.

Frederick remains the hard-working candy maker he has been since childhood.

"Business is booming in the Roaring Twenties of well-to-do New York society," Frederick says. "Even ordinary people are flush with expendable cash, and candy easily dresses up as a luxury item."

"Luxury wasn't ever your style, big brother," Carrie says, a mock frown creasing her brow. "Are you sure you are in the right business?"

"I am," he nods, "and I still consider chocolate a homegrown necessity. But if the people want luxury, who am I to argue?" He raises his hands in a questioning shrug.

Frederick also presents a photograph for Carrie's inspection. Her lovely sixteen-year-old goddaughter works at Maasen & Denzler's on Manhattan Avenue, downstairs from the family's apartment. Her hulking fourteen-year-old brother, whom Carrie will meet for the first time tonight, stands half a head taller than his father.

"What a beautiful family," Carrie says. "Flora has aged very gracefully. And you are no slouch yourself."

"Old man!" Henry pokes Frederick's arm. "When did we all become so ancient?"

"Hey, speak for yourself, my brother!" Carrie quickly rises to her other brother's defense. "We're not getting any older. Though, our children are getting on in years!"

Carrie sleeps at Frederick's that night, squishing her tall frame into the small guest room with the steamer trunk in the corner. The next day, her young niece and nephew accompany her on a round of visits to all the old haunts — the Trinity German Lutheran Church in the morning, the park near Retta's old apartment, the sausage vendor near the river for lunch, the Pratt library, and even the Lutheran Cemetery where an increasing number of ancestors now occupy their spots. When the day is done, she sleeps again in the shadow of the steamer trunk, the lacy curtains stirring above her head in the evening breeze.

Monday brings a visit to Henry's world, to the W & A Fletcher Company where he assembles steamships. He takes her on a tour of one of the ships, the port through which he entered the country and out of which he still frequently sails, the tiny house on Hoboken Avenue where she meets Mrs. Kottebaum, the ancient little landlady. Carrie gladly stretches to fill the whole room back at Frederick and Flora's house again that night. Henry's house is so tiny that his roommate must sleep in the living room on a regular basis; she sees no other place for him to be.

As they chatter, Carrie realizes that for the first time since Meldorf, she has a picture in her head by which to locate Henry, a room in which to put him in her imagination, a desk for the writing and stamping and mailing of postcards from the core of his life to the core of hers.

Charleston, 1942

T HE DAY OF THE CALL starts early, as days on the farm tend to begin. The chickens, the cow, the laundry are all waiting; the red rice and beans bubble on a hot stove for dinner. Witt walks soggy acres in the frigid gloom of a winter downpour, turning over the first soil that will result in truckloads of potatoes by fall. Neither a race against rain to finish the planting, nor a race against rot to bring the crops safely to market, disturbs the peace of his fields.

The day unfolds much as any other day, except for the bone-chilling possibility of snow mixed into the forecast. She finds herself dreaming of July on this January morning. She thinks she will welcome the hotter-than-Hades-by-nine-in-the-morning weather that will greet her by then.

Carrie thinks of her mother, as she often does when a windy chill dominates the Charleston landscape. The waters of the sea run warmer here than in Meldorf, but the storms arise more quickly and run roughshod through the streets. Her mind plays a moving picture of her mother, scurrying from house to shop through the pounding rain, arriving soaked to her skin. Shaking off water like one of Carrie's hens, the mother of her imagination bursts through the door of the chocolate shop, startling the customers who shelter within. Carrie giggles in real time as she remembers her father's reception: "The hurricane arrives!" he proclaims, and reaches to hug his soggy bride.

As Carrie moves the linens to boil beside the beans, her thoughts continue to wander. She is already seven years older than her father when he died, eight years more than her mother lived. She had been away less than a decade when they departed this life for the next, and yet, they somehow still live in her, never gone.

Carrie wonders what her own children will remember when she is gone. She hopes for the laughter in her own recollections of her parents, but fears that memories of her strident, opinionated control may prevail. Being helpless to muzzle the beast for so long does not make the possibility any more palatable, but what can she do now? Only growing wise at a faster pace could have altered the truth.

Her heart stops when the resonant bell of the telephone chimes. She doesn't understand her reaction. Bad news comes deep in the night. A call at noon is more likely business, someone looking for Witt. Shaking off her apprehension, she steps into the hall and lifts the receiver.

"*Hallo*?" Carrie says. A female voice responds.

"I have a call for Mr. or Mrs. Gruening of Charleston."

"This is Mrs. Gruening."

"Go ahead, sir." A male voice comes on the line.

"Hello, Mrs. Gruening. My name is Joseph Amado of San Francisco, California. Is your husband at home?"

"He's out in the fields. May I take a message?"

"No. I thought you might want him close by. I have some hard news to share."

Carrie plops down on the wooden armchair beside the telephone. Her head completely empties of thought, but she still grasps a pencil. She cannot imagine what this man has to tell her, but the room starts to spin around her frozen brain.

"I manage the Embarcadero Hotel in San Francisco. Several years ago, my family become well acquainted with one of the boarders. He ran into serious difficulty and I helped get him admitted to the state hospital at Mendocino. After his release, he went back to New York City, and I heard nothing further from him. I believe he is your son, Henry Walter Gruening. Am I correct?"

Carrie's stomach leaps in her throat at this unexpected revelation.

"Yes. I have a son by that name. What do you know of Walter?"

"I'm sorry to tell you that I had a visit from a merchant mariner this morning, informing me of an incident involving Walter. He made a run from Barranquilla, Colombia to Washington, D.C., carrying a tanker of oil for the U.S. Army. The Germans torpedoed his ship off the Carolina coast. A few of the crew survived, but I'm afraid Walter is not among the living. I am very sorry for your loss."

"Walter … is dead?"

"Yes ma'am. I'm sorry."

Carrie does not think in the moment to inquire as to why she needs to speak with a stranger in California rather than her son's ship commander. Her brain absorbs little information past hearing Walter's location, so close to home. And when she tries to stand, she collapses.

When Witt arrives back at the house for lunch, Carrie cannot speak, and the telephone receiver hangs loose from the wall in the hallway. He replaces the earpiece, lifts her from the floor, and helps her onto the couch in the parlor. He holds her limp body and strokes her hair. His litany of questions seeks assurance as much as information.

"Carrie, what's wrong? Can you tell me?" She gives no response.

"Did you receive a call?" She nods slowly, her eyes empty as if her soul has been stolen from her.

"The call upset you. What has happened?" Her eyes flicker and tears overflow onto her cheeks.

"Is it Henry?" None of the rest of her family would cause this kind of shock. A definite shake of her head.

"One of the children?" He closes his eyes in dread at her slight nod.

"Richard and his girls? Lena and Lynn? Conrad?" No. Not the grandchildren. He has another thought.

"Have you heard from Walter?"

And Carrie slumps over her head into the cushion, and bawls without breathing.

Witt finds a crumpled slip of paper in the hallway under the wooden chair next to the telephone. In his wife's handwriting, he reads:

Manager
Embarcadero Hotel
San Fran . . .

241

The news from the manager of the Embarcadero Hotel evidently had overcome her note-taking skills. But San Francisco? What on earth takes Walter to California?

In a few minutes' time, the long-distance operator locates the Hotel, and after a few minutes more connects Witt with the manager. He relates the same facts to Witt that his wife cannot tell him, adding a bit in response to Witt's questions. Walter, dead, on the *USS Allen Jackson* off the North Carolina coast, an hour or two away from home. A German U-boat responsible for the carnage. The manager of the Embarcadero listed as next of kin on Walter's draft card. Living in California to serve the merchant marines, but unable to work. A note upon release from the state hospital, telling of his intention to return to New York.

Yes, it does seem unusual that in re-registering in New York, he would still list his landlord in San Francisco as the one who would always know where he lives, especially when that gentleman does not, in fact, know his whereabouts. But that's what they said, and he has no reason to doubt the officer who contacted him. Yes, he has that telephone number; hold a minute, and he'll get it.

The commander has little to add. The steamer rounded the peninsula at Miami and started up the coast, a full tank of oil aboard to support the war effort. Within a couple of hundred miles after passing Walter's native Charleston, the Germans interrupted their mission, and Walter died.

Even further up the coast, Henry enters the lobby bar at 120 Wall Street with a halting gait and a slight grimace. Although he technically lives at a different address from his work, his new apartment is in the same physical building, different door, so the journey is short. He yawns, recently tumbled out of bed, not quite conscious after the night he spent. Living in the company of seafaring boarders saps the sleep sometimes. He needs to set up the bar for the busy day ahead, but first, coffee.

The pot gurgles, already warming. The manager of the business he inherited at his brother Louis' death has made the early morning ride across the river from Brooklyn, arriving in time to make the coffee before Henry's appearance. He's a good man, always taking care of priorities. Any minute now. Ah! Breathing deeply as he fills a thick white mug with the muddy brew, Henry begins to feel once more that hope and humanity might be possible for another day. All else could be forgotten in the quest to awaken.

Settling on a stool at the counter, he lifts the mug to his lips, then quickly clanks the heavy porcelain back down on the bar. The scalding liquid burns his tongue. Patience, man, patience. At this temperature, the cure will kill him. He spreads the day's *New York Times* in the space beneath his elbows, absently blowing into the mug as he reads. None of the words are, strictly speaking, news. The incidents are a continuation of the unfortunate wallpaper of his entire life—international posturing, shooting at each other, jockeying for power.

Henry usually remains philosophical about current events. He has evaded disaster long enough that he has little other choice. Born fourth in the line of brothers, he recognizes easily the patterns of top dog, underdog, dog fight at the international level. He knows the dangers of travel right now, but he goes anyway.

Still, his affable nature fails to obliterate the entire awful truth. He may not embrace the 'what is the world coming to?' stance of his late parents. The world has been this way all of his life. But he knows enough to understand that years of flirting with war will eventually unmask the devil. Posturing almost always leads to fist fights between brothers, and bombs between nations. The U.S. always shakes its fist, but this time refrains from entering the war until Japan attacks their base in Hawaii. His country will have their revenge. The only questions are when, and how.

Henry drains the mug, folds the paper, and prepares to face the day. Too many deep thoughts before breakfast. Back to the bar. Olives need stabbing and lemons need twisting, glasses rearranging and bottles restocking. War and rumors of war will have to wait until later. Until later will not wait.

The envelope sits in sinister silence by the cash register.

> *Walter dead off Carolina coast STOP*
> *Carrie in trouble STOP Please come*
> *now STOP Witt Gruening*

War crashes full force into the bar, immediate and threatening. And Henry sails for Charleston on the next ship out of Hoboken.

The sea coughs up no body, but grief still rises on the waves of the tide. Brooklyn empties into Charleston in an effort to stem the damage. The family gathers close together under the blue tinted light of Saint Matthews

German Lutheran Church to mourn the dead the water claims. The descendants of the Denzler brothers sit shoulder to squared shoulder inside the box of the wooden pew. Their stoic dark suits are slightly shrunken since the weddings where they were first worn. Retta's grandson joins them, and even Richard arrives to help shoulder his mother's burden. The comfort of having him on her one side, Witt and Lena on the other, comes as a pleasant surprise amid her grieving. She settles into a temporary ease, still buffeted on enormous crests of anguish and crashing down into the ocean floor in search of her forever-gone son.

Back at the farmhouse, dark hallways echo with emptiness. Fewer and fewer guests occupy the abundant beds, until one visitor remains. The neighbors bearing gifts of hearty casseroles and fruit salads taper off in the wake of the departures. Letters continue to arrive in the post, bearing the sympathies of the aunts, the sisters-in-law, the nieces, the letter-writers of the family. She hears from Bridget, of course, and even has a note from Rosie Chapelle. She reads and rereads and weeps convulsive tears for weeks. When all the others leave, Henry remains. Her brother is the right one to stay on at the farm.

Charleston, 1942

I WANTED TO MAKE everything right with him," Carrie wails.

"I know," Henry says, his brevity carrying the fullness of understanding.

"I had no idea he had even been to California, much less lived there."

"Wanderers have to wander. He had been everywhere he could possibly go. My kindred spirit."

"And the State Hospital! My boy must have been hurting to be admitted to the California version of Bull Street, and I never even knew?! How can that happen? Did he get better? Was he alright?"

"He did get better and he was alright." She darted a sharp glance in Henry's direction.

"You say that like you know."

"I do know. I saw him in New York. He stopped by the bar and we toasted his recovery together over strong coffee and a ham on rye."

"And you didn't tell me you had seen him? Henry! You know how worried I have been." Henry might have laughed, had he not been able to see genuine disquiet in her eyes. She has spent better than half her life worried. Anxiety to be together nearly tore them apart; the same had been true with her sons.

"He swore me to secrecy. He had hurt you so much, and wanted to stop the pain."

"But how could it hurt me to know he doing alright? What have I done, that he is so afraid of me? That he . . . was so afraid of me." Her lips tremble.

"Walter was not afraid of you, Carrie. He wanted to avoid causing you grief."

"I would prefer him not cause me grief, too! But that ship has sailed at this point, Henry. Literally. I have been such a fool to believe I could protect myself — or him — by willfully ignoring the coming and going of his life. I cannot imagine what extravagance of folly prompted me to let him die without really knowing him." Her shoulders shake with sobs. Henry rests his hand in the middle of her back.

"I hold his story in trust," Henry says. "I agreed to honor his request for silence. But with his passing, the decision for sharing the details of his life transfers to me. And truth heals more than silence. Alcohol was a big problem for Walter, Carrie. He lived as a hopeless, unrepentant, life-threatening drunk. He hid the problem from you behind that fish-eating grin of his. But then something happened that a smirk couldn't cover, and he left. He thought the burden of having him gone would be preferable to the burden of being a disappointment to you."

"But Henry . . ."

"Hush, dear. This story is not an easy one. Let me tell you."

Carrie shifts in her chair, shudders, then settles.

"As you know," Henry continues, "Walter took his mariner training in Galveston, while he still technically lived at your address. He received an Able Seaman certificate, a designation that opened up job opportunities to him that he could not have as an Ordinary Seaman. Did he explain all of this to you when he left after high school to take the training?"

Carrie nods, and Henry continues.

"When he returned to Charleston after his training, he started working on ships sailing out of the harbor here. He officially lived at your address, but I'm sure he traveled most of the time. I've worked those jobs and they are good work. He probably sailed forty-two weeks out of the year."

"He sailed most of that year," she confirms. She missed him, but household tension lowered in his absence.

"On his leave, he spent many evenings away from home. Do you remember?"

"Yes. I always wondered about that." And she also wonders how Henry knows.

"He spent a lot of time at White Point Park, where his crowd gathered at the Battery, by the Harbor. They embraced a whole different culture in that area, one that provoked both the neighbors and the police. One night a man died in the park, and Walter spent the night in jail."

Carrie draws a deep breath. She remembers the horrible row and his hasty departure. She has never dared to ask more about this story, but she has to know.

"The death had nothing to do with him; he told you the truth about that. A few hours later, they arrested another man and released Walter. But Walter knew the new suspect; they were friends. Close friends. Walter had added the man's initials to the Rock of Ages tattoo on his back. Relationships were casual among that crowd, but Walter developed a great amount of — um, fondness — for the fellow."

"A man? Why would he tattoo a man's initials?" Most men would choose the monogram of a girlfriend, or a simple "mom" in inky script. Carrie breathes heavily, as if she cannot take in enough air.

"A man. Walter fell in love, Carrie. He loved the man who did the killing." He pauses, giving her time to catch up. When she finally looks up at him, he continues.

"The death itself resulted from self-defense, not murder. The so-called victim beat one of the White Point lot to within an inch of his life, and Walter's friend saved their friend's life by quick defensive action. Not that the police saw it that way."

Henry can see that Carrie has disappeared inside herself, but the story has to be told. He forges his way ahead, knowing the pain he causes, but sure of the truth's ability to heal the wound it inflicts.

"Walter knew his secret would come out in the publicity over the trial if he stayed, so he hastily arranged a train to New York. He fled the same night, leaving his abandoned family, his incarcerated love, and his own integrity behind in his wake.

"That's when the drinking began in earnest. You let me know you thought he had come to New York, but I heard nothing from him for the longest time. I learned of his whereabouts after his arrest early one morning, about three months after his arrival, for public drunkenness. His life was in danger from alcohol poisoning. I discovered then that he listed me as his next

249

of kin in his lodging agreement. The authorities called me to retrieve him in his poisoned misery.

"He simply could not live with himself. If he had been officially on the rolls of the merchant corps, he probably would have gotten himself banished before he established himself in New York. And much later, he did have to repair his reputation when he returned. In the moment, I called on some of my own influence, and arranged for him to go to the west coast.

"Do you remember the postcard I sent you from Bryant Park, the one showing the statue of Goethe that they moved from the Metropolitan Art Museum? They installed the piece a few feet from the bench where we sat and talked during your visit a dozen years before." Carrie nods, as if encased in fog. "I bought that card the day I put Walter on the train for San Francisco, and stamped and posted it when he left. But I had promised silence.

"When he arrived in California, he lodged at the same hotel where I stayed when I traveled to the west coast, a nice place, clean room, beautiful view of the bay. The manager, Joe Amado, had become a friend of mine. He and his family knew that Walter's body encased an injured soul, and took him into their circle. Joe is the one who called you when Walter died."

Henry pauses again for a moment, then continues to speak into silence.

"Walter was unable to work for nearly two years," he says. "His condition deteriorated until Joe truly feared for Walter's life without intervention. He finally called the authorities and had Walter committed to the California State Hospital in Mendocino."

Carrie finally looks at him again. She needs to know this part of the story, too.

"I know," Henry goes on, "that you have a picture in your head of 'Bull Street,' the original 1800s era South Carolina Lunatic Asylum in downtown Columbia. The name changed several times over the years, but the reputation as an eerie shelter for the dangerously insane has remained constant. People are not presumed to be there to receive effective treatment.

"From what I know, the Mendocino Asylum functioned more like a mountain retreat in Northern California, located between San Francisco and the Oregon border. From the beginning, the hospital intended to rehabilitate the criminally insane, not warehouse them.

"Before Walter's admission, the stock market crash that led to the Great Depression had swollen the hospital population, as respectable business executives in mental distress sought shelter from their troubles. The campus expanded to meet the growth, rapidly replacing overcrowded conditions with new buildings. A residency program for psychiatry encouraged practitioners to engage in the latest treatment protocols; even in its earliest days, the hospital shined a beacon on new recreational therapies like music and art. They even had fishing excursions and a pair of baseball teams for the patients."

Carrie's face relaxes, if not into a smile, then at least into a less pained expression. She likes the sound of a place like that to help her son.

"Whatever the likenesses and differences between what you think you know of Bull Street and the program in which Walter participated in California, Mendocino helped him. He struggled, of course, and fell off the wagon, as they say, several times. But they taught him what he needed to know to get well. He made a life and held a job. I saw him a number of times, and he was thriving.

"When he left California, Walter moved into the Seamen's House YMCA in Manhattan. A lot of sailors lodged there, still do. He stayed for several years. The high rise — designed by the same architect as the Empire State Building, by the way! — rests right at the harbor, where the men can literally walk down to the water to go to sea, and walk back home again when they return. The amenities must have reminded him of Mendocino in some ways. A swimming pool, a gymnasium, a cafeteria, and a library all provide effective alternatives to the city of bars down on the streets. He shipped out from that port for his final journey, to procure oil for the American war effort from the port at Barranquilla, near Cartagena, Colombia."

Henry rests the narrative at this point. He waits as Carrie sits, silent tears streaking the contorted features of her face. After a full five-minute eternity, the question bursts out of her.

"Did I kill him? I didn't really know him, and I will regret that failure every day for the rest of my life. But did that distance lead him to his death?"

Henry is already shaking his head. He pulls her close and tucks her weeping head up under his chin.

"No, no. You were not making the decisions that took him down the path he lived. He made those choices."

"But I failed to create the shelter he needed to avert his ways."

"You played the challenging hand you were dealt very, very well. Not perfectly, but well. You loved him. You know how anxious you were in dealing with children. You had the same anxieties about anyone you loved. You possessed us whole in your zest for connection. The more love, the greater the need to own us. When Witt Gruening came along, you finally loved someone completely without consuming him; he simply refused to be anything but entirely himself, and you couldn't move him around the game board like the rest of us. Well, Witt and our Mutti, both of them wired as forces in their own power."

"I've been missing Mutti. I don't know how she let her boys go, forever."

"She loved us. She also fiercely wanted independence for us. Her principles demanded she let us go, so we could thrive. You embraced the opposite principle, controlling us to keep us close."

"I did so much harm." Sobs shake her anew.

"Time, and maturity, remedies harm."

"But for Walter, time is up."

"That's true. The two of you fired shots at each other for all those years, and it took a war to make you call a truce. But I have to believe that he knew how much you loved him, Carrie. He came back home to die."

Henry returns to New Jersey eventually, of course. For a year or more, Witt willingly finds the money to pay the steep price of long-distance telephone whenever Henry is stateside. Brother and sister rehearse the facts together, and express the feelings again and again, and again.

Carrie eats little and wastes away, her body bearing the brunt of punishment for her neglected tendering of love. She begins to wonder whether Amalia possessed wisdom in grief. She begins to believe that Amalia correctly assessed the world when she decided that the only thing to do about it was to leave it behind. Carrie bobs up to the surface again, a cork at the waterline of a great sea, lost in the enormity of time and the immense timelessness that forms her entire existence.

Many people mistake her quiet for peace, but in fact she knows no peace. She fails to breathe in the light scent of the tea olive that spring, to notice the overabundance of pink azaleas lining the edges of the house at the farm. Usually, that kind of beauty causes her inward spirit to soar with a feeling of home. Some see her return to her chores and are inclined to declare her mourning over and complete, but she knows nothing will ever be whole again. She will simply pose on the crest of a wave until she slides into another of the endless troughs that form her life. She arrives, battered and bruised from her journey, at an infinite sense of nowhere.

Walter's death is sad enough for endless weeping all by itself. But after the tragedy of his death breaks the surface of her grief, she weeps for so much more. She weeps for the death of her mother. Her father's passing, so far away that those days held a tinge of the surreal, but few tears, resurfaces. Now their absence inundates her soul. She experiences more exquisite pain than she finds possible in the depths of her imagination.

She weeps for the absence of Retta, the force who directed her young life toward a brotherless existence and then filled in all the motherly gaps for all the others who found themselves motherless in a new world. She weeps for August, gone too quickly and too young, for

Frederick, her rock, and Louis, her mystery, all gone before her.

She bawls and sobs and smashes her fists into the pillows for the loss of her twin baby boys, so much missing time, so much lost potential, so much sorrow. In retrospect she recognizes how little access she had to that grief. It simply could not pierce the fog of her medically assisted crash into the abyss of helplessness. She whimpers and crawls to Witt in a cycle of repeated apology for those small bodies buried at the back of the farm, ushered into heaven by Witt's own parents.

She screams in frustration with herself as memories rush into her consciousness. She wasted time with Richard, drilling him about his motivations and whereabouts. Then, supposedly avoiding further family upset because she had 'learned her lesson,' she wasted time again. Instead of finding a way to actually converse with Walter, she simply stopped asking questions. She alone bears the fault for knowing nothing until the time for action passed. She needed to learn how to ask, not to quit asking at all! The changes she made were as necessary as she believed, but they all shifted her pilgrimage in a faulty direction.

She even cries over Amalia. Poor, poor, Amalia, whom she had viewed as willfully, stupidly helpless and weaker than sand, on whom she had gazed from her superior perch amid steely will and moral judgment. In these impossible moments in the bowels of destruction, Carrie can no longer afford the illusion that she is any better than her nemesis. Eye to eye with each other, they are equals in their battles against demons.

And when the tears seem to be over, she goes into herself, where she lives during all of the major changes in her life. No one else knows where she has gone. Witt, who knows her best, stands faithfully beside her as she journeys, but no one fully knows the hell she passes through. Each day full of empty, agonizing knowledge only leads back to knowing that the one to whom she most needs to reconcile is gone forever. She is powerless to reweave broken relationships. No connection can bridge the distance of death.

In all her days of longing, she never imagined a place impossible to reach. But she finds that place, where she can touch nothing and nothing could touch her, and she lives there. In her life of losses, she has often believed that she understood the words "gone forever." Now she knows she never had the slightest idea the depths those words could reach. How will she make her peace with him, now that he is well and truly gone?

Charleston, 1943

I N ORDER TO INHABIT the rearranged space of her new life, Carrie must stop. She understands in her soul, wordless and living beyond the boundaries where sensible people think to curtail their travels, that her heart will lead her forward, if only she will follow. But first, she must stop the spinning, the whirling, the constant circling of a mind in motion. In stillness, she finds the space to rebuild. The stillness comes from a familiar source.

Near the anniversary of Walter's death, the Saint Matthews German Lutheran Church places a plaque to honor him and the three other members whose lives ended in the war. Carrie, predictably, sobs. But Witt no longer tenses with worry as her shoulders shake. She sees clear-eyed relief in his face. He knows she has braved the brink of death and is returning to life. The organist plays the hymn that has become a theme running through her life, with fresh meaning each new era:

> *What language shall I borrow*
> *to thank Thee, dearest friend,*
> *For this Thy dying sorrow,*
> *Thy mercy without end?*
> *O make me Thine forever,*
> *and when I fainting be,*
> *O let me never, never,*
> *outlive my love to Thee.*

And where love cannot be outlived, it must eventually move to action.

Carrie does whatever she can to mend fences between herself and Richard and his family. She resolves to call them faithfully on their birthdays, placing the names carefully on her calendar as reminders, and stops expecting remembrances of her own special days. She blazes the mail routes with long chatty letters and lets go of the expectation that Hallmark moments will magically appear in her post. She misses him, maybe even more than before his brother died. But she rises from her Amalia moments ready to take responsibility. As has become her habit, she takes her musing to her pen.

Maybe Richard needed and deserved a different kind of mother, Carrie writes. *My lifelong disinterest in children got in the way, of course. I worked hard to change when the children were mine, but change arrives slowly, and too often from the wrong direction. They all needed a fully present mom, and plenty of supportive, nurturing space to become themselves. Rich, especially, needed strong messages of approval to help him grow. I suppose all children need those basic things. I am grateful to Mutti for knowing what to do for me. Without her, I would have remained a truly terrible mother. I suppose even adequate is better than awful.*

But for so long the only way of giving people appropriate distance, in my mind, was to stand apart from them physically. The comfort I felt when Rosie Chapelle sat between me and her husband at that first meeting at the store represented my ideal, my model. I felt the expectations of others keenly, and needed the freedom as a child to struggle a bit in the wake of those expectations. My strong need to push back on tradition needed space in my life.

But when I started mothering, I had little understanding that the hazard of smothering a child's spirit comes from insistence on control more than from physical proximity, or the lack thereof. I didn't think of myself as either controlling or smothering. But limited self-awareness is allergic to truth. Some of the most difficult lessons in my life emerge from situations where control turns into alienation. Richie is among the prime examples.

Perhaps heaven decreed it best that he take care of his mother-in-law in her widowhood. I should be grateful, and perhaps one day I will be, for her ability to give him what I lacked. Perhaps we both benefited from the wide berth he demanded in his young adult life. Something about him elicited the controlling side of my nature. When I look back, I can see myself as he must have experienced me, a woman more concerned about her own well-being than nurturing her child. I fear our natures, and stages of maturity, would never have meshed in a way that inspired mutual support.

And strangely, the pieces of this puzzle now all fit together. Naturally he moved all the way up to New York. She laughs. *He probably thought he would please me by reconnecting to my former home. I wonder if he ever actually met any of my remaining relatives? Or when he could figure out how to care for an elderly woman, maybe he thought he would impress me with his dedication to caring for his mother-in-law. Irony is rich. I'll have to ask someday. But not today. We will take a gentler beginning into this new chapter.*

She chooses the words that will lead to healing, the stories that can rebuild a common base between them.

"Richard, do you remember the barn, over at the Geddes farm, the one you wanted to watch go up?"

"Watch the barn go up?" Richard says, "I wanted to build the thing! But your dedication to safety prevented me from doing anything besides watching. I knew you were anxious something bad would happen to me."

"Well, I shouldn't have been. That's what I wanted to tell you. I kept you back, too safe and too often, and I'm sorry. My fear may have stunted your whole life."

"It's alright, Mama. I found ways. Don't you worry about me."

"My terror kept me from telling you, lest you follow my wicked example, that my brother Henry and I went to a construction site in Meldorf when we were about the same age you were then. We went in the evening, after all the workers had left for the day. And we climbed on the wooden beams right up to the top of the third story, and made it our pirate ship. We leapt from beam to beam and pretended to swish our swords and raise our flags on the mast. I understood your desire to climb up that structure; I just couldn't overcome my fear."

"Mama!? I never would have guessed that of you. Onkel Henry maybe, but you?"

"Ah, yes, your mom fancied herself a great adventurer! I would have sailed the seas with Henry if I could have made that an option. My biggest frustration as a young adult was the expectation that I stay home to 'keep house' as they say, and raise children who baffled me."

"I'm sorry, Mama. That sounds sad."

"I'm not sorry—not now. I'm so proud of you kids. But feeling that I had to give up on everything I wanted prevented a good start for us as mother and son. I'm sorry you paid the price for that. You didn't owe it."

"But Mama—" Carrie holds up her hand to stop the interruption.

"For that matter, the debt never should have existed. But my fear worked to your detriment. I'm sorry."

"I did find ways, Mama. I never thought I'd be telling you this, but you know when they finally got around to opening a store out by the farm? I must have been about twelve or thirteen. My resourcefulness grew exponentially from the eight-year-old me! That summer I figured out that if I told you that Dad needed me, and actually went to the fields to help him in the morning, then I could spend the afternoon helping to build the store, and you never even asked my whereabouts."

"You little sneak! I guess you really are your mother's child!"

"I think Dad knew I went over there, but he never let on, and he never asked. We'll have to see what he remembers. That's where I learned to bang nails into boards and balance on beams. I spent an entire week on top overlooking the marshes, helping to put a roof on that building."

"What a resourceful child you were, indeed, Richard. You managed to get what you needed in spite of me, and that's a good thing. No wonder you are such a resourceful man."

"Why, thank you, Mama!" Richard's head pops up in surprise. "I'm glad to know you think so. And it's fun to hear about parts of you I never knew before. Thank you for that, too."

He will never be her Charleston boy again, but she relearns the hard-won path of curiosity and finds ways to stay up to date on family news. Theirs may not be the life she had imagined, living down the street or across town from each other. But when she ceases to impose her dreams on the life that actually exists, she learns that she still can be the grandmother she wants to be.

She becomes the Oma who sends cards for every occasion, sometimes paper-clipping a surprise dollar bill inside. She becomes the grandmother who sends items of interest clipped from the newspaper to Maryland, scribbling a light greeting in a little note. She learns that Catholic rites are not so different from her well-ingrained Lutheran practices. She makes notes of upcoming activities at church and school, and remembers to ask about them again later.

Maybe most important of all, she keeps more of her opinions to herself than she ever did before. Every now and again she wonders why they think 'this' and how they manage doing 'that,' but her mouth closes on the words that lead her where she does not want to go.

Richard spends the first half of the 1940s in Maryland in the business of war. After Walter's funeral, he surprises Carrie by leaving his daughters, their mother, and their grandmother, in Charleston. Carrie, bound up in grief, finds herself too distraught to enjoy them as fully as she would have desired. And Carrie knows he reasons that Maryland is too close to the nation's capital for his comfort over their safety.

But she still feels his decision, and their presence, as a gift to her. The girls stay long enough to get to know their cousin, though they enroll in Ashley Hall and not at the public school with Lynn. They stay nearly long enough for her to settle back into life and enjoy the fact that all the granddaughters do, for a time, live close by.

When they return home, she notices them by their absence.

Carrie's smaller reconstruction project is rebuilding connections to her brothers' families. She is grateful for her trip to see them two decades before, because she knows they have a remembered picture of her in their heads from which to begin. She sends a big box of oranges to each of Frederick and Flora's children that Christmas, and to each of August, Louis, and Minna's shared grown-up families, with a note to each family:

December 3, 1944
My dear nieces and nephews,

When your fathers and I were young, Father Christmas came every year and put an orange in the toe of each sock we left at the foot of our beds on Christmas Eve. We would wake up to 'extravagant' gifts in those stockings, like new socks and underwear, a new pencil for school, maybe even a carefully wrapped chocolate leftover from holiday stock. But every year, we looked forward to the sweet delight of the orange in the toe. Oranges still make me think of Christmas.

Enjoy in abundance these reminders of the childhood we shared, and the love that created you all. I think of you often, and remember your families in my prayers every night.

Merry Christmas,
Tante Carrie

Soon, a package arrives from Charlotte, Frederick's daughter and her goddaughter. Inside she finds a note, taped to an odd-shaped bundle of tissue paper.

Dear Tante Carrie,

Thank you for the oranges. I loved hearing about my dad's childhood Christmas. Even without knowing your tradition, my children are also growing up with oranges in their stocking toes. I'm sure my grandchildren can look forward to the same!

I thought you might enjoy having this little scrap that I found hanging on the wall in my parent's home when I cleaned to put the building on the market. My dad always told me that your gift came here in his trunk from Germany. He misplaced it for a while as it lay crumpled at the bottom of his steamer trunk after we moved to Manhattan Avenue.

But when my folks moved back to Columbia Street, above the original Maasen & Denzler's expansion, he found your old gift again, and I can still remember his delighted laughter! He had the whole thing framed behind glass "to protect it," he said, and then it hung on the wall in the corner of my parent's bedroom until my mother died and all of our family things moved on. I tucked this little treasure away, thinking I would send it to you, but forgot until now. I hope you will cherish the memories, as he did . . .

Carrie unwraps a thick wad of tape and tissue to reveal words embroidered in green thread with imperfect letters, the lumps still visible in the fabric where the knots line the underside: *Mehr Licht!* She holds the stitching to her breast with a sigh. Her first impulse is to hang the small piece on the wall, next to the sole surviving photograph of her family together in Germany. Instead, she carefully places the cherished reminder of her brother on the bookshelf, beside her weathered copy of *Goethe's Correspondence with a Child.*

Charleston, 1944

CARRIE'S TALENT FOR engaging children is shallow, but for a grandchild, she learns. The little girl is almost seven when Walter dies. By then, Carrie knows to dig deep into her own childhood experiences for inspiration. When she begins to pick up the shattered remnants of her life and reassemble her world, Carrie finds a wordless comfort in her granddaughter. As if she pulls an actual list out of her apron pocket every morning, she slips easily into the rhythm of reliving her own childhood with Lynn at her side.

Sunday morning, they go to church. Lynn, still too young for confirmation, loves attending Sunday School, everything from the stories to the stickers.

"Did you know," Carrie asks her on the way home, "that your Opa and I were married on an Easter Sunday afternoon, right after church?"

"Did you wear a big white dress?"

"Goodness, no, we couldn't have afforded a big white dress even if that had been the style," Carrie exclaims. "I wore my Easter Sunday dress, sage green with a narrow waist and a high, lacy collar. We had to wear horrible contraptions called corsets then to make our waists skinny. I hated those things! I would have preferred work pants, like your Opa wore on the farm!"

"But not for your wedding!"

"No, not for my wedding. For my wedding I wore that beautiful dress and a corset. And shoes daintier than my usual work boots. And a hat! You should have seen the hats we had. Fancy monsters, is what they were. I wonder . . ."

"What, Oma?" They pull up to the old farmhouse.

"Let's go look in my wardrobe." They rummage in the back of the wooden armoire, yet to be cleared out for their upcoming move.

"What are we looking for, Oma?"

"A box, about this big." She stretches her rounded fingers about eighteen inches apart. "I found it! Open this box, Lynn!"

Lynn takes the box and places it on the bed, carefully lifting the lid. As she peeks over the side, her face erupts in an enormous grin.

"Oma! Is this the hat you wore on your wedding day?"

"It is. Can you imagine I've kept it all this time? The dress wore out decades ago. I am surprised the hat is anything more than a pile of dust!"

"Oh, it is very fancy."

"Ruffles and ribbons, bows and feathers on a hat were the height of fashion in 1901. Your Opa's mother, Mama Catrina, wanted me to have something very special for my wedding day. I already had the dress, and she had the hat made to match, and quickly, too. She ordered it only a week before we were married, after the train arrived in Charleston. Look at the enormous thing, and the little veil! I surely could not have worn it to the theater. If the preacher had not been in a high platform of a pulpit, no one would have been able to see him around me!"

Lynn put the bonnet on her own head.

"I feel beautiful in this hat, Oma."

"The point of this hat is to feel beautiful, little one. No other reason exists for wearing a creation like this one."

"I love it."

"Then you shall have it. I need to clean out my things to move to the new house, and obviously I no longer wear anything like that creation. I wouldn't count on your mother letting you wear it out of the house, though. The style is a bit odd for a young girl."

"That's alright, Oma. I will love having something from you in my new bedroom."

Carrie smiles as she and Lynn work together to wrap the ancient relic once again in tissue paper and return it to the round, flat box, a treasure for a brand-new bedroom. She believes Lynn too old for tea parties, but maybe, just maybe, they could build a new tradition of grown-up afternoon tea around that old hat.

A few days later, Carrie mulls over the evening's menu. "Hey, I'm thinking I'd like some crab for dinner. Shall we call the grocer to see what they have, or shall we find a place to catch our own?" Carrie is already dressed in her sneakers and pedal pushers, the classic wardrobe for crabbing, but she still asks.

"I love crabbing!" Lynn practically shouts. "I will change into short pants right now!"

They gather what they need from the barn and set off for salt water. Carrie lugs a metal bucket and a net on a long pole. Lynn carries a collapsible basket, shaped like a box and fashioned of chicken wire, hanging on a rope. When the rope relaxes, the box falls open. They tie a chicken neck left over from last night's hen into the floor of the basket and lower the contraption into the water. The box opens flat against the sandy bottom, exposing the bait to the hungry crabs.

They wait quietly, poised on the tiny bridge above their prey. Finally, finally, a mid-sized blue crab approaches her lunch. At exactly the right moment, they pull the rope and close the basket before the little crab knows she is caught. Then Carrie holds the basket half open, while Lynn scoops up the crab and deposits her in the bucket.

"I got one!" Lynn shouts as she secures their first catch. "How many do you think we need?"

"Well, your mother and father are joining us for dinner tonight, so I think we need at least a dozen." Eighteen crabs later, they retrieve all their gear and go home to put a big pot on to boil. Into the roiling water go small red potatoes and half ears of corn, adding beer and onions and hot red pepper for spice. When the vegetables are tender, the crabs swim in, and dinner quickly arrives at the table, with stacks of extra napkins to sop up the juices.

Carrie has the depth of experience and imagination, of course, to be seriously adventurous, the swell grandmother, but she does impose limits. Using her own childhood as a model brings to mind some interesting possibilities for joint grandmother and granddaughter activities, but she rejects many of them. Dangerously exciting jaunts to the tops of rafters, or diving to the bottom of the sea, are too much responsibility for one grandma, so she takes them off the list.

Fortunately, Lynn genuinely seems to enjoy the mundane activities of life if she can do them with Carrie. A trip to the henhouse to fight the little mamas for eggs holds as much entertainment value for Lynn, as the same frightful venture once held for Lena, and for Carrie herself. Coordination of hands for milking the cows and goats invokes hilarity and a huge mess at first, and a great deal of satisfaction at real accomplishment in the long run.

Even the laundry becomes a race against time, the laundresses rewarded for efficiency by lively card games and endless rounds of tag before moving to the next step in the process. No longer a measure of work accomplished, every activity becomes a structure around which to gather memories before returning to the practical tasks.

Science fills many days, although that would make what they do sound like work. Quite the opposite is true. They pull out the bucket of seashells from the beach after the latest stormy night.

"What do we have here?" Carrie asks.

"Over one hundred specimens," Lynn answers, in a very serious voice. "I counted them yesterday."

"Have you divided them into groups?"

"Not yet. I can do that while you finish making breakfast, then we can use the table after we eat."

"Sounds like a plan. Eggs sound good?"

"As long as I don't have to steal them from the hens. I know how to gather them now, but I still don't like it."

"Nope—we have fresh, no-fuss eggs available this morning. You get started and I'll call you."

Carrie bustles about the kitchen while Lynn lifts the shells one by one to the end of the kitchen table, sorting them into piles of similar shapes. She is about half done when breakfast arrives at the table.

"Mmmm. Thanks, Oma. Could I have strawberry jam for my toast?" Carrie finds the jam in the refrigerator and hands her granddaughter a spoon for scooping. The fresh scent of strawberries wafts across the table, and Carrie recalls the mess they made putting up the jam last spring. Every swipe of the rag on sticky counters and floors is worth this delicious moment.

"What are you predicting from your work with the shells so far?" Carrie inquires.

"I think we will have more of the fan shape with little ridges than any other kind this time. And I think the prettiest ones are the little pink ones that open up into a tiny butterfly. They're delicate, though, so we have to be careful." Carrie nods her affirmation as the child assesses the situation.

After breakfast they stash the dishes in the sink for later and finish sorting their collection.

"Where did you put that book we checked out of the library?"

"On the shelf," Lynn says. "I'll get it." She retrieves the battered volume, a well-used field guide to coastal marine life.

"Find the section on shells and let's see what we can find out about the critters that called these beauties home."

"Right here," Lynn says, pointing to a picture. "This one belonged to a clam."

"And this one belonged to a scallop," says Carrie. "Look, the lines are vertical to the hinge. The ridges are deeper, and the color, pinker."

"I love scallops!" Lynn says. "Do all shells hold food?"

"I don't think so. Although I suppose some people would try to eat almost anything!"

"What about these?"

"The cone-shaped ones and the ones with a big swirl on the outer edge and a tiny little curve at the core both belong to types of sea snails. See them here, on this page? What do you think? Would you eat a snail?"

Lynn wrinkles her nose. "Maybe. I think some people do."

"I think I'll stick with scallops and clams — oh, and shrimp and oysters and crabs — they all have shells, too."

"The book says that shells are skeletons. They don't look like skeletons."

"You are thinking of a skeleton as bones inside the body, like humans or cats or even fish have. Remember, we saw the gigantic whale skeleton when we went to the Charleston Museum? Shells are skeletons that are on

271

the outside. They protect the little animals that live inside them." Where Carrie acquires such knowledge is a mystery.

"I can see how these cone-shaped ones and the snail shells could give protection," Lynn muses. "But what about the scallops and the oysters? Do they not need protection because people are going to eat them?"

"What does the book say?"

"That those are—bi-valves? Two of them go together as one shell, and the animal lives between them. Are these little butterfly shells bi-valves, too? They are still stuck together in pairs, but the scallop and clam halves are separated."

"I think they must be. What shall we do next?"

"I want to use the tiny butterflies to decorate a candle for my mother's birthday. Can I do that?"

"Will you be very careful about the dripping wax?"

"I learned when it dripped on me that it's hot! I will be very careful because I got hurt last time."

"Smart girl." And just like that, they are on to another project.

Retirement from the farm begins in nervousness but melts into joy. Witt spent so many years devoted to the soil and the people of the land they worked. The place is wholly his, body and soul, in spite of the rent he pays to farm it. Carrie worries he will miss the rhythm of planting and harvest, sowing and reaping. And indeed, he still has his farm mind forward when he talks about the weather.

She fears they will break in half when they leave the sprawling farm house, its double porch, upper and lower, its wafting breeze cooling the rooms. And a stream of tears does flow as they clear the rooms of memories. She frets that her lovely, peaceful man will become restless without his daily chores to complete.

But Witt transitions eagerly to the tiny house near the Stono River, the first property they have ever owned. Carrie realizes she has been holding her breath when she breathes deeply again. Any purpose he loses from moving off the farm, he recovers in doting on his granddaughter, defying her parents to spoil her rotten.

He becomes a gift-giver, a language recently developed. When their children were young, Witt adopted from Henry the habit of sending postcards from his travels. But he seldom brought them gifts or even candies, except in his seasonal disguise as Father Christmas. Love alone always provided gift enough from him.

Now, he transforms himself into a shopper. Every venture into town sees him sneaking out of the candy store holding a single caramel or salt water taffy in a little paper sack tied up in a pink ribbon. Every Sunday's hour in the pews finds a rock, or a feather, or a shell, hidden in his ample palm for his wee sweetie. Even the chore of buying a new shirt or a sack of nails pulls him to the toy shelf, a treasury of stuffed bunnies and wooden games.

Nothing is too much for this child, including every minute of his time. Witt has always loved children, but even for him, he is besotted. Carrie grins, knowing that she is nearly as bad. Or as good, depending on the point of view.

"What are you two pirates doing today?" Carrie asks her husband as he leaves to retrieve their granddaughter.

"We are going into town," he replies, a sheepish smile filling his eyes.

"And what new trouble are you going to get into?" Carrie laughs.

"We're going to the barber to get my hair cut, and to the hardware store for some brackets to put up those bookshelves you want in the living room."

"Ah—translation: we're getting a lollipop from the barber and picking out a new treat from the toy shelf at the hardware store. I'm listening."

"Caught again!" He dissolves into laughter, knowing he laughs at the truth. She shakes her head, sure that Lena will forever bear the responsibility of his indulgence. But she doesn't mind. Lynn needs a few treats now that her baby brother has arrived to distract all the grown-ups from her queen bee status.

"Will you stop by the grocer and pick up some vegetables to add to the roast I'm making for dinner?"

"Oh, you mean get you some sugar to bake cookies with our granddaughter?"

She rolls her eyes. "Whatever you hear, you old goat! Be back by lunchtime?" He nods. "And save enough appetite to take in some actual nourishment!"

"Yes, ma'am." He clicks his heels together in a mock salute. "Whatever you say, ma'am."

"Um-hmm. Like that's the way it's going to be."

He leaves her to her humming and whistles as he goes.

Charleston, 1946

C ARRIE ACTIVELY pursues Henry in these days, freely and without constraint. But her quest is no longer a means to control the outcomes. Rather, she is eager to soak up exactly the joy he pours, equally freely, into her life. He continues to call her through the years, at random times and on no occasion at all. And the postcards continue, so even when she cannot reach him, she always knows where he is.

> Sister –
> Cartagena is my second home this month.
> I find Walter here, his last city, his last port.
> Love from your brother,
> Henry

She carries each new card in her apron pocket for a time, taking it out to read in odd moments. Then, she slips it into the next slot available in the postcard album Henry sent his namesake, her Walter, all those years ago. When did she learn to provide the narrative between the written words, the penny postcard version of the long letters he promised so long ago? Now, she hears the longer version, unspoken and unwritten, that he trusts her to understand. She hears his voice in the message beyond the few words, spilling over into her imagination in the full account:

I am thinking today of you and of your youngest son, as my shoes touch the soil that he last walked upon, and gaze on the sights that he saw in his last port, the adventurous mecca of Cartegena. I wonder how you are doing, as you think of him, because I know you do, every day.

The colorful clothing of women in this city, a joyful antidote to German Lutheran brown and drab olive, fills my soul with gladness. The delicate sweetness of fresh fruit lifts me to new appreciation, and the aroma of the street seller's succulent meats wafts over me and calls me home to the streets of Brooklyn on Sunday afternoons.

I wish you could taste and smell what's here, beyond the Colombian coffee that ties our lives together in your morning cup. I feel you beside me when I duck into the local church, rich in statues and the musty smell of old hymnals and prayer books. I visit, as you know, mostly to escape the tropical heat. But I find cool respite for soul as well as body, and you would understand that gift . . .

She pauses in her reverie, smiling at the flight of her own imagination. But she knows the gift is real. He writes a penny's worth of words, intending that she extract a ten-dollar message. Fondness carefully braids into understanding in a miracle of accurate translation.

All these years later, the ache to be beside him has eased a bit and yet, contrary to all the distance between them, they are closer than ever. They understand each other in ways they could not have done when they were younger. They talk about those days sometimes. And now, when their conversations pause, the silence carries no tension, for the bond between them extends beyond all words. They might wish otherwise, but neither of them had gained enough wisdom in their youth to weather the conflicts that plagued them as young adults.

January 4, 1946
Dear Carrie,

I thought we had probably talked about everything over the course of the last few years, but I thought of something this morning that I never told you. Since I'm shipboard (Argentina again), I'll put pen to paper instead of calling. I never told you how happy you made me, beyond words, that you came to visit us during that spring in the early 1920s. Witt proved a wise and generous man when he gave you that gift. Everyone enjoyed getting reacquainted again, and no one loved that week more than I.

When we were children, I fell crazy in love with you from the moment you entered the world. I never helped care for you, of course. We had to count on Frederick to help Mutti; I was hopelessly a child. Fortunately, I think he saw us as his twin littles from the very beginning. I will miss him every day for the rest of my life. How grateful I am that we had that one last time for the siblings to be together. Even old crotchety Louis proved a joy to have along. We all were mature enough by then to take things as we were, and make our peace.

What I missed (and you're going to laugh at this ridiculous-sounding statement!) is that neither you nor I ever got any older than the other. Do you know what I mean? Neither of us ever gained significantly more experience than the other, so neither of us possessed wisdom enough to make the necessary changes for a smooth transition into adulthood together.

We were more like twins than true big brother and little sister. If one of us could have had the other to follow, we might have done better. I still adored you, but I felt constantly nagged, as if I could not possibly live up to your expectations. I felt called upon to justify to you why I could not be who you wanted me to be, doing what you wanted me to do. In my reticence to be controlled, I experienced your demands as bullying, but I stood down and stayed quiet rather than speaking up.

Now I understand the insecurities, and the similar lack of wisdom, that prompted your behavior. But when we were young adults, I experienced you as a very sweet pain in the neck (or elsewhere?!) that I didn't quite know how to handle. I believed silence to be my only option. I had not yet learned how to interact with you as an adult. I had only gotten so far as knowing how to get around you, even if it made you mad. And it usually did. I'm sorry. Not so much that I made you angry (siblings do that sometimes!) but that I judged you so wrongly.

Frederick used to tell me that if I had an urge to change you, then I needed to think about changing how I approached you, because I couldn't change you, only myself. I couldn't hear his wisdom. Mutti and Vati tried, too, but they were so far away — what could they possibly know about what I needed to do? Even Retta tried to talk to me, but by that time all the old folks were impossible, and I steadfastly refused to listen to any of them! I held fast to the hope that if I waited patiently enough, then surely you would see the error of your ways and get back to the old you. Ha!

Then I heard you tell Amalia that you weren't going to do her chores any longer, and I had to stop and consider that strategy. You told her what you were doing, not what she should do. I heard some echoes of Frederick's advice in those conversations, and now I know you were listening to Bridget. She and Frederick were simply telling us the same things; I guess their version of events must have been true after all! And how grateful I am that we had Bridget and Frederick, because your willingness to try to follow that counsel may be the only thing that gave us a chance at being connected as adults.

When you left Brooklyn to marry, we were still so young. Of course I celebrated for you, and yet I also grieved your leaving deeply, so sad to think that we might never again find the joy we shared as children. I knew you would understand, and yet I never found a way to tell you. I loved laughing together at our silly selves during that Roaring Twenties visit. I wish we could have understood more while we were living through our troubled times, but I think such knowledge escaped possibility. We simply needed more growth, more experience, and by that time, far less physical distance.

Eventually, I found a way to stay connected that let me share my true self without being overwhelmed by your need. And eventually, you began to understand the mettle that helps me stand. We returned to giving and receiving love based on mutual agreement rather than my way or your way. But for an interminable moment, I doubted deeply whether we would ever claim that space, and our disconnection kept me so sad.

I know that visit gave you a chance to reconnect with both Frederick and Louis before they died, and my gratitude is boundless for that renewal. The three of you were real to each other again in a way you would have missed if you had not been face to face. Everyone wants one more conversation, one last hug. I'm beyond grateful for time together for the four of us.

But my gratitude goes far beyond the apparent. During that visit, I reached out to you as an adult free of the fear of losing you. I felt apprehensive on my way to meet you, but soon discovered that the old bonds still tied us together. I found myself full of hope that the new bonds we were creating would continue to weather whatever problems we could devise. At forty-three and forty-five years old, the two playmates finally found their way back to each other. Ahoy, mate! What a wonderful feeling that is, one I feel every day even twenty years later.

Well, my thoughts have eaten more paper than the simple note I meant to pen. I don't want you to die of heart failure at the surprise that I can actually produce such a missive, so maybe I'd better bring my thoughts to a close for the day. You are and will always be my very best friend – and I love you!

Your brother,
Henry

Carrie is moved to tears, but not to surprise. She knows exactly what her brother is expressing, and she knew everything before opening the envelope. Her only surprise is seeing the words so bold in ink on paper. But she knows him, and she knows herself. And she has her brother back at last.

One dreary afternoon not long after this letter arrives, when the rain will not cease and the humidity is 100%, Carrie goes in search of relief from the Charleston heat. A first-floor guest bedroom on the northern side of the house captures her attention. She opens the tall windows onto the porch and invites in whatever air is stirring. She begins to sort the contents of the room for their upcoming move. Searching through the wardrobe, she finds Mutti's old leather bag, the one Carrie lugged onto the ship at Meldorf and off of the train in Charleston.

At the bottom of the case is a small cardboard box. Full of wonder and a lingering dread, she carefully sifts through the papers inside. Her confirmation and marriage certificates. Her German passport and U.S. immigration documents. Her mother's death certificate and the undertaker's bill. A photograph of herself between childhood and womanhood, taken at a studio in Brooklyn to send to her mother. Cards and letters postmarked in Germany. A few feathers and pressed flowers, memorializing experiences long flown from her mind.

Below all the other papers, she finds a letter in her own handwriting, unsent, and long ago forgotten. The date at the top is the week of her train trip to Charleston with Witt in 1901. She takes it to her desk, and scrawls a note above the date: *'Finally mailed March 8, 1946.'*

April 18, 1901
Dear Henry,

I wish I could tell you that I have moved on in your absence, but I am not able to accomplish that gargantuan feat. I am not brave enough. For all my bluster, I cannot summon the courage to write you the letter I so desperately wish to receive from you.

When you left me alone in Meldorf, my heart broke into two jagged bits. Half of my soul got on the ship with you, whether you wanted to take it or not, and the other half jerked in exquisite agony inside my own body. The painfully poignant effect of being torn in half made me sure, both that I would never see you again, and that I must follow you immediately. Jealous that you were going to live your greatest adventure, and terrified at the thought of living without you. Terrorized in fear for your very life, and writhing in grief at your abandonment.

I feel that way today. Leaving you behind in Brooklyn raises all the same questions. When will I see you again? Will I ever see you again? Today, I feel both the impossibility that we could ever be reunited, and horror that we would not.

Does anyone else ever feel such angst on the eve of her wedding, the terrible ache of agonizing grief? This quandary cannot be normal. Yet the wisdom of ages gives me faint hints that to grieve the changes of such a joyful time is part of the human condition. I am off on my adventure, and all I can think of is leaving you behind.

Carrie gathers all the other papers back into their storage place. But this old letter, she slips into a new envelope, then neatly prints Henry's address. She scrawls a note on the sealed envelope: *'Look what I found!'* She affixes a stamp and drops it in the post.

May 2, 1946
Dear Carrie,

I still have every letter you ever sent me. The girlish ones you sent from Meldorf, which you never knew found me. The furious notes you scrawled when I had offended your loyal countenance in Brooklyn. The chatty and informative epistles you sent from Charleston, so typical of the Denzler women, the letter-writers. (Though, I did notice the distinct absence of details about the feeding and diapering of your infants. Your foremothers would be horrified at your omissions!)

I learned to read between your lines, as you learned to read between mine. Thank you for having the courage to put a stamp on your fierce affection after all this time, and mail your love to me. I love you, too.

Henry

Charleston, 1946

C LOSER TO HOME, Carrie picks up the strings that bind her to her daughter, her plucky determination poised to arrange all the bonds into freedom. She finds a willing and experienced co-conspirator in Witt, who asks at every parting when the grandchild, now grandchildren, can visit again. For now, she concentrates on their mother.

Today, the two women dress in their Sunday best, to partake of afternoon tea at the Francis Marion Hotel on King Street. Practically next door to their church, across from Marion Park and the new library under construction on the opposite corner, the hotel occupies the elegant, special-occasion corner of the block. Carrie chooses tea to celebrate the motherhood of her favorite daughter on this Mother's Day. The tea ordered and the cucumber sandwiches on their way, they finally have time to talk.

"She frightens me sometimes," Lena says, ducking her head as if confessing her shame.

Carrie laughs.

"Of course she does. You may spend the rest of your life afraid. Fear's a natural condition when you have charge of a child."

"But how do I know whether I am doing it right?"

"If you are raising her to be exactly who she is meant to be, then you are doing it right. But often time marches on before you figure out how to really support your children. I'm still not always sure about what I'm doing, and my baby is all grown up and has babies of her own." She pokes Lena's arm affectionately on her way to retrieving another scone.

"I used to be sure I was doing a good job," Lena says more seriously, "all the same ways you supported me as a child. And then her baby brother came along, and she's been an absolute pill."

"But that makes perfect sense," Carrie says. "For so long the three of you made a solid unit. Then, during the war, you two were on your own. She commanded all the attention as the first grandchild on both sides of the family, and the first child of her generation among all of her mother's closest friends. You made special arrangements for her to go to kindergarten when she was too young to enroll, because you worked there. You made special arrangements for her to go to camp with you when she was too young to be an official camper. She's used to being a special feature at the center of all the adults in her world. Jealousy and rivalry come naturally to a person, even a very young person, who has reigned without competition."

Carrie watches Lena's body relax as she listens. She reaches over and refills their cups of oolong.

"The trick, I think," Carrie goes on, "is to reassure her of your continuing love through this experience of upheaval. We see a second child as an unsurprising turn of events, especially after a husband has been away in a war. But for Lynn, returning to your normal ways represents a major disturbance in her expected chain of events. She needs to know she will always be the perfect her, no matter who else comes along. She needs to know that we all have love enough for the whole family, without taking any love away from anyone."

"I guess you're right. I sort of miss our tiny household, too. It's been a major adjustment — or maybe I should say a Lieutenant Colonel adjustment! — to have Conrad at home every day again, and then this new little interloper came to live with us . . ."

"Yes, post-war babies popping out all over everywhere. Junior's arrival jolts her understanding of the world, but the experience is far from unique. Give everything plenty of time. And give her attention. Love works wonders. She will find her way."

"I'll try. I hope I can do well enough." Lena pauses in her thoughts, turning her curious eyes away from her shrimp salad sandwich and toward her mother. "How did you cope, Mom? How could you keep up? We came along like clockwork. You didn't have much time to learn before the next one arrived."

"I made a lot of mistakes," her mother says. "I suffered a world of hurt, honestly. But I kept moving, hoping I would eventually find the right direction. Your father is wonderful with children, a real natural, so he made up for a lot of what I couldn't, or lacked the skill, to do."

"But you were my whole world as a child! I can't believe you ever thought you were not good at being a parent."

"My failures were fact, not opinion. I had a very rough start to parenting. Before I had you kids, children were neither of use nor of interest to me. They were little snot-nosed, stinky nuisances, in my opinion. But you grew on me. I adjusted. I learned some really tough lessons. And here we are. I'm curious, what do you think made me an adequate parent?"

"You turned me into a kindergarten teacher!" The words out of Lena's mouth are sure and immediate. And timely. She resigned from Mrs. Buncombe's when the second baby came along, but she dreams of opening the Avondale Kindergarten, in her own home and under her own control, in the new neighborhood. She and Conrad are already discussing an addition to the back of the new house to give the school a dedicated space.

"I did what?" Carrie could not have been more surprised at her daughter's assertion. "I don't know anything at all about kindergarten! And you were born a teacher!"

Lena pauses, then reaches for her teacup.

"But you let me follow my dreams and interests," Lena says thoughtfully, "and those interests led me to sharing the wonders of the world with children. Plus, I suppose the German blood helped. We did invent kindergarten, after all."

"But what does becoming a teacher have to do with me? You made all that happen."

"I guess the biggest example is the way you encouraged me in Girl Scouts. The Scouts offered the most adventurous life imaginable for a girl. When I got old enough and wanted to do all the things they were doing, you signed me right up. When they were going canoeing or hiking, or shooting an arrow with a bow, you encouraged me to participate, even if whatever I wanted made you nervous." She giggles. "And I know I made you plenty nervous sometimes!"

"Oh, yes, you gave me some gray hairs in those days! You were basically well-behaved, but at your core, I think you may have been a devil child. You were willing to try absolutely anything. The wonder is I avoided apoplexy and lived through your childhood!"

"And yet I always knew I had the freedom and permission to try new things," Lena says. "Even when we wasted perfectly good ingredients, you let me experiment in the kitchen. Even when I tracked mud into the house, or built a home for a wooly caterpillar in the middle of your good living room rug, you encouraged me to learn firsthand about nature. Even when I was perfectly awful at things, drawing or painting or acting in plays, I could count on you to let me try whatever interested me."

"That reminds me of another sign that your worries of inadequacy are for nothing!" Carrie says. "Lynn wanted to dance as a little girl, so you stitched into the night, one sequin after another. She always had two left feet when actually dancing—and still you carried on, because she adored the costumes." Carrie laughs, and Lena joins her.

"Well, yes, her love of satin and lace always outpaced any grace she might have mustered. I am relieved to leave that stage behind us!" She interrupts herself with another thought.

"Another thing to your credit—you always joined in the activity when I showed any fear of tackling it on my own. Like the time I wanted to go to the Girl Scout convention in Miami—you remember—the one that met on the cruise ship in Miami Harbor? I saw you gulp when I raised the possibility. But next thing I knew, you had volunteered to chaperone all of us so we could go. You set an example of bravery in the face of new experiences." She pauses for breath before she goes on.

"And do you remember when I started doing chores on the farm?" Carrie's eyes say she knows exactly which story is coming. Lena presses on. "Those chickens presented the greatest danger ever known to a child, and I had to learn how to gather eggs from under the hens. I almost fainted with the fear that their huge monster beaks would peck me to death. You calmly pulled my little hand into place under each hen, extracting the eggs safely and expanding my range of courage."

"You should have seen me when I first married your father," Carrie breaks in. "Your terror of those birds pales next to mine!"

"And I'll always remember the year I got married. You and Dad were planning to move back out to the farm, to save the expense of a town house after we all finished school. I had recently graduated from the College of Charleston. Richard lived in New York by then, and Walter sailed away about three-fourths of his life in search of adventure. We were all launched. Conrad and I met only a few weeks before. And even though I worked at Mrs. Buncombe's school, and had applied for the Girl Scout job, the two of you looked at me and looked at each other and said, 'I don't think she's quite ready yet.' And you renewed the lease on Bee Street for one more year to give me time to get settled. That simple gesture cost way more than I realized at the time, and backed me up in a huge commitment to what I needed."

"You're right, that's exactly what we were thinking, but I didn't know you were aware."

"I knew then, and I am grateful now. I hope I can do half as well for my children as they grow up—the best thing for them is not always the convenient thing for me."

"You've got the gist right there! That's what motherhood is about. And you're so smart—you have continued your adventures into adulthood and taken your children along with you. I admire that." As Carrie recalls watching Lena calm a fussy infant, she considers how much Lena resembles her father—a natural at engaging with children. *She gets all that ability from him,* Carrie thinks, and then adds in her quiet mind, *but maybe I played my part, too.*

"I love you, Lena."

"I love you, too, Mom. And thank you for tea."

As they make their way back down the street to the car, Lena turns toward the library construction site.

"I can remember when The Citadel West Wing occupied that spot," Lena muses.

"Yes, you were about Lynn's age when The Citadel moved over to Moultrie Street. The new location seemed to have endless land back then, ten acres for the marching grounds alone! They moved a whole, what, not even two miles into the country? Now, downtown engulfs the campus. I don't think they got as far away as they meant to."

"I look forward to having the library here. I have a lot of catching up to do. Time is what marches now, and it's going so quickly."

"Wait until you get to be my age. Time gallops!"

"How long do you think the country will take to truly recover from the war?"

"For us," Carrie says slowly, "not nearly as long as we would have taken had we stayed in Germany. I have been grateful every single day that my brothers were not fighting for that foolishness. Losing Walter is life-altering and awful, but I have the comfort of knowing he worked against an evil regime. I don't know that I could have survived that kind of loss to supporting the Nazis. Germany will always be my motherland, but that home feels like a foreign country. I don't know how we let that atrocity happen."

"I hear that a mere 325 students and living graduates of The Citadel were not involved in military service for this war. The place must have been emptier of Southerners than when Union troops occupied the place back in the 1860s. You don't think of an arsenal being empty during a war."

"You're a deep thinker today."

"I am grateful to have Conrad settled back at home, safe and mostly sound. But I also wonder what he's doing with the war in his head. He's made five big scrapbooks in the past year, albums of pictures and letters and memories. He's even talked about donating them to the Charleston Historical Society as the record of an ordinary citizen's involvement. He's taking his experience very seriously, but I'm not sure his projects are bringing him peace."

"So, war weighs heavy on your mind."

"I think about war a lot these days," Lena affirms with a quick nod, "and peace eludes so many. I hope his haunting truths are really dissolving, and not being filed away to resurface later."

"In my experience," Carrie says quietly, "peace depends on how closely one can engage the truth without allowing its fire to consume you. A little like Moses and the burning bush. Recovery takes a healthy dose of miracle."

Lena nods again, more slowly this time. "Let's pray the miracle moves into our house in the new neighborhood," she says. "Something is not quite right."

"Junior slept most of the time you were gone, the little rascal!" Witt says as the two women enter the front door. "Easy assignment, but no fun at all. I completely missed play time."

"Where's Lynn?" Carrie's eyes sweep the room.

"Outside. I haven't heard from her in a while. She's too busy thinking up projects to spend much time with the old guy."

Lena shakes her head. "Her father's child," she laughs. "If he didn't have some sort of scheme going, I would check his pulse. Thanks for watching the children, Pops. Your wife and I had a grand old time, and the peace and quiet provided me an oasis."

"Glad to have them. But they were pretty subdued. I wish they had been a little more fun!"

"You'll get your chance. Eventually they will show you the full handful they have the potential to be!" She pauses. "Say, have you been out to the old property to check on Pebble Cemetery lately? We drove by last week on the way to the railway cut off, and the property looks like a wildlife refuge. Does anyone ever clean it up?"

"I haven't been back to the farm in a while," Witt replies, "but I guess I might need to do a little project of my own. I can't have Diedrich and Catrina wandering around in the weeds. My parents were more civilized than that, and would be distressed to be stuck in the conditions you describe. Would you mind if I ask Lynn if she'd be willing to help?"

"Fine with me, Pops. They're her family, too."

South America, 1947

WHEN HENRY CALLS looking for adventure, he tells Carrie to apply for her American passport.

"Ahoy, mate! Are you up for a voyage? Hope Lines out of Ecuador scheduled me for a maiden voyage in three weeks, a circle tour, starting and ending in New York. The ship combines extensive cargo holds below with passenger cabins above. I've made you a reservation for a cabin. Do you want to go?"

"You are asking me if I want to travel out of the country? Are you serious? Of course I want to go!"

"We will pick you up in Charleston," he says, "three weeks from tomorrow." *As if*, she thinks, *the Charleston Harbor is simply another trolley stop downtown.*

Does she want to go!? Carrie calls the passport office even before Witt comes home for lunch. By the time he arrives, she is half packed, at least in her head.

"I'm glad I have no objection!" Witt laughs. "And in fact, I'm happy your brother wants to take you along. All my life I've lived in Charleston, and I still can't get my sea legs. I've heard of these new ships and thought of taking you somewhere special. But thinking of even a week on the water turns my insides an inglorious shade of green."

"You don't mind if I go? I will be away six weeks."

"I would be delighted if you would go! Your brother makes a generous offer."

"Then my mind is made up," she proclaims, and the packing begins in earnest.

Charleston Harbor is not, in fact, a regular port of call on the itinerary. It fits into the schedule only because Henry uses his winsome influence to get the city added to this particular voyage. Witt hauls Carrie, her old leather bag, two smaller bags, and her new hat box to meet Henry on the dock.

"I hope she's coming back," Witt quips. "She's taking more baggage than she brought from Germany to Brooklyn!"

"My shoe size was smaller then," Carrie shoots back. "My clothes took up less space. And I owned no fancy hat for dinner." She sounds mildly perturbed, but the two men smooth things over in a hurry.

"You have your passport?"

"Yes, and Henry has my ticket."

"Good-bye, then, sweet wife. I look forward to hearing all about the journey."

Henry escorts his sister to her cabin, then excuses himself. They will have time together, but embarkment takes the whole staff to manage. She has a seat at the captain's table for dinner, and he will try to join her.

"What made you decide to make this particular voyage?" the captain asks, after making introductions.

"I would have gone anywhere with Henry," Carrie admits, "but this particular itinerary attracts me for a number of reasons. My late son shipped out of Barranquilla for his last voyage. Henry says Santiago, or I suppose properly Valparaiso, is one of his favorite ports. And I swoon to think of sailing where Magellan went all those years ago, even if we make the trip in reverse."

"That's quite a variety of interests," the captain says. "Does the considerable length of the journey bother you?"

"Not at all," she says. "Henry and I discussed flying me in. I want to be onboard for all the ports, of course. I could have driven to Atlanta, flown to Miami, then to Panama, then back to Cartagena. But why would I? By the time I do that, I barely beat you to the port at Cartagena anyway."

"Travel by ship provides more relaxation, honestly," he says, "and you can let us do all the work!" After a lifetime of housework, that option sounds as heavenly as she always believed it would.

The initial days at sea pause only briefly for a stop in Miami and another in Puerto Barrios to take on fuel and provisions. Henry, as quartermaster, has charge of those details, and she sees little of him. She talks to other passengers, or retires to her cabin to read one of the several books she packed for the journey. She has a biography of Ferdinand Magellan along, Charles Darwin's account of his voyage on the *HMS Beagle*, and a couple of novels to keep her occupied. And she has her journal, and all sorts of questions.

An early morning arrival at Cartagena, Colombia, allows Henry to finish his duties about the time Carrie rises for breakfast.

"Today we visit Walter, my dear. I don't know exactly where he walked in his last days here, but I do know he was here in the city."

"How are you so sure he spent the time here in Cartagena, and not in Barranquilla, near his anchorage point?" Carrie asks.

"Simple," Henry says. "He left before Carnival, and that festival is the only reason he would remain in Barranquilla. Any extra time he had before sailing, he would have spent here. He took after his mother, interested in the history and the beauty more than the industrial detail."

"I missed a lot of him, didn't I?"

"Yes, you did. But you can still know a lot, because I can share."

They disembark and head for the fortified parts of the city. First on the agenda, the Castillo de San Felipe. Henry clearly has been here before.

"The Spanish began construction on this fortress back in the seventeenth century. Obvious from its location up here on the hill, they meant to defend the city they were building at the same time."

"That's old!" Carrie comments. "Charleston prides itself on history, but has nothing to show this far back!"

"Indeed," Henry says. "They built an extensive system of underground passages into the fort. The acoustics allow no secrets. Any movement alerts one soldier to the presence of another, and the protectorate to the presence of an enemy. The design is quite a marvel."

"I remember this place from your letter! But words did not convey the immensity of the structure. I am quite impressed!"

"I love the way the hallways reveal secrets. I think about that when I sit in the churches and wonder how many secrets are stored away in their shadows."

"And how many of them are ours?" Carrie says. "When will we simply start to say things aloud and skip over the secrets?"

"But for those who can't see their way to saying things aloud, at San Felipe one can always whisper, and make things known in quiet ways!"

From Castillo de San Felipe, they make their way to the treasure the fort protected, the walled city of old Cartagena, rising with the cathedral, stately and majestic, at its center. Today, a new bride in the court-yard, her veil billowing around her to encase her new husband, enhances the romance of the scene. The streets, crowded between imposing structures, teem with life. Henry and Carrie find a small jewelry shop tucked under the sloping eaves, and Henry purchases a tiny, newly-mined Colombian emerald mounted on a thin gold band.

"From Witt," he says. "In memory of Walter. He says he saved enough money by not coming on this voyage himself that he can certainly buy you a gift!"

"This ring is beautiful!" She can think of no other words, but these seem to fit the occasion.

They weave their way through the shop-lined streets to the sanctuary and monastery of San Pedro

Claver. The Jesuit missionary, born in the sixteenth century and known as the patron saint of slaves and seafarers, spent much of his life in this spot, where the sun begins to fall on his bones now at rest.

"We have to get back to the ship before long," Henry says, "but I think we have time for one more stop. Where would you like to go?"

"Getsemani, of course! I've wanted to visit ever since you brought me that postcard."

"Ah, yes, the barrio. That plain old neighborhood is worth a visit. Ten-minute walk from here. Let's go!"

Henry takes off at a pace that leaves Carrie panting after their long day, but she still prides herself on keeping up with her brother, so she pulls in right beside him. They slow in tandem as they turn the corner into the neighborhood. Here, the entire world unfolds in the block before them, instead of at a distant horizon. The colors are close at hand, permeating walls and gardens in splashes of beauty. The music and art have direct access to the senses. The chattering voices, young and old, bring to mind more of the present and less of the past. The rest of the day has been history; here they walk firmly toward the future.

From Cartagena, the ship sails half a day and then enters one of the marvels of human invention. Carrie followed the progress of its construction through newspaper articles and photographs. The Panama Canal has been open for a little over thirty years, and has transformed trade in this part of the world. Where ships carrying mail and cargo had been forced around the southern tip of the continent to through the intersection of one ocean with the other, the canal offers quicker, less turbulent passage.

Carrie has been through the new Pinopolis Lock and Dam in Charleston, a small operation which helps her understand the mechanics of the canal, but also dwarfs her vision. She expects a single, industrial lock and dam across a narrow isthmus, a simple water bridge constructed within a few hundred feet from beginning to end.

She quickly discovers that the Panama Canal encompasses a series of three locks and dams spaced out over miles on a massive lake, a daylong and beautiful sail. She watches, fascinated, as the "mules" (so named for the original sources of energy) hook onto the ship and pull it through the narrow locks. Then she enjoys the view as the ship moves on its own power to the next passage point.

When they exit the Canal Zone, they traverse the coasts of Ecuador and Peru, then continue down the coast of South America, hugging the long, slender country of Chile.

Since the beginning of time, or at least European colonial time, city squares form the centers of commerce and residence on this continent. Every stop has a plaza, usually bordering a church on one side, and homes and shops on the others, an oasis in the middle of a city that blossoms around the colonial center. In Valparaiso, every sector seems to have grown a separate square, one for the cathedral, one for the government offices, one for the largest store in town. But the level land with sufficient space for squares is limited to the area below the hills, close to the water.

On the ridge where they stand now, nothing is flat, and nothing is square. They arrived here through the technology of a "funicular" device called, a hillside elevator of sorts, originally powered by pulleys and mules rather than the electricity added more recently.

At the top of this particular hill stands the Baburizza residence, built a decade after the historic Chilean earthquake. The interior, Henry says, is full of polished oak panels, carved mahogany handrails on every staircase, decorative iron gates to match those on the exterior, and fireplaces encrusted with carved molding.

Not that Henry, of course, ever goes inside. But the exterior of the home would certainly support those rumors. They see a fancy tiled roof, art deco iron fittings, and sculptures worked into the outer corners. Carrie cannot help wondering whether the Croatian businessman, who had entrusted its design to Italian architects, might have completed the international theme with funding from the United States. Henry says that the golden age of Valparaiso trade ended when the Panama Canal opened in 1914, but she has her doubts that the money completely stopped. She suspects the owner of this magnificent home might have received generous payment for the copper and nitrates that were Chile's biggest exports during the war effort.

This palace dwarfs in comparison to the city, spreading in every direction, sweeping down toward the shipyards and upward to the horizon, perched over even higher peaks. Buildings dangle off the steep slopes, barely clinging to their foundations. Most of them were rebuilt after the earthquake in 1906. At that time, much of the city fell into the water, and the rest was pushed in

301

to fortify the remaining land. All of these homes and businesses belong to this century.

The buildings radiate every color in the rainbow, yellow, pink, red, green, orange, every conceivable shade of blue. Carrie needs no conversation to understand why Henry chooses this city, nestled in a wide cove and open to all manner of adventure, as his favorite in the world. She could have explored here for days had the ship's horn not called them back on board.

The touchpoint with Walter's last days and the acquaintance with Henry's travel experiences fade into the past behind them. The sister and brother now sail together into territory where neither of them has ever been. Continuing down the long coast of Chile, the ship enters the Magellan Strait.

Carrie neither knows nor cares why this particular sailing follows the old route instead of returning home through Panama. She reads about Magellan's travels until late in the night, but puts her book away and sits out on the deck all day, basking in the same glorious scenery that greeted the medieval explorer on his journey.

The sandy beaches of Cartagena and crowded peaks of Valparaiso turn into desolate mountains and tiny fishing villages as the ship wends around the old passage between Pacific and Atlantic Oceans. The way rambles long and slow, but Henry assures her that she prefers the Strait of Magellan to the dreaded Drake Passage, directly south of the continent.

"Much easier on the stomach," he says. "I turned as green as Witt the one time I sailed in that area, and I do have good sea legs. When the oceans crash together, they create quite a ruckus!"

He joins Carrie to enjoy nature's bounty every time he can. In fog, rain, and brilliant sunshine, the sights are worth the trip. They even abandon the dining room to take their lunch onto the decks, balancing plates of sandwiches on their laps.

"I cannot imagine the precarious journey he made," Henry says. "The water is not difficult. But remember, they were dependent on wind power, not steam. A captain cannot conjure wind out of nowhere by command; the ship must wait for a stiff breeze to arrive."

"That statement hides a lesson in it somewhere," Carrie responds. "I suppose the accommodations were less luxurious, as well."

"Oh, the ships were tiny," he says. "Crew members would have been stacked on top of each other, and of course pleasure seekers would have been disallowed; the whole team consisted of working sailors. They had to be entirely divested of any notion of comfort!

"I noticed you reading Charles Darwin," Henry goes on. "His *Beagle* followed some of this same route when he traveled to the Galápagos Islands for his most famous research. His interests ran more toward wildlife than land exploration, but the discomforts and inconveniences would have been the same."

"Two very different stories in very different times, yet so many common threads," Carrie comments. She reaches for the glass of iced tea at her elbow.

"Ernest Shackleton's treks to Antarctica also link to this region," Henry says. "Did you follow him?"

"Ah, yes! I remember well. His journeys occurred during my baby-birthing years. The accounts made me so jealous! I read everything the *Courier* printed about him. But he had something to do with Chile?"

"When the expedition got into so much trouble, he retreated to Punta Arenas to plot his crew's rescue. We are going right to where he worked."

"Even if I see no evidence of these people at all, I am thrilled to breathe the same air they took in!" Carrie sighs happily. They reach, at exactly the same moment, for the cookies in reserve for dessert.

"I've done some research into the whole Los Lagos region, where we will spend some time on shore," Henry says. "We can certainly stop and let you breathe the air! But when we arrive at Castro, we have two sites we should see, the palafitos and the church."

"I know the word church."

"Palafitos are stilted structures, both homes and businesses, on the shores of the Chiloe islands. They are anchored on land, but hang out over the water. The architecture is unique to the region, and they tell me they are quite picturesque."

"Alright. We shall see them. But why the church? We have seen every church in South America, haven't we?"

"We've seen quite a few," Henry laughs. "But these particular churches are special. Jesuit missionaries built about seventy-five of them, all over the islands. One of the largest is in Castro, near Punta Arenas The Jesuits worked in partnership with the indigenous people of the area, resulting in structures that still stand today, after years of battering by humidity and harsh weather conditions. We'll see what we find."

"Ah, I love a mystery!"

Castro reveals a special kind of charm. Like Valparaiso, a variety of colors splash the scene. She notices a few docks hanging over the water on their wooden legs, and wonders if those are the palafitos Henry told her about. Unlike Valparaiso, the mountainous horizon reaches high above the rooftops, lending the city a small-town appeal. The church looms at the top of an enormous hill in the center.

For the first time in their journey, Carrie is a little doubtful. Contrasting with the church's coat of pleasant creamy yellow, the twin spires are painted an odd shade of—is that purple? The combination seems to lack a certain sophistication. She stands too far away to tell, but also unsure that the trek up that mountain will be worth the effort for a closer look.

Henry has no similar hesitation. He's going up.

"Come on, Carrie! Time to solve the mystery!" What choice does she have? The man has issued a dare!

Without a funicular, the way is arduous, accompanied by the ever-present temptation to complain. But they make several stops, and, using the switchback design of the roads, the two of them finally reach the sanctuary. The lovely yellow gleams in the sunlight, but the spires are indeed painted bright purple, along with the steps, the foundation, and the top of the dome at the far end. What an odd choice. Well, they are here now, they may as well go in.

Standing barely inside the door at the very back of the sanctuary, Carrie understands why they are here. Unpainted wood, stained with a matte lacquer, covers every inch of the sanctuary's interior. Paneled walls and columns, carved bases to shelter the statues, molding to define the joints between sections, narrow slats arching into the ceilings, even the dome at its core, each piece fitted together like a puzzle determined to keep out the rain.

"They used boat-building techniques," says Henry, interrupting Carrie's thoughts. "The indigenous people used the abundant wood sources in the area for everything. The European footprint, a cross shape with a dome centered over the sanctuary, combines with pure indigenous skill to create something special and unique. This place is really something, isn't it?"

"This place is magnificent," Carrie stammers. "Simply . . . magnificent.

From the silence of the church, they wind their way up a little further to the end of the quiet street. Henry has directions from someone who came this way before. He spots the palafitos immediately and points, directing Carrie's eye downward toward the shoreline.

Tucked above the row of trees that lines the street below, perched on the far side of the glassy canal, vividly painted porches line up like long-legged birds on a clothesline, dipping their feet in the water. One after another, as far as they can stretch their necks to see, a hundred little dwellings rest, reflected in the water.

Carrie is glad she made the climb. Nothing will ever be ordinary again.

Charleston, 1947

SCHOOL STARTS NEXT week and your days will be spoken for, Miss Lynn. What would you like to do on your final Friday of summer vacation?"

"Could we go to the beach, Oma?"

"We could do that." One of her favorite things about grandparenting is saying 'yes' so often.

They stop by the house to make sandwiches and grab a bottle of fresh lemonade from the ice box. Even at the beach, people get hungry, and hungry people are not happy people.

School starts on Monday, and their rhythms will change. But for now, they have plenty of time to make one last trip to the ocean. Carrie thinks of the bicycle rides to the sea in Meldorf, she and her brothers, before everyone started to leave. She counts it a blessing that she had no idea what her life would turn into. Those days were so precious. And these are equally so.

But all those days in between—well, she doesn't like to think such serious thoughts, and yet, those were the days that made her. Those were the days that taught her and tested her. Most people use "those were the days . . ." to introduce sickly sweet nostalgia that may or may not be strictly grounded in reality. But Carrie knows she would not be Carrie if the days in between could have been avoided. She needed all of them.

"Do you have your swimsuit on under that romper?" Carrie asks, and Lynn nods vigorously. "And do you have your shovel and pail?" Another nod. "And what about your towel?" Lynn's face fades to alarm and she runs back to the linen closet to find the missing item, then returns.

"Good girl! I think we're all ready. Opa, are you and Junior set for the beach?"

"Check. Check. And . . . check!" Witt's contagious enthusiasm radiates joy.

As they set out toward the beach in Witt's Roadster, both adults don sporty sunglasses in defense against the bright morning. The turn south onto Folly Road relieves the glare. The baby sleeps, and Lynn reads her latest book from the library. Carrie feels fat and lazy as the heat shimmers up off of the road, and finds relief in the slower pace and the light breeze when the roadbed switches to sand and oyster shells.

"What are you doing tomorrow?" Carrie seeks idle chatter, not deep conversation.

"I thought I might see if Conrad wants help installing those shutters for their house. He'll be going back to school, too, and we'd best get them done before his busy season starts. The job is not hard, but I think four hands will make the work much easier than two."

"I'm sure you are right about that, and I bet he'll take you up on your offer. I could help with painting. Charleston green, I assume?" Charleston green is so dark it looks black to outsiders.

"I'd imagine so," Witt answers. "I wonder whether he will want to paint them before they go up, or after. I think they take a better finish if you do them before, and that's what I'll tell him if he asks. You can get all the edges completely covered that way." Witt shrugs. "But they're his shutters. We'll do it his way."

"They are already loving that house," Carrie says. "Our tiny cottage works fine for us, but they need a larger place. Lynn takes up more space as she grows, as does the entire family. I think they really enjoy being able to spread out."

"I'd imagine so."

"You have quite the imagination today, Mr. Witt!"

He chuckles. Sometimes life does not require very many words.

"Did you pack the leftover cookies?"

"They're in the bag with the sandwiches," she says. "I ordered potato chips from Van Dusen's grocery this week, so I brought them along, too."

"Thank goodness for Mr. Crum and that fussy Mr. Vanderbilt!" Witt exclaims. Carrie sputters in her attempt to guffaw.

"What on earth are you talking about?" she asks.

"Potato chips," he answers. "Mr. Crum cooked for a restaurant in Saratoga, New York. Cornelius Vanderbilt ate his lunch at this establishment one summer day, and complained about how thick and soggy the fried potatoes were. Mr. Crum, determined to prove himself to Mr. Vanderbilt, cooked up a batch of the thinnest fried potatoes you've ever seen. That's how we got Saratoga Crisps, the first potato chips. You never heard this story?"

"Never. Is it true?" Witt has a reputation for stretching the truth a wee bit.

"Truer than rain," he replies. "You're accusing me of not knowing my potato stories, of all things?"

"Well then. You learn something new every day."

"Yeah—we owe our favorite snack to a little-known mixed blood Black and Indian man, Mr. Crum. The Charleston elite would be appalled to know."

"The Charleston elite would be appalled at a lot of things," she retorts. "Maybe it's better that everyone doesn't know all the facts."

"What are you reading back there, Lynn?" Witt asks the question because the backseat has been entirely silent for several miles. He wonders if Lynn, too, has dozed off for a quick nap in the hazy air.

"*Mrs. Piggle-Wiggle* by Betty McDoo . . . McDen . . ." Her reply from the back seat is immediate.

"McDonald?" Carrie prompts.

"Yes, McDonald. By Betty McDonald."

"Are you enjoying the book?" Witt asks.

"Oh, yes! It's a very funny one. Mrs. Piggle-Wiggle helps children with all kinds of silly problems. I love her."

"Well, that's good," Witt says. "Funny is fun."

"Oh, Opa, you're funny, too!" Lynn pauses. "I want to read *Make Way for Ducklings* to my baby brother, but he keeps being asleep. The pictures make it more of a baby book, you know."

"The one by Robert McCloskey?" Carrie asks. She really would have made a good librarian.

310

"That's the one," Lynn replies. "All of these books are brand new. I can hardly keep up!"

"That's our girl," says Carrie, wondering at the breaking news that Lynn wants to read to her baby brother. Might detente be on the edge of possibility? The war has ended, after all. But what about the aftermath?

Carrie puzzles over how she feels about the war. The atrocities committed by the leaders of a country she once considered her own are overwhelming. The photographs of prisoners stacked on top of each other in their bunks like so many piles of bones horrify her, as they do her German compatriots around the world. She shudders as she speaks.

"Witt, how will we ever reconcile ourselves to the harm done to the world by our own motherland? I don't know what to do with myself when I think of it."

"I can tell you what I think. I'm grateful my family left for the United States when they could, and well before the worst began. I'm grateful your brothers sailed when Bismarck came to power, and naturally I'm grateful you followed them." He pats her knee and she takes his hand in hers.

"Draft dodging may be a crime in Germany," he goes on, "but evading service in a party that can do that kind of damage is preferable to the greater crime of participating in mass murder. But you have to decide within yourself how to respond."

"Oh, I agree with every word you say. But I also loved the breezes and the seabirds of German shores, always my motherland. I cannot find my way around the fact that millions of people who were guilty of no crime at all were put to death in my name."

"You get to decide whether they speak for you."

"Then I decide they do not speak for me, that they are not Germany."

"May it be so." They fall into silence as the last mile of their route passes slowly by their windows, buoyed by the bumps of shifting sand.

The road from town runs out in an extra layer of oyster shells piled up on the sand, where they can leave the car. They park on the land side of the berm that marks the boundary between the land and the tides. The shells are hard on little feet; Lynn grabs her towel and begs to be lifted over them. Her grandfather, of course, obliges, while her grandmother totes the baby.

Safely on the other side, they take in the footprints that still line the shore. The marks are erased every night by the ebb and flow of water with the moon, and renewed every morning by the return of human creatures to the wilds of sea and shore.

Folly Beach illustrates possibilities in the absence of human effort or planning. Bright sun bouncing off white sand, a mess of reeds and discarded shells defining the line of the tide, sparkling water and foamy peaks stretching across to the distant motherland, and civilization out of sight behind the dunes, nothing visible for miles except what God has made.

Last week they were here with the whole family. This week grandparents and grandchildren alone enjoy the vista. Junior, dressed in nothing but his diaper and a madras bucket hat, wields his spade and metal pail as if to show off the expertise of an eighteen-month-old castle builder. His grandfather, resplendent in plaid swimming trunks that clash mightily against Junior's hat, reclines on a towel in the sand beside him. Opa offers occasional construction assistance and keeps watch as deconstructive waters lap closer and closer to the site of the build. Dark glasses shield his emotion as well as his vision, but everyone knows those eyes are smiling.

Carrie has Witt's habits memorized. He still keeps a journal on a tiny black-bound calendar that provides barely a half-inch of space per day. After all the years of observing rain and sunshine, keeping watch over the crops by day and night, his long habit of recording each day's weather persists. The tiny spaces allow for little else, except perhaps to note the most important event of the day.

Today, the entry will likely read: *Warm and sunny. Folly with the children.* His whole day, in two phrases. Tomorrow the words might reflect a trip to the garage, a visit to another retired farmer, or shutters successfully installed. But today, the children are everything. Warm and sunny.

Carrie walks down the beach with Lynn. Last night a thunderstorm rolled into this very spot. She heard the clapping chaos and saw the lightening zig-zagging through the sky from their little house off Savannah Highway. But even if she had not heard and seen, she would still know. An abundance of beautiful shells forms a line across the sand, mixed with water-tossed garbage reeds from the risen tide.

313

She and her granddaughter start the day splashing in the lapping water, darting up the beach like little hermit crabs. Then they return more slowly along the shell line, rescuing and preserving the most beautiful abandoned specimens. Their bucket holds treasures to wash and sort, identify and discuss this afternoon while little brother has his nap.

Right now, Junior expresses only hunger. His squawking catches the attention of the few others who walk the beach, causing some to smile and others to look away with irritated scowls. Witt returns to the car and retrieves lunch, neatly packed into a wooden fruit crate from the grocer. Lynn helps Carrie unpack the food onto a faded old quilt from the vehicle's trunk, spread out on the sand.

"Buh!" the baby declares.

"Peanut butter?" Witt translates. "Here you are, little guy. Would you like some lemonade? He lifts the jar, dripping with condensation in the heat. The boy gurgles enthusiastically, and Witt pours a round for them all.

Happily crunching the cookies and chips, tummies fill and irritations ease. Carrie can see that nap time fast approaches. She briefly considers packing up and heading home. The trip would be easier before sleep arrives. But her favorite part of the day, always shared between her and her granddaughter, is yet to come. So as the baby curls into a satisfied ball of happy, she tosses Witt a towel to shade the boy, and aims a slight, silent jerk of the head at Lynn. *You have to take advantage of the time,* she thinks. *You never know.*

Up the beach, Carrie becomes hopelessly tangled in thin cotton string, white except for stains from briny water, smooth except for grit from their beachy fingers. She and Lynn stand silent, working together to extract her from her bonds. This moment is their favorite beach time fun. After they sort and tame the cotton cord, Carrie walks back down the beach carrying the chaotically wrapped bundle in her hands, gradually releasing the string. When her ten-year-old companion calls out to her, she stops and turns.

In this moment, silence vying against the cry of the gulls and the crashing surf, eternity rides the waves, one generation tumbles into another. What others might ignore comes into sharp focus. The white cord droops, forming a new mess in the breeze. Carrie gathers the bundle back to her heart, and waits. The wind plays in her hair, granting freedom to a few tendrils that escape her usually tidy pins, like her mother's used to do. The birds signal their friends, a harsh sound, equal parts greeting and warning. The water pulses its ancient tune, the rhythm matching the passage of time. The world stands ready for this moment.

The girl shouts "Now!" and runs with abandon toward her grandmother, wafting a bright swatch of magic high in the air. When the two women, one old and one young, come even with each other, their twin silver necklaces glimmering in the sunlight, the younger one lifts the kite even higher. She runs for all she is worth on the sandy floor of eternity. She grasps the cord tightly. She pushes for one final, exhilarating measure of speed. And then, the child lets go.

The kite dips. Then it wobbles. And then, finally, firmly guided by Carrie's hands, it catches the wind and soars.

Acknowledgements

Any author, even a newly minted one, knows that a book never happens in isolation. Thanks to:

- The Universe for challenging, coddling, calming, cheering and providing peanut butter. You know who you are!
- A Writers Room for showing me how, telling me I could, and leading the way through the maze to publication.
- Kay Bender Braun and Jiahong Bender, both family and proofreaders for this project, for examining every single space and spot of ink.
- Lindi Lewis for capturing so much in the beautiful cover. We finally got our timing right!
- Joe McGowan, Rhonda Habel, and Claudia Gold for reading every word, carefully, with encouragement, and often more than once.
- Eric Rodgers, my one-man production crew, who held my hand, then made me do it myself.
- Kay & Richard, Joe & Rob, Edye & David, and Elizabeth & Nelson, for hospitality and a port in the storm.
- The Holland America cruise director who, on the way to Antarctica, gave a lecture on the history of the company. I think his name was Ed.
- The makers, then and now, who crafted the poetry, sang the song, created the ancestors, and birthed the children who populate my life.
- The angels who helped find all the pieces and kept saying they wanted to read this story.
- *Soli Gloria Deo.*

-LLB, November 23, 2025

Further Information

For this author, reading and writing are all about learning. Some of her favorite reading for this project includes:

Jones, Robert Alston. *Charleston's Germans: An Enduring Legacy*. Bublish, Incorporated, 2022. *Lives of German immigrants in Charleston, SC.*

Hawes, James. *The Shortest History of Germany*. Published by The Experiment, 2019. *Concise history of Germany, perfect for readers who want to cover a big story in a short time.*

Minetor, Randi. *Historical Tours: The New York Immigrant Experience*. Globe Pequot, 2015. *Tour guidebook, but enjoyable at home, too, with lots of wonderful information on the topic.*

Riis, Jacob. *How the Other Half Lives*. Dover Publications, 2015. *Photographs of New York tenement life from the muckraking journalist and social reformer.*

Ziegalman, Jane. *97 Orchard*. HarperCollins, 2024. *Social history of turn-of-the-century Lower East Side New York, through a series of immigrant families who lived at one address over time.*

Two of her favorite children's books from the 1940s, still in print in new editions:

Robert McCloskey. *Make Way for Ducklings*. Viking Press, 1941. Caldecott winner, 1942 (library.commonwealthu.edu).

Betty McDonald. *Mrs. Piggle-Wiggle*. J.B. Lippincott Company, 1947 (www.isfdb.org).

And one of her favorite hymns:

The hymn quoted in chapters 9 and 34 is a verse of *O Sacred Head, Now Wounded*. Text attributed to Bernard of Clairvaux (1091-1153), and translated into English by James Waddell Alexander, 1830. This text is commonly set to a tune by Hans Leo Hassler, 1601, and was harmonized by J.S. Bach as part of the *Saint Matthew Passion*, 1727. It is in the public domain.

Author

LOUISE LYNETTE BENDER bears the names of her grandmothers, whose family stories inspire her work. She is a fourth-career writer, now retired from faith community, non-profit, and educational pursuits. She lives twenty-one stories above the Mississippi River in Saint Paul, Minnesota. She still misses the little white junkyard dog who lived with her, but has two young adult daughters and a son-in-love within a few miles. When she's not writing, Lou reads. Or knits. Or travels. You can find her at LLBenderAuthor.com.

Postcards from Onkel Henry is Lou's first novel. She is already at work continuing the tradition as she opens the world of *The Viking Aunties*.

www.ingramcontent.com/pod-product-compliance
Lightning Source LLC
Chambersburg PA
CBHW050011120726
47903CB00006B/1723